There were six people here, two of them arguing loudly and irrationally, two others inserting inflammatory comments, and at least five packing guns.

Garrett and McCracken, of course, had the usual firearms that went with their sheriffing business. Arnold Clenting had some kind of fancy hunting rifle, looked foreign made; Bennie Senderson was carrying a humbler .22 rifle. Billy Ray Clenting was carrying a little pistol which she kept pointing around to emphasize her statements, until McCracken put a heavy, admonishing hand on her wrist and gave her a stern look. No gun was evident on Ronald Gump, but Garrett figured it was there, all right, concealed for use as necessary... to promote his own interests.

Also By This Author

All the Bad Stuff Comes in Threes

Baby Skulls and Fowl Odors

After the End: The Sumbally Fallacy

The Climbing Dog Affair

Karen Weinant Gallob

Earth Star Publications

Map illustration by Roxanne Carpenter
Cover design by Ann Ulrich Miller
Cover photo by Cheyenne Gallob

The Climbing Dog Affair

Karen Weinant Gallob

Earth Star Publications
P.O. Box 1213
Cedaredge, CO 81413
www.earthstarpublications.com

FIRST EDITION

July 2016

Library of Congress Control Number: 2016945313

ISBN 978-0-944851-46-3

Printed in the United States of America

This book is for Linda B. Thompson,
the best of true friends

I also want to mention: Keiko, Diesel, Daisy,
Sweetpea, Biscuit, Panda, Hutch, Lucky
(ask Doug and Judy), Dirt, Onyx, Bubbles,
Buttercup, and Julia Caesar

Semper Fido

Cast of Characters

THE DOGS

Sneaker (Pom, Yorkie, Papillon mix)
"My little dog — a heartbeat at my feet." Edith Wharton

Buddy (Red Heeler, Border Collie)
"I used to look at [Buddy] and think, 'If you were a little smarter you could tell me what your were thinking,' and he'd look at me like he was saying, 'If you were a little smarter, I wouldn't have to.'" Fred Jung Claus

Sheepdogs: Sassy, May, Speedball, Sic'em, Little Belle, Corky, and Cupcake.
"If dogs could talk, it would take a lot of the fun out of owning one." Andy Rooney

Killer (Pit Bull)
"When a dog runs at you, whistle for him." Henry David Thoreau

Cuddles (Pit Bull)
"Why keep a dog and bark yourself?" Proverb, Source Unknown

Lucky (bird dog of some kind; can't tell by looking)
"Outside of a dog, a book is man's best friend. Inside of a dog it's too dark to read." Groucho Marx

THE LAW

Sheriff Pat Garrett
"The barking of a dog does not disturb the man on a camel." Egyptian Proverb

Deputy Leigh McCracken
"I loathe people who keep dogs. They are cowards who haven't got the guts to bite people themselves." Author Unknown

Detective Asa Hobbs
"Dogs are getting bigger, according to a leading dog manufacturer." Leo Rosten

Also, **Receptionist Edith Oviedo and Deputies Red and Louie**
"Politics are not my concern... they impress me as a dog's life without a dog's decencies." Rudyard Kipling

THE POLITICIANS

Ronald Gump

"Life is like a dog sled team. If you ain't the lead dog, the scenery never changes." Lewis Grizzard

Bennie Senderson

"My dog is worried about the economy because dog food is up to $3.00 a can. That's almost $21.00 in dog money." Joe Weinstein

Billy Ray Clenting

"Women and cats will do as they please, and men and dogs should relax and get used to the idea." Robert A. Heinlein

Arnold Clenting

"Those who sleep with dogs will rise with fleas." Italian Proverb

THE WIDDERS

Carol Haddon

"The disposition of noble dogs is to be gentle with people they know and the opposite with those they don't know. How, then, can the dog be anything other than a lover of learning since it defines what's its own and what's alien." Plato

Maureen Macklenburg

"If you think dogs can't count, try putting three dog biscuits in your pocket, then give him only two of them." Phil Pastoret

Gritty Anderson
(and don't forget her elderly mother, Alma Weinant)

"Every dog has his day, unless he loses his tail, then he has a weak-end." June Carter Cash

Eileen Garcia

"To err is human, to forgive, canine." Source Unknown

Also: Deb Smith, Betty Oglehozer, and **Letitia Dash** — *"One dog barks at something, the rest bark at him."* Chinese Proverb

THE VEDRUSSIANS

Will Yelets

"A door is what a dog is perpetually on the wrong side of." Ogden Nash

Maarika Yelets
"I always like a dog so long as he isn't spelled backward."
G. K. Chesterton

Also: Zhora, Misha, Luka, Grisha, Marianna, and Lada
"I wonder if other dogs think poodles are members of a weird religious cult." Rita Rudner

AT PEASEFORD VETERINARY CLINIC

Dr. Edgar Clary
"I care not for a man's religion whose dog and cat are not the better for it." President Abraham Lincoln

Annabelle Clary
"Breed not a savage dog, nor permit a loose stairway." Talmud

Dr. Junee Bailey
"A house without either a cat or a dog is the house of a scoundrel." Portuguese Proverb

Sophia Bailey
"What counts is not necessarily the size of the dog in the fight; it's the size of the fight in the dog." President Dwight D. Eisenhower

Cole, Vet Tech
"If you get to thinking you're a person of some influence, try ordering somebody else's dog around." Will Rogers

ALSO PRESENT AND OF EXTREME IMPORTANCE

Jim Patchit
"When you feel dog tired at night, it may be because you've growled all day long." Source Unknown

Lew Harris
"In my day, we didn't have dogs or cats. All I had was Silver Beauty, my beloved paper clip." Jennifer Hart

Jenny Threewinds, Sheriff Garrett's beloved
"I wonder what goes through his mind when he sees us peeing in his water bowl." Penny Ward Moser

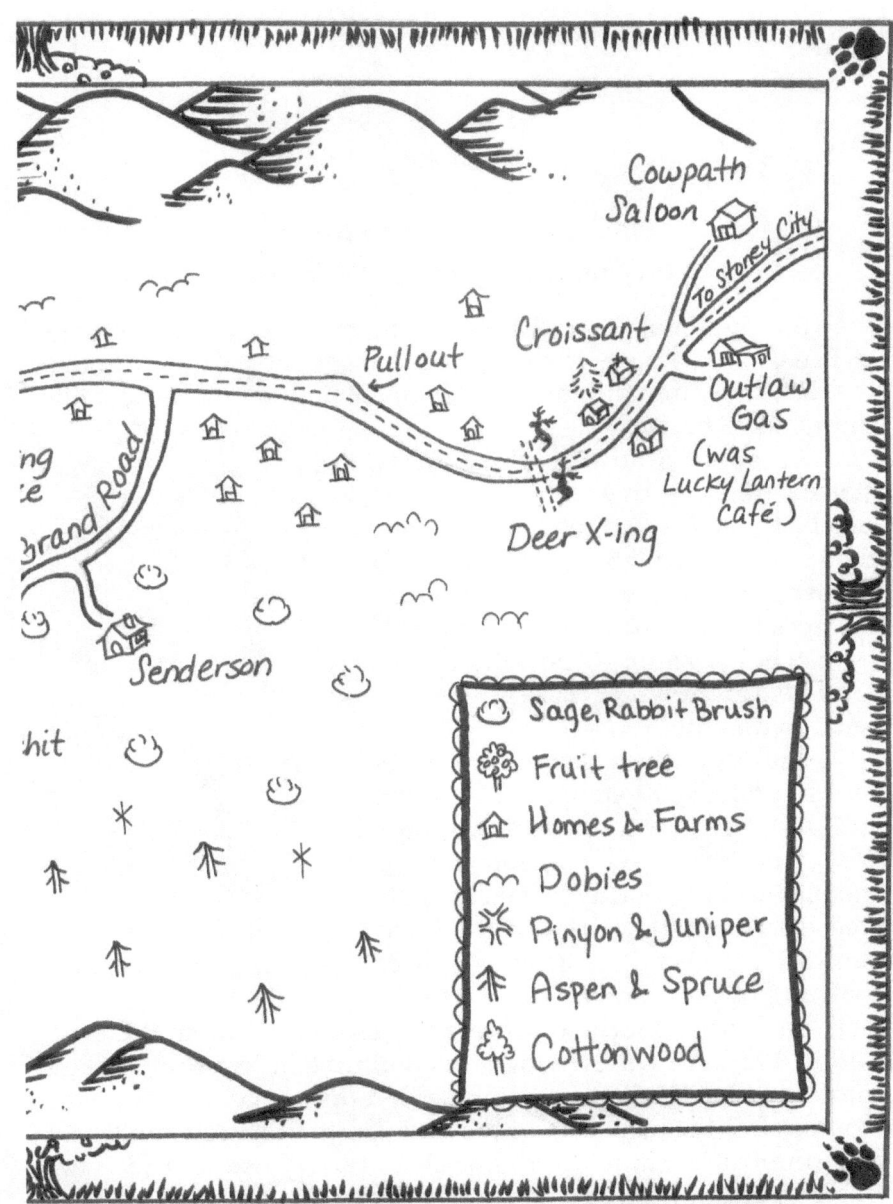

Preface

Before You Start to Read,
You Should Know These Things

Buddy is real. That's him, all right, on the cover. He belongs to Lee Cook, who says he is a "hell of a cow dog. Draw a line in the dirt, show him the cows, and he won't let them cross that line until you're ready."

At about four months, Buddy started climbing trees. He can leap as much as six feet to get into the tree, then climb on up (going backwards) to sixteen feet or more. He climbs for fun; he loves to chase squirrels and birds. If he catches a squirrel, he kills it, but once he caught a bird. He had no idea what to do with it!

The day that Lee showed us Buddy's talents, he stepped over to the tree and said in a conversational tone, "Hey, Buddy, there's a squirrel up there." Instantly Buddy leaped into the tree, alert, sniffing in all directions. No squirrel. Disgusted, he gave us a dirty look and hopped down.

Lee credits Buddy with breaking his tobacco habit. When he adopted him, he was driving home with the little puppy tucked into his jacket. He wanted a chew of Copenhagen, but he was driving and the pup was in the way, so the tobacco spilled all over the truck. Fumbling the truck to safety, Lee told his new dog, "Buddy, we are better men than this," and he hasn't chewed since.

Lee works at Delta Animal Health. People often enter the store, point excitedly outside, and say, "There's a dog up in your tree out there!" Lee responds, "Don't be silly. Dogs don't climb trees."

****

Sassy and May are real, too, as are the other sheepdogs who, in this book, go by pseudonyms. They belong to our good friend, Jolie Clark, a diligent practitioner of the magnificent art of training these amazing dogs. Jolie helped me with the sheepdog scene in this book. I thank her so much! (By the way, the particular DIMA whistle described in the book is real, too—it belongs to Jolie.)

****

One more *real* thing: Vedrussians. Vedrussians are the Earth's good guys. They believe in an alternate view of human history, in which gradually over the last 3,000 years their kind have been "put to sleep" by dark forces. They are now awakening and each is prepared to take a hectare (2.471 acres) of land upon which to create a paradise on earth, which will help to bring light back into our world. The movement is worldwide, but Russia is the place where they last prevailed before the darkness came, and it is now leading the awakening. The Vedrussian concept is so popular in Russia that it is a recognized option for self-identification on the Russian census.

The Vedrussian movement is connected to the Anastasia/Ringing Cedars movement. Anastasia is a gorgeous, nearly mythic, blond woman who, like a prophet, is guiding the return of light into the world. The cedars (Siberian pine, *Pinus siberica*) are found in the taiga (subarctic evergreen forests) of Siberia. Their purpose is to bring in the Light and when they are ready, to ring. The ringing means the tree should be harvested and its parts dispersed (as pendants, etc.) to carry the Light around the globe.

Two other helpful terms are *dacha* and *dolman*. *Dachas* are the little plots of land which were distributed for free to 35 million Russian families in the twentieth century. Anastasia urges that they are the land that is to be cultivated as "kin domains," the hectares that are to be paradises on Earth. As for *dolmans*, they are neolithic tombs, mostly in the Western Caucasus; they are large, upright stones topped with flat stone tables. According to the movement, long ago, enlightened priests resisted the dark forces, and these priests have withdrawn into the tombs for eternal meditation, but remain accessible for consultation in certain instances. There is currently an expanding tourist trade for visits to the *dolmans*.

So, where did I come up with all this? I first encountered the Ringing Cedars and so-on in *CAFE*, the anthropological journal of Culture, Agriculture, Food, and Environment, in an article by Veronica Davidov called "Beyond Formal Environmentalism: Eco-Nationalism and the 'Ringing Cedars' of Russia (*CAFE* 2015 37(1): 2-13)." Following that up, I read some in the ten books by Vladimir Megré, the Russian merchant who first discovered the cedars and Anastasia (and had heavenly sex with her and a child by her). If you are curious to know more, google "The Ringing Cedars" series by Megré. You can also just google any of the other terms I've mentioned above; believe me, the information will pop up.

Now, on to our story, which does involve Buddy, sheepdogs, and some fictional Vedrussians who are settling near our special town, Croissant.

The Climbing Dog Affair

Karen Weinant Gallob

1

BY THE TIME SHE HIT THE BRAKES, Junee Bailey knew it was already too late. Her eye had just caught another "Vote Ronald Gump" sign when bang! The little sucker bounced off the hood, slumped to the road, and lay still in the headlights, staring up with its accusing, glazed and dying, soft, brown eyes at the steam hissing its way free from her damaged radiator and passing the bent, crushed metal above. Junee shot her eyes to the back seat where, for some reason, Sophia continued to sleep, unaware of this snag which had sharply broken their momentum. On the other hand, Sneaker's eyes were wide open under the hair that sprouted all over her tiny forehead, but it would be difficult to say if the crash had actually alarmed her, since she showed her emotions with her entire body, and Sophia had all but the little dog's fur-fattened face swaddled in a blanket that was clutched unyieldingly to her chest. Returning her gaze to the deer, now obviously dead, Junee lowered her head to the steering wheel and mumbled, "Shit. Shit, shit, shit, shit, shit, shit, shit."

According to her GPS, they would have been at Dr. Clary's in less than fifteen minutes. In self-defense, she assured herself that she hadn't been wool gathering. No more than two miles back, a large herd of deer had burst across the road and she had successfully avoided every one of them. After all, she was coming here from a dairy practice in upstate New York, a state where deer on the road were not a rarity. Plus, after that herd crossed, she'd slowed way down, alert and ready. No, this buck had attacked her. Well, that's what it felt like. She was in a cut that had been made to bring the road through a little adobe hill, and, wearing the necessary camouflage for a late summer dusk

1

against dobie and tumbleweed, the fellow had leapt from the hillside and attacked her van. And lost. She looked at the crumpled body and shuddered. After all, one reason she had become a veterinarian was because she was quite fond of animals. She wanted to see them "live long and prosper," as Spock would say, and now the initial thump was still resounding in her ears and making her a little sick.

She lowered her forehead again to the steering wheel and began to take deep breaths to clear her mind. It wasn't fair. She had been so innocently driving along, pleased with herself for having decided to drive the extra couple of hours that it would take to reach her destination once she had reached Stoney City from Denver. The drive had been beautiful, rock formations and canyon, aspen and spruce. Why, who wouldn't want to live here? Maybe she would actually want to buy Wheezer's clinic, after all. She hadn't met old Dr. Clary yet, but she referred to him in her inner dialogue as Wheezer because that's how he sounded on the phone. Old. And, she had to admit, also maybe because she wanted to keep up a little barrier, not get herself too attached to the idea of buying here. After all, the main reason she wanted to look into this area was to find that woman, get the issues between them resolved after all these years. The clinic, blue sky and all, was being offered for an alarmingly low price. It might be difficult not to be tempted into buying it, just because of price alone. Like a drifting mall shopper spotting an item not really needed, but at such a bargain price. Wheezer said the price was low because he needed to retire for his wife's sake, and the offer did not include the house and fields behind it. Just the clinic. Well. She would have to see. Probably not her cup of tea, but then maybe she could use it as an investment, build it up—after all, the old guy had probably let it run down over the years—and get it going and sell it for a profit.

Those had been her thoughts as she drove. Then the GPS had taken her out of the mountains, away from the aspen and spruce, and dropped her in elevation. Not pleased, she thought maybe it wouldn't be so difficult, after all, to resist buying the clinic. She watched as the foliage went from thick, lush green to fussy straggles of serviceberry, buck brush, and little stands of scrub oak, which then yielded to the sage, rabbit brush, and dobie hillsides she was seeing here. There had been a few stands of pinyon and juniper, and the occasional creek bed offerings of cottonwood. She had just passed a large nest of irrigated fields, some with adequate water to stay green, others baked crisp yellow in the high altitude's unyielding August sun. No, this did not appeal to her. It was not the Colorado she remembered. She had done pre-vet in Boulder, skied everywhere: Breckenridge, even Steamboat. From vet school in Fort Collins she had found time to wander the high trails and climb mountains with Ethan. When he was alive.

The thought of her lost Ethan made her slump even further as she drove. This landscape looked so drab, the dobie clay. She had decided it wasn't even colorful. She had gotten weary after the long drive; Sophia was no company; all she did was play games on her iPhone and sleep. Just as she wondered if she might have to pull over and catch forty winks herself, the signs started to show up. There were a lot about this guy, Gump, kind of like Burma Shave signs, slogans in sequence. "Google Gump and you'll get it." "Gump says to Know Your Neighbor!" And so-on. They were entertaining, and helped her stay awake as she watched for the next one. Then a huge and colorful billboard popped up just before she passed through Croissant. "You need a Billy Ray of Hope!! Now is When Experience Counts the Most!! Vote Wisely! Vote Clenting."

"Well, all righty, then," Junee told herself. "Clearly an election is in the works. Wonder what they're running for?"

Just then a modest little black and white sign came up on the right. It said, "You can bet on Bennie for County Com...." The rest of the sign appeared to have been damaged by weather. Junee smiled to herself. She knew it originally must have said, "County Commissioner," but she chuckled that maybe the guy was running for "County Communist." Who could tell, in a place that was shaping up like this one was?

Then all the deer had crossed in front of her. Then she had slowed and made her way through them. Then the Gump sign followed by the sickening thud. Then she had put her head on the steering wheel to delay having to figure out what to do next. She decided that maybe she had been hurt in the deer encounter after all, because her head felt heavy and she could see lights flickering behind her lids. Well, whatever. Right. Junee Bailey, you still have to cowboy up, as they probably say around this

place. Raise your head; you've had worse; face the music, and...
A sharp rapping on the window and her head shot up of its own
accord.

What appeared, looking closely in at her, was one of the
uglier faces she had seen in this life. Round, yes, but with big, jug
ears, a pointless mustache straggling across the upper lip then
drooping tiredly down each side of the chin, the mustache itself
pulled askew on the left by a large, puckered red scar beginning
on the left cheek and working its way out of sight toward the
neck. The face was very close to the window, and its voice was
saying, "Are you all right, Ma'am? Ma'am, are you able to open
your window?"

Junee Bailey suppressed a shriek. Her whole brain rattled
with, 'Open my window to you? Not in this lifetime.' She cast
her eyes feverishly around the van for a weapon. The man stood
up, stepping away from the car door. He looked thoughtful, and
finally Junee was able to gather her wits. A sheriff's badge on his
chest blinked in the light. Light. The flickering behind her lids
was not from her having been injured. It was from the patrol car
that had pulled up behind her.

2

EMBARRASSED, JUNEE WAS TALKING even as she pushed her door open. "Sorry, Sir. I'm sorry. I'm fine. I really am. I was just thinking... trying to think... you see, this deer hit me and I was trying to think what to do... "

The man, a tall, lanky type, had continued to look thoughtful until she said, "...this deer hit me... ", then he grinned, spat expertly across the road, and said, "They do that, don't they?"

Her flow of speech interrupted, Junee said, "Do what?"

"They hit you. They kinda come out of nowhere, no matter how careful you're drivin' and lookin', and they hop right into you."

Surprised and confused by the unexpected empathy, Junee stammered, "Yes, that's what this one did."

"Sure nuf. Well, let's get 'im drug off the road before he causes more trouble. Wanna help me?" He didn't wait for a reply, but walked to the dead animal and grabbed its hind legs. Scurrying to catch up, Junee got behind it and pushed, and without much more effort from them it flopped into the bar ditch.

Straightening up, the sheriff dusted off his hands and tugged at one large ear. He was looking past her. "Well, so what do we have here?" Junee turned to see Sophia standing barefoot in the middle of the road, still clutching the half-smothered dog in the blanket.

"Oh! Oh, that's my daughter, Sophia. She was asleep in back and... "

Again, the sheriff interrupted, his eyes twinkling but his voice sober. "No, I meant the little bug-eyed creature that's got hold of her. Kind of worries me that your daughter might need rescuing."

Feet firmly planted, back straight, chin up, Sophia addressed the sheriff with all the solemn demeanor that could be mustered by a media-educated seven-year-old. "Look, Mister. This is my personal canine, which I have with me at all times." She unrolled the dog onto the road from the blanket. It responded with relief and pleasure, its ears popping up on the shaggy head, its tail waving happily skyward. It eyed the rapidly darkening area beyond the road with immense interest. Nodding at it, Sophia continued, "Yes, Sir, this animal is named Sneaker. An appropriate name, as well you can see."

The sheriff could no longer suppress his grin. "Appropriate, Ma'am? Perhaps, if one is to consider that he might be the size of my sneaker. As for your own shoe, I believe him to be too large."

Sophia snorted. "Mom's sneaker. And she's a girl, not a him. And also, she is not only little, but exceedingly sneaky. Sir."

As if on cue, Sneaker, who had been doing a bit of dancing and shifting to ease the tingle in her overly loved, squashed limbs, now raised her head and began to edge to the roadside. In alarm, Junee recalled that even though they were in the country, it was, after all, a road, and a car actually could come down it. "Sophia, you must get Sneaker on her leash. Now!" Turning to the sheriff, she began, "Sheriff, I... "

"Right. My name's Pat Garrett." He held out his hand. "And you might be... ?"

"I'm Junee Bailey, Sheriff Garrett. I'm a veterinarian; Sophia and I were just going to Dr. Clary's clinic. Perhaps you know him? He owns the Peaseford Valley Veterinary Clinic? We are considering purchasing it. But what to do now!"

"Right. Well, I think first things first. We need to get this van off the road. From the look of it, you better not be drivin' it very far, but maybe it can go far enough to reach the turnout just down the road here. Sophia and her canine can load up with me, and you give 'er a try, see if you can follow. Then I'll get you to Clary's from there—it ain't far."

She might have been nervous about letting Sophia ride with someone who was still a stranger, cop or not, but she had little choice without making a scene. Sophia had already snatched up Sneaker and was clambering into the sheriff's car. With a sigh, Junee got back into her van, which grumbled and fizzed, then with a final whoosh of steam began to roll, creeping behind the sheriff as he set a considerate pace down the road. In her rearview mirror, Junee examined the retreating slice of roadway that was the cause of her trouble and uttered a last imprecation. "Damn this place already," she said, then turned her face to struggle with the windshield crack that ran exactly across her field of vision.

3

NOT NORMALLY A GARRULOUS MAN, Garrett reached without comment for the two suitcases Junee pulled from the van. Not ever a dependent woman, Junee shook her head and said, "It's okay. I've got them." Then she hesitated before opening the sheriff's car door, looking back. "Will I need to do something tomorrow about that deer carcass, report what I did or something?"

Tugging at his mustache, thoughtful, Garrett said, "Nah. You know what? Old Bennie Senderson, the DOW man in these parts, he lives just up the road here. I'll let him know, and he'll deal with it." He slipped the car into gear and started to pull onto the dark road when his radio crackled, causing Sophia, in the back seat, to sit forward, alive with interest, and Sneaker, now beside her on the seat, to focus on her mistress. The voice on the radio was crisp and officious.

"Car 101. This is Riversmet."

Garret sighed. "Go ahead."

"Sheriff, my guess is that you are already up in the Croissant area. We need you to respond to a possible hit and run."

Garrett's annoyed grunt was audible this time. In the first place, he could have stayed all night with Jenny, which is where he always wanted to be anyhow, these days, but he had to testify in court early tomorrow. He figured he could save him and Jenny having to get up crack of dawn by just running on down this evening, checking on stuff at his own house, and getting some paperwork done at the office. These good plans had seemed only mildly interrupted by this woman and her deer accident, but now a "possible" hit and run? What the hell did that mean? And in the second place, how did they always seem to know more about his business than he did?

"Dispatch, I need the address of the R. P."

"Yes, Sir. Reporting party is at 2440 Old Grand Road, Croissant. Near you, right?"

Garrett ignored her question. None of her business. To the radio he said, "Copy that," then turned to Junee. "Look, I'm sorry, Ms. Bailey, but we're gonna have to take a little detour before we can get you to the vet clinic."

Before Junee could respond, Sophia's head appeared across the back of the seat, her eyes big with excitement. "Why, that is perfectly all right, Officer. We are here to offer our services in any way that they may be needed."

Lips grim, Junee turned to her daughter and snapped, "Sophia Bailey, you sit back down and buckle your seat belt."

They turned left shortly onto a graveled road that twisted its way west, climbing, then dropping again into the dark. The sheriff was quiet and the isolation of the area made Junee feel anxious. She turned to look back, and saw a full moon edging over the mountains to the east. Already it had begun to illuminate the landscape; she could see now that they were working their way past farm land, irrigated pastures, and an occasional house or old barn. Then there was another one of those signs, a small, unobtrusive one. Not much money in that particular campaign. It simply read, "Bennie Senderson. Best Choice for Commissioner."

Venturing to break the silence, Junee commented, "Looks like there might be an election coming up."

Garrett, lost deep in contemplation as to whether he dared propose marriage to Jenny, struggled to the surface, trying to find a context for this woman's comment. "Uh… yeah. Sure is."

"All the signs," Junee continued. "I seem to be seeing a lot of signs for county commissioner."

Now back in the present, Garrett nodded. "Right. I guess from what Jenny says, uh, Jenny's my… " he hesitated. My what? This was the problem. He and Jenny were too old to be called girlfriend and boyfriend, weren't they? That sounded not only juvenile, but obsolete. Untangling his tongue, he finished, "… my friend. She lives here in District 2, which is this Croissant/Peaseford area. Anyhow, I guess the race here is hotly contested this year. Not so much in District 1, which is the county seat, you know, Riversmet. And District 3, on down the line, that just has one candidate. So she's a shoo-in. But up here there's all sorts of economic issues, coal and agriculture and so-on, and these three people are really duking it out. See, we're passing old Senderson's place, just over there to the left. He's one of the candidates.

"Oh." Junee peered out the window at a well-kept log house set back from the road on a small rise. As it receded behind them she could make out a tidy lawn, flower beds, possibly gnomes and a flamingo. Sitting forward, she added, "Doesn't his campaign have much money? His signs are so small."

"Well, he's an old-timer. He's probably pretty careful with his funds. I suspect he relies on face to face interaction with all the people he knows around here."

"Didn't you say Senderson was… Is he the one you're going to call about that deer?"

"Yeah, he's the Department of Wildlife man for this area. Has been forever. I kind of think he was employed here even before the park system built the Croissant Reservoir."

"Wow," said Junee, not really sure of the significance of the statement, since she didn't know anything about the Croissant Reservoir. Was it that little puddle of water she'd passed before entering Croissant? She seemed to recall a sign. Hmmmm. Deciding not pursue the reservoir issue, she said, "What about the other candidates? I saw a lot of signs for Gump."

"Yeah, there's Gump. He lives on up the road a ways here. Just before your vet clinic. Jenny doesn't think much of him."

Uncertain what to say to that, Junee was quiet. Glancing back at Sophia, Junee could see that, as usual, she was taking everything in. Garrett spoke again. "There to your left, that's Jim Patchit's place. He's another old-timer, big buddy of Senderson." As Junee glimpsed a log cabin which, unlike the earlier one, seemed not to have had any attention paid to it since the *Mayflower* crossed, Garrett slowed and pulled into a short driveway, saying, "And here we are. 2440 Old Grand Road." He parked along the circular drive that fronted the white frame house as several women emerged from the front door and hurried toward him across the yard.

Junee got out of the car when the sheriff did. She couldn't

resist. "As they say," she thought, "The apple didn't fall far from the tree. I'm just as nosey as Sophia."

Garrett cleared his throat and began, "Someone here reported..."

A large, bottle-blond woman with a face that would have made mashed potatoes look pretty reached the sheriff before the others with long, ground-devouring strides. She grabbed his hand and shook it vigorously. "Howdy, Sheriff. Howdy. Glad you come. You know, I seen you way earlier goin' up Pinyon Point, headed for that Jenny's, and I just told Gritty, here, we needed to get you stopped in case you was headin' back down to Riversmet, 'cause you oughta have a look here while them tire tracks is still fresh."

"I see." Garrett squinted at her. "Maybe I do recall right. Aren't you Mrs. Dash? Letitia, is it? Are you the person who called in a hit and run?"

Pushing in front of Letitia, a slightly younger and smaller woman also grabbed Garrett's hand. "I actually reported it, Sheriff. You probably know me, too. Maureen Macklinburg. I'm a reporter."

Garrett momentarily wished for his detective, Hobbs. Hobbs had an incredible memory; he would recall this Maureen Whatever and whatever it was that she reported. Garrett couldn't, and he sensed she would be offended about that, so he just said, "Well, very good. Can you tell me what happened?"

By now at least a half dozen women had congregated in the yard, including one who had briskly rolled herself out in a wheelchair. Maureen said, "Well, I didn't really see it. Carol, here, will have to tell you. It was her that saw him hit Sassy." She pushed forward a small, chubby woman in a flowing caftan. Junee stared. Who were all these women? This one appeared to be only in her mid-twenties, and she sported thick, shiny black hair and eyelashes that ravished even in the dim yard light.

Carol started, "Uh," and Garrett said, "Sassy?" and Maureen said, "Sassy's Carol's dog. Her best one. Tell him, Carol!" Garrett cleared his throat and looked at Carol expectantly.

"Well, uh, this is my place, and I have sheep, Bennie and I, we both have sheep, you know, Bennie Senderson, down the road there. And we both have sheep dogs. Trained dogs. And tonight was the bimonthly meeting of... well, I guess you'd call it bimonthly. We meet every two weeks, the one kind of the business, grief meeting I guess you'd call it, and the other we think of as a kind of get-back-into-the-world meeting and we go to a movie or something." She looked for support to the other women, now closely clustered together behind her. Junee realized all the women were wearing black. WTF? What was this?

"So this was the business meeting, here at my house. For this month. So, we were done talking and I had just handed around some dessert when..."

Sophia burst out, her voice bouncy and full of jolly good cheer. "So, who are all you people? You all look like witches. Are you all witches?"

Junee gasped. "Sophia, hush. Don't interrupt." She dropped a heavy hand on her child's shoulder, but she thought, "My question exactly."

Everyone's face had turned toward Sophia, all taken aback, but it was the woman in the wheelchair who chuckled. "No, kiddo, we're just women trying to keep from becoming witches. We're all widows. All of us here have lost our husbands, and we're sad, so sometimes we feel like witches. So we get together to try to feel better."

A ruffled, red-eyed woman with an unhappy mop of brown hair flying loose from its seams gave a healthy sniffle and said, "We call ourselves the Black Widders. My husband, Lester, he got shot less than a year ago, and there isn't a day goes by I don't yearn for him purely to death."

A woman beside her patted her arm, saying, "You're gonna be okay, Deb. Time will heal."

Deb gave another large sniffle as someone passed her a tissue, and she mumbled, "Time might heal, but I won't forget. I will never forgive Arnold Clenting. Billy Ray should've never married him in the first place. She... "

The wheelchair woman spoke crisply. "Later, Deb, honey. Now we must let Carol tell the sheriff what happened."

Garrett, taking in the conversation with some amazement, quickly righted himself to say, "Yes, please do, Ms.... ?"

"Haddon. I'm Carol Haddon. Anyhow, some time during the meeting Sassy had asked to go out; she gave her little yip at the kitchen door. Sheriff, my dogs are good dogs. They don't run, and I don't restrict them much. They know where they're supposed to be, and I trust them not to stray. So, while I was handing out dessert, I realized Sassy hadn't come back, but I wasn't worried. I thought I'd just go to the door and call her on in.

"Well, I went to the door and I saw her across the road, snuffling around in the grass, like dogs do, there by the mailbox. Everyone was getting ready to leave anyhow, so I stepped on out, right over there, by the road, and said, 'Come on in, Sassy. Bedtime.' And she looked up all sweet-faced and obedient and started toward me, and..." Carol's voice broke as she choked back tears.

The big blond woman growled, "All the rest of us, we saw what happened then. That car, it shot up the hill like it had just been waitin' in the holler down there at the bottom, other side of Jim's. Heard the motor grindin' and roarin'. And Sassy was tryin' to come to Carol, and Carol put her hand out and shouted, 'No! Wait, Sass!' but the car, well, it was a truck. It kept comin' and the dog kept tryin' to reach Carol and..."

Maureen cut in. "What we saw, Sheriff, was that car swerved toward Carol and the dog. We all saw it. We saw it just miss Carol, and the bumper, I guess, it caught Sassy. But we saw that woman swing out, right toward Carol, and she was just inches from Carol when she roared off."

Garrett said, "I thought you said 'him' earlier. Was the driver a woman or a man?"

A little babble of voices resulted in disagreement, so Garrett interjected, "Well, did anyone get a make on the vehicle?"

Again, a discussion until a woman, who might have been judged plain had she not revealed a huge, glowing, conspiratorial smile, turned to Garrett. "Well, sheriff, aren't we something? We are agreed it was a small pickup, blue, probably old, but none of us knows if it was Ford, Chevy, or what. Gritty saw a bit of the license plate, UBS something, but that's pretty general, too, I'm afraid."

"I can show you the tire tracks," the large blond said.

Tugging his mustache, Garrett said, "All right," but Junee interjected. "But where is Sassy?"

"Oh, we worked a blanket under her, got her to the porch there. She cried a little, but we wanted to watch her awhile before we called Doc. You know how hard it is to get him out at night. And it's gettin' worse. I blame that Annabelle."

Sophia jumped in. "Who's Annabelle?"

Maureen did a double take; she hadn't noticed the little girl. "Oh, that's right. You aren't from around here. People around here know Annabelle. She's Doc's wife. Real weird. Cold and stand-offish."

Before Sophia could ask more, Junee said, "Could I have a look at Sassy? I'm a veterinarian. I left my instruments back, well, there was an accident, and they're back in my van, but maybe I could see something of how she is."

Curiosity crossed Carol's face, but all she said was, "Oh, I see. Well, by all means; I'm sure it won't hurt if you have a look at her." She led the way, and everyone started to troop along behind, but Garrett said, "I think some of you wanted to show me tire tracks. I'll get a light, and you women except Carol follow me to the road. I may have questions."

Carol and Junee pulled the blanket, bringing the dog into the light from the porch bulb, and at Junee's request Carol fetched a flashlight. Sassy lay on her side, panting. Junee shone the light into her eyes, pulling aside the lids, then opened her mouth, examining the gums. "Not too pale," she thought. "What a pretty little thing. Maybe Border Collie mix." Gently, she felt around the little dog's body, probing for sore spots and finding a few, then she noticed larger abrasions on the right stifle. "See these, Carol? I'd like to see what she does when she tries to walk. Could you go over there and encourage her to come to you?"

Junee carefully lifted Sassy to her feet as Carol took a position a few feet away, patted her knee, and coaxed, "Come now, Sassy."

Holding up her right leg, the little dog tried to negotiate the space on the remaining three, whimpering as she stumbled, but Junee stopped her at once. "That's enough. Here, come and hold her while I look at that knee of hers." They bent over the dog and Junee palpated her right leg. This caused Sassy to cry and snap toward the vet, but Junee knew what it was and stopped at once.

"Carol, I'm feeling drawer motion at that joint. I think she has a ruptured cruciate ligament. Otherwise, she's probably okay. Her color is good; her eyes are clear."

"Well, I... Well, thank you. I don't know what else to say.

Oh, poor little Sassy! But at least she's alive."

"Of course, but that tear is so painful to her. She needs to go in to the clinic. The sheriff was just driving me there when, uh, who was it? Maureen? When she called. I had an accident, you know, hit a deer, and Mr. Garrett offered to take me on to Dr. Clary's. Would you be all right with me taking her in with us?"

"Oh. Well, surely. But do you think you can get Doc to see her tonight? I know he'd see her if he knew what happened, but I guess... well, I think Annabelle kind of blocks him off after hours. Tries to protect him from so much work, I guess. Or something."

Junee was shocked. "Well I... well, I... He is expecting me. Surely he would see this little dog."

"Oh, he will. He will. He's a very kind man. It's just that Annabelle...." Her voice tapered off.

The sheriff was standing with the women, gazing at the dusty gravel road and rubbing at the back of his neck. "No, Ma'am," he was saying, "I don't like the look of it either, but so far there's no evidence that a crime was committed here. Even if we could find the pickup, the driver could just swear that he or she swerved to avoid Ms. Haddon and accidentally clipped her dog."

Overriding the chorus of voices that greeted this decision, Garrett stated firmly, "I will promise to make a file on this, to be ready in case anything else comes up." Then he looked up with some relief to see Junee approaching.

It was only after they got Sassy loaded and the widows were leaving that Junee realized that Sophia hadn't been directly in the middle of things for quite some time. "Sophia," she shouted, anxious again. "Where are you?"

A hushed voice came from the shadows under a well-branched, tall fruit tree on the east side of the Haddon yard. "Shh, Mom. I'm here. You be quiet and come over here to look, but shut up and be quiet, okay?"

Tired and anxious to reach Clary's, Junee grumbled, "No, Sophia, just come on. It's time to go; come on now."

"I won't, Mom. You hush and come here. And be quiet. Don't scare it, okay?"

Wearily, Junee trudged toward her. What a day this had been, and it didn't feel close to getting over yet. She was resisting an urge to shake this daughter, grab that darned Sneaker, and drag them both to the car. Sophia was pointing up, pointing at the tree, pointing at the full moon behind the tree, or... at what? What was she pointing at?

Then Junee saw it. Well up in the tall tree, several branches high, was a dog. It was looking down with great interest at Sophia and Sneaker, and it seemed very pleased with itself. Sophia's face was filled with wonder. "It's a dog, Mom! I saw it climb that tree. I really did see it! It's a dog, and it climbed itself all the way up into that tree!"

4

"OH, THAT'S JUST BUDDY, Jim's dog. He's been climbing trees since he was a pup." Carol had been making her way back to the house after waving at her departing guests when she saw Junee and Sophia standing transfixed under the tree. For the first time since Sassy had been hit, she smiled. "You know, we're kind of used to him around here, and I guess you're going up to Clary's, so you'll probably see a lot of him and Jim there. Jim and Doc are big pals, and Jim likes to hang out over there. He's pretty proud of this dog, so I'm sure you'll hear all about it."

"But how does he *do* it?" Sophia was still agog "Can he come down?"

"He jumps into the tree where he can get purchase. He can jump, well, maybe six feet high. See that hollow above the trunk there where the branches take off? He jumps there, then braces his feet between branches and limbs and climbs on up. It's fun to watch, because he walks up backwards."

"But can he get down?" Sophia insisted. Then, to the dog, "Here Buddy. Come on down. Come on, boy."

"He'll come down when he's ready, or when Jim wants him. I don't think he'll come for you, though, honey. He's very much Jim Patchit's dog."

Junee, also, was still staring at the dog, who smiled back. "What, um, I mean, is this the only tree he can climb?"

"Oh, no, he'll climb anything. Apricot, globe willow, cedar... He climbs for fun, but mostly he likes to climb up after squirrels and birds. He goes up wherever he can get purchase. This is his favorite tree, though, because it's right here between Jim's and my place. It gives him a good view of what's going on."

The sheriff had approached. "I heard about this dog from Jenny. First time I saw him, though. He's quite a dog, ain't he?"

This comment returned Junee to thoughts of her need to get to her original destination. "He really is! But I guess we'd better not hold you up, Mr. Garrett. Come on, Sophia, let's get poor little Sassy to Dr. Clary."

As they pulled out of Haddon's drive, Sophia said, "Wow! That dog was awesome!" Junee agreed, but her fear that Sophia would start up with a string of endless comments, as she sometimes did with respect to the wondrous phenomena she often encountered in her unfolding world, proved unfounded. To her mother's relief, she settled back against the seat and all that could be heard after that was a stream of tender muttering as she fussed over Sassy. All else being quiet, Junee studied the landscape as it rolled past. To her right were dry adobe hills, unappealing to her. She knew that in this area they would call them dobies, and have ATV races on them. It made her tired.

A road took off to the left, clearly marked as Forest Road, and sure enough. In the moonlight she could see stands of pinyon and juniper thickening as the land rose away from the road. Seeing her looking toward, them, Garrett said, "There's some kind of settlement on past those trees a ways. I don't know what they are, survivalists or a religious group or what. Then in a few minutes you'll see Gump's place."

"Okay, thanks. I'll watch." The silence broken, she ventured a question. "What did you think of those widows back there, Sheriff Garrett?"

He shot her a glance. "Well, probably helps 'em to be around other people in the same pickle."

"Yes." Junee watched as the road twisted against the trees. "Yes. You know, I'm also a widow."

"You are? Oh, I'm sorry." His face said that he was, so Junee continued.

"His helicopter went down over the Persian Gulf. Ethan's. There were no survivors."

Again, Garrett said, "I'm sorry. Hell of a deal."

"Well, it's been almost seven years now, so the shock is past. You never get over it, though. Maybe if I stay here, I can check out the widow organization, see what they're like, maybe try to join."

"Could be supportive, I guess."

A short silence, and Junee thought to herself, "Supportive, maybe. And maybe a lead to the woman I'm looking for." The forest was giving way to pasture land again, and out loud Junee said, "Did we pass Gump's?"

"Ah, hell, it was just back there. I forgot to show you. We're coming up on the vet clinic now. Down there to the right."

With that, a voice piped in from the back. "Yes, Sir, Sheriff Garrett, I do believe I see it. Thank you. Sassy, we have almost arrived, and you will be cared for at long last."

Junee sighed, but she did lean forward to look. The sign beside the gate was partially faded but she could make it out. "Peaseford Valley Veterinary Clinic." And the place, well, it didn't look all that bad. A short gravel drive, a large, graveled parking area, a paved walkway leading to the entrance. It was a brick, ranch style building, nothing fancy, somewhat rambling. She could just make out some dog runs to the side. In the back, there were some outbuildings of some sort. There was a small lawn; there were several trees, and she couldn't resist a quick glance up to assure herself that they didn't contain dogs. "Jeez, I am tired. I am getting like Alice down that rabbit hole." The thought amused her.

The clinic was pitch dark, only a tiny light over the entrance step. Garrett pulled at his mustache. "You know, Ma'am, there isn't a chance in the world that you will catch Doc down here this time of night. You want to drive on up to the house? We could try, and if that don't work, there's a little motel in Peaseford might help out for one night."

Junee looked at the clinic with longing, and then across the road where a large white house topped a small hill. There were lights on at the house. Clarys should be expecting her; she had called earlier. But then, it was late now. Maybe at least late for people around here. What to do?

"But what about Sassy?" came the back seat voice, thick with indignation and alarm. "Sassy needs a doctor and medicine, not a motel."

Junee sighed. "She's right. Let's go disturb the vet."

Garrett had developed an odd little smile, but he said, "Well, we can try." Slipping the car into gear, he set off across the road and pulled up the Clary driveway, stopping at the walkway to the front door. A thin curtain was drawn over the lighted window and, dimly silhouetted against it, were two people in easy chairs, perhaps talking or reading. Maybe TV.

"Oh," Junee was pleased. "It looks as if they're here. Why don't I just go give a knock first, then maybe we can get unloaded and you can be on your way. To Riversmet."

The sheriff still had an odd expression on his face. He rubbed at the back of his neck and looked at the house. "Well, give 'er a try, I guess. Can't hurt."

Junee slipped out of the car and hurried up the walk, eager to bring this evening to a close. She knew there was a lot to get through yet—greet the Clarys, admit the dog and get her some pain medication, try to get settled in the apartment Wheezer had promised, and so-on.

There was no doorbell, so she knocked. One of the figures inside took a sip of something from a cup. From this closer perspective, she was sure it was Wheezer. He leaned back, apparently unable to hear the knock. The woman, his wife, was apparently reading, and continued to do so. Junee shrugged and made the next knock good and loud, pounding really. The people inside seemed to continue as before, oblivious.

She tried a third time, louder if possible, and longer. The silhouettes sat and sipped and read, read and sipped and sat. Defeated, Junee turned to trudge back to the car, her hands spread in surrender. What could she do? Wildly, it occurred to her to just unload Sophia, Sneaker, Sassy, and her suitcases and sleep under a tree in the Clary yard. Then she realized she really had only one choice, and it gave her no way to help the poor dog tonight. The motel. She had almost reached the car when she realized that Garrett was standing beside it, arms folded, watching her.

"So no answer, huh?"

"I guess they can't hear me knock."

Garrett snorted. "They hear you. Doc doesn't want to bother Annabelle. They're ignoring you. I had hoped it wouldn't come to this." He walked around the car and reached in the window, flipping on the flashers. They swept across the front of the house, illuminating the people inside in bold relief, and Garrett strode up the walk, tossing a firm "follow me" over his shoulder. Junee scampered behind.

When he reached the front door, he shoved it open. It wasn't locked. Sticking his head in, he bellowed, "Damn it, Doc, you stubborn old S.O.B., this is the sheriff, Jenny Threewind's boyfriend. I got you a hurt dog here, and a new vet. Now answer the goddamn door."

5

OMG, THIS WAS NOT THE WAY she had planned it! Driving across the passes from Denver, she had visualized herself professionally shaking hands with a twinkly-eyed, rather elfin old fellow. For some reason, she imagined Wheezer had a nice white beard. Later, as she drove from Stoney City, she courteously called the clinic to keep her fellow practitioner informed of the time of her anticipated arrival. She got his answering service, who said the clinic was closed, but that they would let him know. This had led her to hope there might be an invitation into a cozy kitchen, a jolly, roundish veterinary wife to match the bearded elfin man, cup of coffee offered, perhaps a cookie for Sophia, although lord knows the child didn't need the sugar.

Holy crap! There was nothing professional about this meeting! The door the sheriff had slammed open went directly into the living area where the couple had been sitting. Both chairs were now empty; the woman had disappeared completely and magically, and hulking across the floor toward them was no elfin old man. This guy was as tall as Garrett, but not lanky. No, he was solid except for the belly emerging from his large T-shirt and overhanging his belt. He had a beard, all right. A two-day stubble that looked cranky and needed shaved. His head was almost as bald as Garrett's, sporting only some grayish tufts that bravely clung to the territory they had staked out above his ears. "Well, you damn sonuvabitch, Sheriff! This is one helluva way to treat your neighbors. Shouldn't you be out lookin' for some real criminals?" He was raising his hand.

Junee instinctively reached for Sophia, who she knew would have trotted up the walk behind them, but as she looked down she realized her daughter, cuddling Sneaker, was grinning like a Cheshire cat. Now she realized that both men were chuckling. The doctor's raised hand was taking a frayed shirt from a peg near the door as Garrett was saying, "I think I found my damn criminal all right. Ain't there some kinda law says a man's gotta tend to his business once in a while? Like I said, we gotta hurt dog out there and a new vet here that's probably smarter than you ever were, even though she ain't got no medical stuff here to work with."

The doctor jammed his arms into the shirt, then extended a paw toward Junee. "You must be Dr. Bailey. I'm real glad to meet you. What held you up so long?" And, tilting his chin toward Garrett, "And how did you get tangled up with some no-good son-of-a-gun like this?" He buttoned his shirt, started loosening his fly, turned his back to them and proceeded to tuck in the shirt tail.

To his back, Junee said, "I hit a deer. The sheriff came by just after I hit it."

A brief struggle and then the zipper sound; turning around, Clary said, "Hell, that's too damn bad. Both counts. Hittin' a deer, gettin' stuck with the sheriff. I expect he was headed back down country from Jenny's. The man is just like a ping-pong ball." Garrett grunted. Somebody else with their nose in his business. Now fully dressed, Clary started herding them all out the door and closed it firmly behind him. "I'll just follow you on over to the clinic in my truck. Wanta ride over with me, Sis?"

This question, directed at her daughter, surprised Junee. She hadn't been sure that Clary even realized Sophia was there. Sophia, however, was on it as usual. "I am not 'Sis,' Dr. Clary. I am Sophia, and I, also, am pleased to meet you. This dog, which is not the hurt one, is Sneaker."

"Oh, Soapy, you say. Well, bring that thing that pretends to be a canine along and we can discuss whatever it is you did to deserve a moniker like Soapy." Before Sophia could object, he started across the lawn, so she trailed behind. Only now did Junee see Doc Clary's age. What she hadn't noticed in her initial surprise as he lurched across the living room was that he limped. A lot. He shuffled toward the battered vet truck, dragging his right leg with some effort. Was it his knee? Sciatica? Suddenly she experienced an unexpected pang of sympathy. This man was real, not a fiction. She watched as he helped Sophia scramble up into the high interior of the truck, then drag to the other side and pull his own body in. Turning to Garrett, she baffled him with the statement, "I will never again call that man Wheezer."

They unloaded Sassy and set her on the exam table, her pain and worry causing her to pant frantically. Junee ventured, "I think it is a ruptured cruciate, Doctor."

Quickly exploring the dog with his large hands, Dr. Clary said, "And I think you are right. Let's give her something now to help her rest; we can deal with it tomorrow."

Junee felt surprisingly at home as they worked over the dog. Surprising, because the exam room and the waiting room were one room, all decidedly tatty. Having interned at Angell Memorial in Boston, she was used to a high level of strictness and formality, but still, bottom line, here it was: a place dedicated to treating and repairing sick and wounded animals. It felt right. She could see the surgery, too, through the open door behind Doc Clary. She couldn't help herself; she was starting to like this place.

Sophia tagged after Doc as he put Sassy in her cage, assuring herself that he was doing it right. When they returned to the waiting room, Doc said, "Well, it's been a long day, Dr. Bailey. Sheriff. I bet you two could stand a spot of coffee, and I've got some beer here for the kid."

Sophia and Junee both gasped, Sophia squeaking, "Beer!"

Garrett chuckled and Doc Clary said innocently, "Oh, did I say beer? I meant root beer, all right, Soapy? Let's get that, then we can all visit a while."

With that, Garrett said, "Honestly, Doc, it has been a lot longer day than I'd planned. If I can trust you with these two, I'm gonna unload a couple of suitcases and get on my way on down to Riversmet."

"You're sayin' Riversmet, right? Not Miss Jenny's? Gonna finally tend to business?" Doc was grinning; he just couldn't resist a final poke.

Shaking his head, Garrett replied, "Give me a break, you old coot."

After the sheriff left, Junee finally got her coffee and cookies. Doc sat her and Sophia down in the waiting room. Just behind the exam table were cabinets and a refrigerator filled with samples of animal tissue and manure, vials of blood marked for the lab, vaccines, drugs, and apparently a variety of snacks. While the coffee brewed, he rummaged around in the fridge area to produce a generous sampling of venison jerky, some sliced cheddar, a stack of Ritz crackers, a sack of ginger snaps, and a bottle of root beer. He coated a paper towel with disinfectant, gave the exam table a swipe, and set out the food.

Junee was ever so grateful for the coffee and surprisingly happy to work on the snacks. It really was cozy, this room! Sophia had perched on a chair that was too high for her, thus freeing her legs to swing as she swigged pop, ate cookies, and took in her surroundings. Bowls had been produced for Sneaker. She gave the water a cursory lap and haughtily sniffed the scoop of dog food, then turned her back on it with queenly revulsion. Instead of eating, she stalked the room, greedily inhaling the bouquet of scents from the doggy traffic that had preceded her here.

They didn't talk business. There was a phatic discussion of the weather, of the trip from Denver, of the unhappy event of hitting a deer. Sophia broke it up with a blunt interjection. "Dr. Clary, where are we supposed to sleep? I am getting tired."

Doc laughed. "You're a kid really knows her own mind. I think you're not the only one worn out — mine and Annabelle's bedtime passed quite a while back. Come on with me and we'll see if your new digs are gonna suit you."

The promised apartment turned out to be an addition at the back of the clinic. They entered a door leading down a short hallway from the surgery, then a door that opened directly into a living area. The living area itself was all in one, couch and end tables; a kitchen alcove demarcated by a counter; chairs and table. Opposite the door that entered from the clinic was a sliding door; Doc walked over to flip a light and through the glass they could see a small fenced yard, hollyhocks high in the corner, a rosebush blooming red by the step. Back inside, he opened doors and switched on lights, revealing a big bedroom and a tiny bedroom separated by a bathroom and closets. Junee was fascinated to see that many small touches had been undertaken to make the place inviting: a colorful entry rug; a glass mobile at the kitchen window ready to catch the morning light; and here, on the beds, were handmade quilts. Quilts that someone had spent many hours arranging and stitching. Who had done that, she wondered. They were unique and beautiful. The tour ended in the small bedroom and Doc said, "Well, how's it all look?"

Before Junee could respond, Sophia shed her shoes and, clutching Sneaker, flopped on her bed, declaring dramatically, "Home at last! Oh, praise God, we are home at last! Oh, my goodness, it looks quite wonderful. Thank you, Dr. Clary."

6

THERE WAS BACON. She was starving. Somewhere in the distance, dogs barked. Sunlight pried at her eyelids. Bacon. And voices, one a troll and one Sophia and … She jerked up; Oh! It was the clinic bedroom. Yes, she did hear voices, Sophia's and the troll's not far from her bedroom door. What the hell? The bedroom that was supposed to be part of her private apartment for her stay at the Peaseford Veterinary Clinic? Her feet hit the floor.

It wasn't a troll, but maybe some kind of wizard. He and Sophia were sitting at the table eating, and beside the old man was Buddy, out of his tree. The troll was talking about him. "Yup, he loves to chase squirrels all right, but once he got his comeuppance. He shot up a tree after a squirrel, then slipped and down he went. Hurt his hip. And another time he caught a bird." The troll chuckled, a forbiddingly deep sound. "He didn't know what to do with that bird. Had it, now what! You could see the surprise in his eyes."

Sophia, who had never liked eggs, stuffed in a gob-stopping forkful of fried egg and leaned forward, wide-eyed. Then she spotted Junee. "Oh, hi Mom." The troll jumped to his feet, shoving aside his chair and dropping a slice of bacon, which Buddy accepted with gratitude and grace. He extended a friendly hand, and "Good morning, Dr. Bailey" emerged as a distant rumble from his chest, slowly giving voice to the words his lips formed. It was he who had the white beard Junee had planned for Dr. Clary. "Doc told me about your problem with the car. Figured you hadn't got any groceries yet."

"Yeah, Mom. He knocked and I got a chair and looked through the peek hole and saw Buddy, so I knew it was okay to let him in."

So much for the "don't let in strangers" lecture. Instead, Junee scrabbled in her brain for the man's name. "Mr. Patchit, is it?"

"Yes, Ma'm. Call me Patch. I brought plenty. Sit right there—I'll get you coffee."

"My phone's in the bedroom. I need to know what time it is." Junee turned to go back, but Sophia pointed to the kitchen area. "Clock's right there, Mom. Cool, huh?"

On the wall above the counter a clock shaped like a cat had been affixed, its tail hanging down, its eyes rolling back and forth. It ticked and tocked, and with each tick and tock its tail and eyes moved. They moved in opposite directions. Tick, tail left, eyes right. Tock, tail right, eyes left. It was mesmerizing. Tick, Junee's eyes left; tock, Junee's eyes right... With a shake of her head, she snapped free. "8:20 already! Good grief, I should be able to call a garage by now." Again, she started for the phone, then she noticed the disappointment on her companions' faces. "Uh, yeah, I could eat with you right after I call. But I need to help Dr. Clary with Sassy." She felt uneasy and out of place, anxious to get control of her own situation again. "Mr. Patchit, what auto mechanic do you recommend? I can get my phone, get them called."

Patch and Sophia answered at the same time, Sophia saying, "Sassy's okay; I went to see her; Dr. Clary called Ms. Haddon, and then went out to look at a lame horse, and he told her he'll take care of her dog when he gets back;" while Patch said, "Call me Patch, Ma'm; only one mechanic in Peaseford; Marco; Marco's Motors; I figure he'll fix you up okay; they tow, too; no hurry, he'll get to it when he can; you got all day."

Her eyes swiveling like the cat's, from one speaker to the other, she reached across Sophia and absently grabbed a slice of bacon. One bite distractedly down the hatch, and she thought, "Uh, oh, now that was a sialagogue." Ah! So she was still herself! She hadn't lost her grip—she was still a vet. She still thought in words like sialagogue—the bacon was a sialagogue that had made her drool like one of Pavlov's dogs. She wanted the coffee, too, and the egg, and the fat, round pancake. She looked at the wide grins on the faces of the two characters sitting at the table and felt her shoulders relaxing. What the hell? They were right;

she was here; she was hungry; and she had all day. She grinned back, sat down, and loaded up her fork.

MARCO, THE TOWING MECHANIC, agreed to a loaner car. Junee asked how much, and he said, "Nah, that'll be fine."

What did that mean? Not sure how to negotiate 'fine,' Junee said, "Well, we've got some surgery here, then I'll see if Dr. or maybe even Mrs. Clary might be able to drop me by to pick it up." Marco snorted.

"Nah, Doc's busy and you know Mrs. Clary. Me and my missus will run it up pretty soon."

Well, then. Junee actually felt she didn't know Mrs. Clary, but she thought she might be getting an idea. Well, maybe. Was Annabelle Clary just a woman with her own life and a lot on her mind, or was she some kind of uncooperative, cranky, antisocial veterinary spouse? Junee also realized that she wasn't clear on when "pretty soon" would be, so she left Sophia and Jim Patchit puttering busily away in the kitchen and went into the clinic.

Dr. Clary had already told her that he didn't have a receptionist, just an answering service. "Cole comes over to tend the animals twice a day, then he'll come over for tech stuff if I need him." The clinic was empty, so apparently this wasn't Cole's tech time. Half a dozen dogs and cats and one bird were in the cages. The bird, a magpie, had a splint on its wing. It hopped to the cage front, tipped its head, and croaked. The other animals looked up with interest but didn't set up a hullabaloo; apparently Cole had already tended to their needs for this morning.

She put a hand in the cage to pet Sassy, who whimpered. "Still hurts, doesn't it, little girl. It won't be long now, I don't think."

Junee had gone on into the surgery to look things over when Dr. Clary came back from his call. The surgery looked great. She pegged the Doc as a fashion disaster in the personal department but with major OCD about his professional tools. Everything from scrapers to scalpels was clean and in its place. When he walked in, she gave herself points for being right. Doc had shaved, but his coveralls and battered shoes had seen more than one barnyard since having been washed, and his collar was so frayed it was a miracle it remained attached to the shirt. He seemed pleased to see her, and as they set about repairing Sassy, he described the damaged hoof on the horse he'd just seen, joked about eccentric clients, and asked her about the dairy practice where she'd worked in New York after she left Angell Animal Medical Center.

They were mid-surgery when Marco and Mrs. Marco walked into the room. Doc said jovially, "Hey, there, Marco, you old grease bucket. Still draggin' the missus along to do your work for you?"

Realizing who it was, Junee said, "Oh, you've brought the car." She thought, "What are they doing in the surgery?" She looked down at the sterile, open wound on the sleeping dog and back up at the couple, who both wore coveralls and grimy sleeveless tees and looked as if they'd just crawled through a gulf state oil spill. "Thank you, then," she told them. "We won't be long now, if you'd like to just go out to the waiting area and…"

Marco said, "Nah. We like to watch Doc work. He'd make a great mechanic if he was just smart enough."

Junee shot her eyes to Doc, but he was focused on stitching. "Too bad, ain't it," he said as he skillfully joined tissue with sutures that should have been far too delicate for his heavy hands. "Too bad it ain't possible to find anybody in this whole valley smart enough to fix a simple car."

Seriously? Junee gave up, and now the four of them bent over the ruptured cruciate, commenting on the probable outcome of the surgery ("She'll probably have a permanent limp, won't she, Doc?" "Nah, she'll do okay."), as well as the source of the injury. ("Doc Bailey here says it was over at Haddon's. Thing was, some of them Black Widders was out and they told Garrett it was a pickup truck actually tried to hit Carol Haddon. Swerved and hit her best sheep dog." "Who done it?" "Can't say. Wouldn't put it past Gump, or even Clenting. He's a brute…") And so it went.

Jim Patchit came in from the apartment and tight on his heels were Buddy and Sophia, carrying Sneaker. Peeling his gloves, Doc said, "Hey, Patch." Mrs. Marco said, "Hey, looka that little bitty dog." Before Sophia could respond with her 'size of a sneaker' schtick, Marco said, "Nah, ain't a dog. That's just half a dog. Where'd you leave the other half, Sis?" This last drew a chuckle from the adults, but Sophia was sober and wary.

Chewing her gum with renewed vigor, Mrs. Marco held out

her arms. "Lemme hold it."

Eying the oily mechanic, Sophia gripped Sneaker more tightly, took two steps back, and said, "She's not an 'it.' She's a girl."

Patch intervened. "Now you leave little Soapy alone. She just got here."

Thinking to rescue her daughter, Junee said, "It's okay, and besides, Sophia, Mr. and Mrs. Marco are lending us a car until the van can be fixed. Now we can go get groceries and pick up the rest of our stuff. You need to get ready to go. Shower, change your clothes."

Turning horrified eyes toward her mother, Sophia said, "No, Mom! I've gotta stay here. There's a guy coming here with an invisible dog. He's the only one that can see it. I want to see if I can see it."

Doc said to Patch, "So, Lew's comin' up?"

The slow rumble, "Yeah, him and Bennie. We wanna work on that shed roof out back."

The men continued talking, but Mrs. Marco knelt by Sophia and said, "It's all right, kid. I ain't gonna hurt your little dog. I think she's real cute. And just between you and me," she winked, "I ain't no Mrs. Marco, just like you ain't really a Soapy. I'm Doris Diberry, and my hubby there is Marco Diberry." She extended a muscular arm covered from wrist to shoulder and beyond with tattooed names, hearts, flowers, angels, and skulls, and gently petted Sneaker, then she stood up and directed a louder voice toward Junee. "Anyhow, Dr. Bailey, we better do some key tradin' here. Here's the keys to the little Civic. You got your van keys?"

Rummaging in her pocket for her keys, Junee said, "Maybe we could fill out the paperwork here on the exam table?"

Marco sent her a 'you are a strange woman' frown. "Nah, no paperwork. Got a phone number we can reach you at?"

He wrote her cell number on his hand. Doc looked up. "If she don't get reception here, just call me or Patch." Junee followed them to the door to watch as they climbed into a major tow truck, Mrs. Marco taking the driver's seat. They pulled out, and a little red pickup pulled up and parked beside the Civic. An old man was driving. Another old man. Jeez!

Behind her she heard Doc say, "Soapy, could you take Sassy

and put her in that clean lower cage?" She whirled to object; Sophia was too young to handle client animals. Damage! Death! Lawsuits! Her protest died on her lips. Sophia had set Sneaker down, and Doc was handing her the anesthetized dog. Ever so carefully, her little arms slipped under it. "Support her a bit more right here," Doc said, moving the dog into a safer position. Everyone watched as Sophia, literally on tiptoe, eased her way into the cage room. Kneeling by the open cage, she tenderly slipped the dog onto the newspaper and set up a quiet cooing. Doc had already turned away, but he smiled to himself as he commented, "Regular little dove she is, isn't she?"

Before Junee could think if she should respond, the old man from the parking area came in. He was stooped but had a determined gait, and under his mane of white hair was a strong, heavy head and a face displaying a look of fury. "You know what that sonuvabitch means? I just found out. You know what he means?"

Patch had found a seat on a waiting room chair, and Buddy was walking around the room, holding his nose on Sneaker's back. Patch rumbled, "Which sonuvabitch, Bennie? We got more than one around here. And good morning to you, too, by the way."

Bennie glowered at the dogs. "What kinda squirrel has that damn Buddy come up with now?"

"Dog belongs to your new vet's kid." Junee had stopped dead center in the room, wondering what to do now. They really needed to know that she might be the new vet, but she might not, too. Doc seemed to be peacefully involved with a ticket pad over on the snack area cabinet. Patch continued, "This here's Dr. Bailey; Ms. Bailey, this is Bennie Senderson. I heard you seen his signs." Directing his thrum toward Bennie he said, "Doc Bailey here had a unfortunate encounter with some good venison last night. Wasted it."

The extended hand, a brisk and hearty shake, and "Pleased to meet you, Ms. Bailey," then back to his initial concern. "Anyhow, apologies, Ms. Bailey. I want these people to know what's behind that slogan of his."

Clary pushed aside the ticket book and said, "Whose slogan?"

"You know whose," Senderson growled. "Who else? That asshole, Gump. Sorry, Ma'm."

"It's okay, we've heard worse." Junee was beginning to want a piece of this. "Which slogan?"

"That cute little, seemingly friendly 'Know Your Neighbor' slogan. That slogan. What he wants is to get everybody watchin' everybody else. He wants to introduce something into the county rules and regs so that if you are suspicious of any of your neighbors, for any reason, you can anonymously turn 'em in. Then that will give the law probable cause, and they can come search their place. He says he specifically has foreigners in mind. Says there's too many of 'em in this country; most of 'em are probably terrorists."

Senderson had their attention. "Wait," Doc asked. "What the hell does that mean?"

"Ha!" Bennie growled, then "Ha!" again. "It means I could call up, not tell 'em who I was, but say that I had seen suspicious activity over here at the clinic, maybe that you were selling drugs or building bombs. Or even just that I believed that the reason Annabelle doesn't get out much is that she is an undocumented alien. Then the law, hopefully Garrett, I guess, but the law would have to come up and search your place."

"Whoa!" Patch said. "Just on somebody's word? Somebody who doesn't have to say who he is?"

"Damn tootin'. The guy's dangerous. Gump. We gotta get him stopped."

Patch grunted, skeptical. "Kinda means vote for you, don't it, Bennie? We vote for Billy Ray, we might get that worthless supposedly-ex husband of hers."

Doc added, "Yeah, like I said, that boy's a brute, that S.O.B., Arnold."

Still stirred up, his face red, Senderson said, "This ain't no campaign ploy. Whether I win or not, we gotta stop Gump."

Sophia had entered the room and her eyes were fixed on Senderson. "Sir," she said, "I must ask you, do you have a dog? A dog I can see?"

Trying to change contexts and figure out what had brought that on, everyone stared at her. Then Patch caught on. "Oh, no, Soapy. This ain't Lew. Lew's the one with the invisible dog. This here is Bennie—he has a bunch of sheepdogs, like Ms. Haddon. He didn't bring 'em."

Bennie said, "Oh, yeah, Lew. Him and Lucky coming?" But

Patch was still addressing Sophia. "Lew'll be here in a minute. And you remember what I told you?"

"Yes, I do. You told me three things. First, to never, ever let Sneaker out to run free away from the clinic, or the coyotes'll get her. Second, never tell Mr. Harris I can't see his dog or that maybe it is just pretend. We all just have to understand that for him it is a real dog and he thinks everyone sees it." Patch nodded; this was enough, but Sophia persisted. "And finally, I must never take Sneaker up to see Annabelle. 'Cause Mrs. Clary absolutely and completely does not like dogs."

For the first time, Senderson grinned. "Smart kid," he said.

But, turning away and under her breath, Sophia muttered, "She might not like all dogs, but I bet she'd like a little dog, a little old dog like Sneaker. How could anybody not like Sneaker?"

7

SHERIFF PAT GARRETT WAS AT HIS DESK. He and his deputy, Leigh McCracken, were taking a break, sipping coffee in companionable silence. He was, in fact, contemplating how to say what he wanted to say to her. As usual, McCracken's mass of red hair looked like a storm-tossed sunset on a windy summer night. The time some people might have spent in hair arrangement she directed toward weight lifting, shooting pool, and climbing mountains. She had a wild look. Even so, Garrett knew that this vigor was poured into her job; she was intense about getting it all right. Yes, Garrett was aware of that and appreciated it. He had finally accepted that toward him she directed unwavering admiration, although he personally felt that this high esteem was clearly misplaced. Still, her attitude made up for the fact that it seemed every time he needed to talk to her, her intensely freckled face was bent over her damned iPhone, lovingly texting his other deputy, Red. And so it was now.

And he wanted to talk to her now. It didn't help that he couldn't decide how to say what he needed to say. He didn't have anything concrete to share with her. It was just that, well, he was an intuitive man—Jenny called him psychic—and he was struggling with a feeling he had about his experience in the Croissant area last night. It would help if he could say it out loud to his deputy. He took another sip of coffee, which brought up an unhappy burp of acid. This coffee was a puddle of rusted mud. A-deet (Edith, the office secretary) must have had it sitting and roiling in the pot since yesterday.

Oh, well, nothing ventured... He cleared his throat and McCracken looked up from her text. "The coffee?" she inquired.

"Gotta get a fresh pot outta that woman one of these days. Just was gonna tell you that they postponed that case, the one I hurried down here so dutifully to testify for. Duval's got them back at the table, trying to plea bargain again."

Sympathetic, McCracken said, "Typical."

"I suppose they'll be after me again before too long at an equally inconvenient time. You know, I left Jenny's and came down last night, since they'd set that thing so early today, but I didn't get here till damn near midnight, I guess, in the end. Ran into a little sheriffing business before I could get away from Croissant."

He had her attention. She set aside her phone. "So what happened, Chief?"

Giving her a run down, he described Junee's encounter with the deer and the call to Carol Haddon's. "The thing is, Mac, I told those women there is nothing we can do about that possible hit and run, which is true. There just isn't substantial evidence, even of a crime, but I left with an uneasy feeling. You know, I did see what they claimed were the tire tracks, and if it happened like they said, I'd say whoever it was did swerve, maybe toward Ms. Haddon."

"So do you think it happened like they said?"

"No reason to doubt them. More interesting, though, was Carol Haddon's demeanor. I wish you'd been there. We could compare notes. I'd say she isn't telling everything. She's holding something back."

McCracken gave a low whistle. "Wow, Chief, do you think she knows who might be after her?"

"I don't know. Maybe. But there are other issues I'm having trouble sorting out. Jenny tells me that the county commissioner campaign up in that district is getting vicious. She says they are going after each other with hammer and tongs, and both Gump and Senderson live along Old Grand Road. Clenting isn't that far away, just down by Peaseford. But I don't see how that could affect Haddon, unless she has a relationship we don't know about. The other thing that crossed my mind when I dropped off the new vet is that Annabelle Clary seems to be just as wacky as she always was. She was clearly at the house when we knocked [Garrett didn't mention the nature of his 'knock'], but she didn't come out. No cheery welcoming hellos for Doc's possible buyer.

"Yeah, Annabelle's reputation has come all the way down here to Riversmet. A cold woman, they say. Won't help Doc at all. Hates dogs."

"But other than the fact that she also lives nearby, what would that have to do with Haddon? I have no clue. Unless maybe it was Annabelle and she swerved to hit the dog, and it just looked as if she was after Carol Haddon."

"So what do we do, Chief?"

Garrett tugged his mustache. "That's the problem. I don't see anything we can do. We're gonna have to just keep our heads up, I guess. Keep an eye on those Black Widders, Haddon, in particular. And, I suppose, Ms. Clary."

8

CAROL HADDON WAS STANDING with her back pressed tightly against a pinyon, concentrating. The tree was very old and had had a good life; it was taller than all the rest of the trees in the pinyon-juniper forest surrounding it. It was twilight, the day after the Widder's meeting, and Will Yelets, watching Carol experience the tree, thought she looked even more beautiful than usual in the soft, diffuse light of the setting sun. Her dusky skin was free of blemish; just the right amount of freckles danced across the high ridge of her nose, and those eyes! Huge, deep green, nestled in the gorgeous black lashes. He wanted to dive right into her eyes and die of the drowning. She slid down the tree to sit and whispered regretfully, "I don't hear anything yet. Not yet, Will."

He sat beside her and took her hand. "It's okay, my darling. I have only heard it once, and I don't hear it tonight. We will keep trying."

Encouragingly, she said, "It will know, I believe. If I understand the Anastasia writings, it will know when it is actually filled with the energy of cosmic light and ready to share. And then we shall hear it."

Will Yelets sighed. "Maarika says that only Russian cedars ring. She says that these trees here are not Siberian pine, and that I can poke around on them all I want, but no tree in America will ever ring."

"She would," Carol snapped. "That's what she'd say." The two were quiet awhile, pushing against each other, a simple need for love, but more, seeking refuge from a storm. The darkness thickened around them.

After a bit, Carol leaned away in order to drink him in once more. "Such a funny farmer," she thought. "American and Russian; F.F.A. and dachniki; hippy and Vedrussian." His blond hair spilled from under his duck-billed Bronco cap, crowning the blue eyes that sparkled in the tan face. A silver earring stud shone in his left ear, defying the worn jeans and heavy boots. Around his mouth was a nest of short, downy yellow hair that was not quite a beard and that yielded readily to his quick, friendly grin. She swallowed a lump of frustrated longing. She longed for his tree to ring. She longed for their lives to be simple and together. "Will, why did you ever marry her!"

He held her closer. "We've been over it. You don't ever need to be jealous. It was so, so long ago, almost ten years now! It is you I love."

"You say it, but... "

"We were kids. With Maarika it was lust, not love. At least for me. For her, I think... well, now I think of it as a scheme. Try to put yourself in my place back then—it was all so exciting! An American exchange student in a Russian high school, seeing some of the things my grandparents remembered from their own youth, learning to speak real Russian—maybe I could talk to them when I returned—and most of all, planning to change the world. Thinking I could be part of bringing enemy countries together and so-on. Thoughts like we all have when we're young."

Carol tried to relax in his arms. "Well, you are still a crusader..."

"But, at the time, there was their dacha, their excitement at making it yield—they grew cucumber, cabbage, potatoes, carrots, everything! It is true, you know. The dachas provide 90 percent of Russia's potatoes.

"And then there was their daughter. She looked a little like you, you know... " Oops, this one was going to call for a save. He scrambled. "Well, you've seen her. Just like you from a distance only. Not beautiful, like you! Of course not. But the same size, the dark hair... " He hesitated, hoping that humor might rescue him. "I guess while her parents were getting the dacha to yield a good crop of cabbage, I just decided it was their daughter I should get to yield."

Carol pushed him away. "Seriously, Will." She tipped her head up to watch the multiple branches of the old tree as they were enfolded into the darkness. "It's me that believes in you. She doesn't. There is no reason that American trees can't bring in cosmic energy just as well as Russian ones, and I believe when one is ready, and it rings, you will find it."

"Maybe."

"No, I'm not kidding. I believe in you, and in the cedars."

"I didn't mean maybe you didn't believe. I meant that maybe I will find it. It should be here," he added, his voice worried. "Why couldn't it be one of these pinyons right here? Same genus, and they try to give us pine nuts, and everything!"

"I know." She turned to the tree and fingered the rough old bark again. "I want to cry. I thought it was me who married you."

Will's face clouded. "How could they! How could they recognize what we did in that dacha as a legal marriage? Maarika was fifteen, practically a baby, when her father supposedly married us. And I was a kid, too. I just came on back to America after my student exchange was over and got my high school diploma here and never even realized that something had actually happened, that I had done something binding in Russia. I guess it was like a game to me. Then here comes Maarika, years later, with papers to prove that that marriage was valid, which crushed ours." He let out a whoosh of air and Carol turned to look at his face. Yes, he looked as if he might cry.

"I wish she was in hell."

"Oh, Carol! Don't say that! You will curse us—it will bring dark energy, to this forest, to this tree.... It will curse these trees!"

She could only sigh. "I'm sorry." Again it grew quiet. They kissed, long, gentle, reassuring. Then she said, "But Will, you know this can't last much longer. I am not going to have a place in this community much longer. The Black Widders are soon going to notice that I have a baby coming, and they will hate me. Unless we change something soon, and find a way for me to explain that I am not a widow, that you are not dead, even though when I joined them it felt like you were—oh, Will, it felt to me as if you had died when Maarika showed up! Then I tried to follow you here, but I have the dark skin, the foreign look. I guess the ancient tribal genes came from my mom, damn it, even though she was born right here in America. Anyhow, I didn't think this redneck community would accept me."

Will interjected, "That's a little prejudiced."

Carol shrugged. "Whatever. It's still why I made up the story about being a widow. I thought if everyone believed I was a widow that they would have sympathy and accept me here. I lied to them, and now I don't think I can face them. And honestly, I really do wish that woman was in hell."

"Dear God!" Will tried to kiss her again, to comfort, but she was struggling to stand.

"Don't you see? It's either me or Maarika! You have a child coming — she must free you!"

Will helped her up and held her, his hands on her shoulders. "I will get it done, my dearest! I promise. I will get it done. I keep trying — last night I told her about our baby, and begged her again for release. I made it clear that I didn't love her, that I love you. I thought maybe straightforward truth from me would get her to provide our release. All it did was make her furious. Her face hardened, like it does, and she started to scream. She ran at me, yelling, "*Ty che, suka, o'khuel blya! Eto pizets! Suka blyad! Otvali! Tibe bisdets!*" ["Are you fucking crazy, you asshole! This is fucked up! Mother fucker! Fuck off! You are *so* fucked!"]

Carol's face blazed red. "Stop! You have taught me too much Russian! But what you say... That does explain one thing. Did she drive your truck last night?"

"Yes. Why? She screamed that she had to get away from me, had to think things over, so she ran out and took off. She was gone a long time."

"Think things over, all right. Will, she tried to kill me last night. She tried to hit me with the truck. She barely missed, and she got Sassy. I believe that if she had succeeded and been discovered, she'd have pinned it on you."

9

GRITTY ANDERSON HAD BROUGHT LUNCH for her mother, and now she was in the kitchen washing up. Alma Weinant, her mother, was having one of her good days, meaning she was connected to the present rather than drifting in that undefinable zone of cognitive confusion so often experienced by the ancient elderly. Eager to be involved with the world around her, she was vigorously nagging Gritty from her chair just around the corner in the living room. "Greta Amelia, you have forgotten my pills."

"Mom, the CNA gave you your pills earlier, remember?"

"Oh. What are you doing, then? I thought you came here to visit."

"I told you, Mom, I'm doing the dishes. I'll be in to visit in a minute."

"Don't forget to put the good green plates from Aunt Aggie in the cupboard above the sink."

They hadn't used the "good green plates" in decades. Gritty said, "Okay, will do."

"Haven't we forgotten my pills?" (Alma was, after all, very old, and did repeat herself.)

Gritty rolled her eyes and snarled under her breath toward the sink, "When will that woman ever die!" A practical and straightforward empiricist, Gritty had been educated as an engineer and was not one to mince words. She spoke the truth as she saw it. Not only was she direct and honest with others, but she was also honest with herself, so she didn't cozen herself with excuses for the painful words she'd just spoken.

Her husband, Mel, had finally succumbed to prostate cancer last year and the trouble with terminally ill or overly elderly people is you can never quite know what they are actually experiencing. Pain they can't describe? Depression? Maybe even joy and gladness? Are they getting any good from the trickle of life they have remaining to them, or are they just waiting for release? Worse, to the extent that they are being crushed by the oncoming disaster which is life's end, there isn't much of anything the living can do for them, anyhow. Contrary to the platitudes bandied about by television, film, or the folklore of the distant young, death itself is dark and mean. It is an irredeemable, permanent thing, and in the end you die alone; glorious and Godly exits are a fabrication of those left behind. Gritty believed this, and as a brisk, no-nonsense person, she knew that when she wished her mother dead it wasn't because she wished the worst for her, but it was because she wanted to get it over with; she needed to get this dreadful job done.

From the living room Alma was saying, "Greta Amelia, I need you to run in here and adjust these blinds. Hallie forgot to do them."

"Sure, Mom," a touch of sarcasm, a touch of resignation. Hallie, Alma's best friend from days of yore, was long dead, and Gritty hadn't been able to reach things as high as the blinds since her car accident years ago. She dropped the last of the silverware into the drain and rolled her chair back into the living room.

Alma's old brown eyes were moist with worry. "Oh, there you are! I didn't know where you went. I was afraid you had left, like your dad did. He said we would get through all this old age together, but he left. Do you remember that?"

Gritty sighed and rolled close. This was, after all, her mother. Her mother, lost. She needed to die, but... gently Gritty took the gnarled hand. Alma said, "Lew was here. He said he set a live trap right by the den to catch the little foxes. He baited it with tuna, but they wouldn't go in. He said that they were smart. They would circle and play, but not go in the trap."

Where did that come from? Maybe it was true. Sometimes old Lew Harris and his possibly-existent dog, Lucky, would pay a neighborly visit to her mother. She patted Alma's hand, but Alma was concentrating on something outside the picture window. "I see them right now, those little foxes. They're sure cute, aren't they, how they play out there in the yard? Well, I hope they don't get the chickens."

That did it. Making a show of looking out the window — no foxes, no chickens, only the apple tree — Gritty made a decision. "They're cute, Mom, but you know, we need to get out more. I'm going to give Jilly a call and see if she's around. If she has a minute, maybe she could run up and help us get you into the car and we could go for a nice, Sunday afternoon drive, just like you and dad used to do, before he died." Was that brutal? Well, he was dead, and maybe it would help Alma to accept it if she heard it out loud... of course not. Gritty chided herself. It didn't help her to have people tell her Mel was dead. The Black Widder thing, of having to say out loud, like at an Alcoholics' Anonymous meeting, that your husband was dead, just irritated her. Briefly, she wondered if she really wanted to keep attending those meetings, but her mother's voice brought her back to the present.

"I'd *love* to go for a drive." It was a gush, filled with anticipation. "And of course you don't need to bother Jilly Brown. I think you and I can get me into the car okay."

Good grief, what could she say? Here was her mother, who couldn't rise from her easy chair without help, and who, once up and gripping her walker, could barely lift her legs to negotiate a trip to the restroom, suggesting that her daughter, who hadn't been able to move her own legs in years, somehow work with her to maneuver the two of them into the car. Such expectations there were between mothers and daughters!

At last, the situation struck Gritty funny. "No, Mom, I'll call Jilly. You and I, we're both social liabilities. You're an old codger, and I'm so deficient that I forgot to get my car equipped for any handicaps except for what the driver would need."

This made Alma look anxious again. "But, honey, I can't drive!"

"No, no, that's not what I meant. I'll drive, Mom." Gritty leaned in to kiss the forehead that was still cold, despite the August heat, then reached for the phone. "We do need to get back before your evening CNA arrives, but we'll have fun till then."

AND, TO GRITTY'S SURPRISE, they both did. Her mother had become a weird mix of real knowledge and warped commentary, and it was an interesting challenge just to sort out the truth. They headed directly toward the Dairy D'Lite in Peaseford to buy soft cones, Alma's favorite. When they passed the old Clenting place, Alma said, "There's where that Carl Clenting lives. They say his daughter's trying to run for office, governor, I think, and she's a woman."

"Yeah, Mom. I think you're thinking of Billy Ray. That's his son's wife. Ex-wife. They're divorced, but she's running for county commissioner. Carl's dead; it's just Arnold now. At that place." And, to herself, Gritty thought, how did Alma know about the election? Even half-blind, half-deaf, and stuck in her chair, that woman could keep up with all the community gossip and goings-on better than most of the fully functional folks around here.

"Good thing it's the wife, then. You wouldn't want an actual Clenting for governor. Did you say Billy Ray?" Alma sniffed. "What kind of mother would give her poor daughter a boy's name like that?"

Before Gritty could answer — after all, she was Greta Amelia only to her mother; she was Gritty to her brother and the rest of the community — her mother continued. "You know, that Carl Clenting, he was mean. He had cruel ideas. He was a paid hunter and he worked to make his dogs vicious. Greta, he used to tell your dad that feeding a dog shot meat would make it mean and hungry for the kill. Fed his dogs that way, venison and mountain lion he'd shot, and he'd shoot pet cats, too, and throw them to his dogs. The neighbor cats, but he claimed they were wild. People said he'd throw in live cats if he could catch 'em. Doug and I hated that man."

She sank into her seat, furious at the memory, her face sour. Gritty soothed, "He's dead now, Mom. Old Carl's dead. I don't think his son, Arnold, is that bad."

"Dead like your dad," Alma muttered, "But at least your dad won't rot in hell."

This was heavy stuff, and caused them to lapse into silence for a while. Gritty stole a glance at her mother; her eyes were open, but she was so quiet that Gritty wondered if she'd entered a zone again. Just before they reached Peaseford, however, as if reading her daughter's mind from the earlier discussion, Alma said, "You wondered how I knew about the election.That Maureen Macklinburg called yesterday. That's how I learned about everyone trying to be governor, Billy Ray and all."

Surprised, all Gritty could think to say was, "County commissioner, not governor."

Alma said, "I think you know her, that Maureen. I think she lives down here somewhere."

"Oh, yes. She started the... " Gritty caught herself. She didn't want to get into a judgmental discussion of the Black Widders. Alma would disapprove of them; she would disapprove of the name, and she would most certainly disapprove of Gritty's belonging. She would tell Gritty that *she*, after all, was getting through her widowhood without some club or other. That, Alma would tell her, was nature's way. Plus, the kind of women that would join a club like that were probably just out to find themselves another man.

Having caught herself, Gritty finished her sentence with, "... Maureen started that column in the *Valley Views* paper, the one called 'Croissant Crumbs.'" Gritty recalled how proud Maureen had been of the name. She had pointed out at some length that even though people in the area pronounced the town's name 'kroee-sin,' no doubt because of a certain level of redneck ignorance on the part of the old-time settlers, it still was spelled c-r-o-i-s-s-a-n-t and still referred to a kind of flaky roll. She continued that this roll, so excitingly foreign, was in fact a treat which she, Maureen, truly loved. It was a French word, she had informed them, pleased to have dispensed a fact they might not have known. Croissants, she reiterated, carefully giving it the French pronunciation, were flaky, and thus left many crumbs. Going full steam, she had reached the grand finale, using a word she was sure many of them would not know: 'metaphor.'

"So," she had said, "I decided to make the title of my column a metaphor." She was gratified in her word choice; Letitia and Betty had looked puzzled, perhaps skeptical. Now she wrapped it all up. "Of course, you understand, that the metaphor was referring to crumbs of information, not bread crumbs. I decided my column would be full of important crumbs of information about Croissant." She stumbled briefly, having named the roll, but quickly recovered. "About Croissant." This time she pronounced the name of the town.

Gritty smiled to herself, recalling how Maureen had

finished, triumphant and proud. That had been a while back, but the columns had appeared steadily ever since. Gritty rather liked Maureen. She was a person who might be called a mover and shaker. She had organized the Widders, after all, and coaxed Gritty to attend. Gritty remembered that conversation, too. "Gritty," she had said, "Ever since my Lee got bucked off that horse and tangled up in his rope and drug to death, there've been times when I thought I just couldn't live with it. With him being hurt, then gone and all. I figured it would help if I could join up with others in this community that had my kind of grief, too, you know, lost their husbands and all, and lord knows there's enough of them kind of women around here. Now, my Lee, he barely made it through eighth grade, and I know your Mel, he was a college-educated engineer, but I think the kind of hurtin' we go through, you know, when we lose 'em? That doesn't have anything to do with race, creed, color, or level of education."

That speech had done it for Gritty. She'd been drawn into the Widders. Well, she would never get all that across to Alma; she didn't feel like defending herself on that one. Instead, she just went back to the original question. "Yes, I think the Macklenburg place is up north of town here somewhere."

They got their ice cream, and Gritty asked, "Why did Maureen call?"

"Oh, I don't remember. Something about the governor, I guess, or taxes."

Gritty smiled. Of course she wouldn't remember. Alma's short-term memory had been shot to hell for years. She licked at her ice cream like she used to when she was a kid. Being with her mother made her feel that way, she supposed. Then, just to say something, she asked, "Well, Maureen is a reporter. Was she asking you questions for an article?"

Alma frowned, struggled to remember, then finally said, "I'm getting tired. Could we drive by the old Critchelow place, then go home?"

Okay, curve ball. It was Gritty's turn to frown. "You know, Mom, the Critchelows sold it. Or at least their descendants did. I think Ronald Gump wanted that piece of land and the spring that goes with it pretty bad, but some survivalists or something beat him to it. I'm not sure we can get in there now; probably no trespassing signs all the way."

"It wasn't like that in my day." Gritty wasn't sure what her mother meant by that, but Alma had set her jaw. "We can at least try."

Gritty sighed. "Okay, we'll try. Then we will get you home."

As they drove, Alma provided a contented running commentary. "Oh, there's Doc's place. Doug loved Doc. We didn't know Annabelle too well, though. She's shy. Somewhere around here, though, is where my grandpa had that general store. He'd let us pick a candy. We never got sweets, so we thought about it so long before we picked. One day, I picked a pickle instead. He laughed about that till he cried. Called me a pickle puss."

Chuckling, Alma watched the fields a few minutes, then went on. "He wanted a post office there, but he never could get the papers straight. Not a trace of it left now, is there? Oh, and there's a big sign. That's new." She peered, her old eyes working to get the words from the sign. Gritty slowed, trying to help her. "It says something about grump, or grumpy."

They'd passed, and Gritty said, "The sign said, 'Vote Gump,' Mom. He's one of the ones running for commissioner."

Alma leaned back, pinyon-juniper forest to her right now, and dobies, bare and dusty, to her left. "Oh. Well, that reminds me. That Molly was doing a poll."

This completely lost Gritty. "Molly was doing a poll?"

Annoyed, Alma said, "Yes. You know. That Molly. The reporter. The one with all the opinions, who always talks more than she listens? Well, she was doing a poll. Said she was going to get some numbers on who is voting for who in the governor's election."

Now she had her footing again. Gritty said, "Ohhh! You mean Maureen. So she wanted to know who you planned to vote for?"

"That's what I'm trying to tell you. Plus she talked a lot. Repeated herself, you know. She told me there's a new vet who's a widow, and that she was going to ask her to join that senseless widow's club she has." Alma sniffed. "Personally, I doubt that a woman can be much of a vet. They aren't big enough. Can't manage a cow or horse. But I know you're a woman's libber and will disagree with me, Greta. Here's the road to turn up if you're going to take me to Critchelow's."

There was just way too much in that onslaught for Gritty to think how to respond. This, she told herself, is why I never feel safe in confiding in this woman. Stifling an "I know, Mom," about the turn, she instead asked, "So who did you tell Maureen you'd vote for?"

"Well, honey, Bennie of course. I used to babysit him. He was ornery then, but no worse than the next kid. It looks like he turned out okay, and anyway, those Clentings are crooks."

They were approaching the pull-out on the hill above the Vedrussian settlement when Alma said, "You know, Greta, it was probably a good idea you had when you first suggested we visit the Critchelows, but it's getting late." She peered at the watch with the large numbers that Duz, her son, had gotten for her some years ago, and pretended to read it. "Very late. Why don't we just turn around up there and go back home. I think it would be a little rude to drop in so near to suppertime."

Giving her mother a wry smile, Gritty pulled into the turn-out. This was the last that was said until they passed some cattle in a field shortly after going through Croissant. Sleepily, Alma commented, "Those are your dad's cows, you know. He says there's a problem. They are not licking their calves as much this year. He says it is because they need more protein cake."

Gritty reached across to pat her arm. "We'll try to get some, then, Mom. Some protein cake. Maybe tomorrow."

Alma nodded, her face quiet, her voice dream infested. "Yes. Maybe tomorrow."

10

WIDOWS OR NOT, this was a weird bunch of women. At least, that was how they appeared to Dr. Junee Bailey. She had been doing her nod-and-smile thing for some time now, while secretly plotting her permanent escape. She yearned for her poor van, still in Peaseford at the Marcos', hopefully being repaired. Had she come in her van, she might have faked an urgent veterinary call and been free. As it was, Maureen Macklenburg, who had initiated this visit, had insisted on driving her. Maureen had urged, "I heard you are a widow, Ms. Bailey." (Where had she heard that, anyhow? And why did they insist on Ms.? Couldn't their tongues twist around Dr., the correct title, or were they that stuck on Doc Clary as the only real vet?)

Maureen had continued, "You will find so much comfort in being near kindred spirits. I will pick you up at 6:30, sharp." And just like that, Junee had been entrapped. Anyhow, at first she had felt happy about going. She had the idea that the woman she had come here to find might be part of this group. Now that she was here, though, it appeared that this was to be a false hope. Only two women here were even close to the age range Junee was looking for. The one was the chubby, anxious-appearing Carol Haddon, owner of Sassy, who was dark enough to be Latino, but was, well, too dark, too foreign, too young, too.... Maybe she was Arabic. At any rate, Junee was sure she was not the one. Intuition.

The only other young-enough woman attending was an incongruously sparkly brunette, her green eyes peering from oversize glasses, her hair in a sort of messy chignon, a top-tail with stiff sprigs bursting free and flying wildly in every direction. Her small frame was encased in jeans and a maroon hoody, both comfortably bulky, and she shot a crowd-killing smile in whichever direction that she cast her gaze. Not that one, Junee grumbled to herself. That one didn't fit her idea of the person she was hunting. Probably not Latino. Or Mexican. Whatever. Not her. Intuition.

That was it, just a very small group, eight in all counting herself. The others were each old enough to be her mother. Or grandmother. Betty Oglehozer, a chickadee of a woman with a tight, feathery cap of white hair, fluttered into a seat beside Junee and rummaged in a large, canvas purse that bulged with brown pill bottles. Her hand located the objects of her search, emerging with a worn photo of "my Merl," as well as at least two dozen more photos featuring grandchildren, great-grandchildren, and more. Junee began politely with, "Oh, my, and who is that?" which was answered with something along the lines of, "Why, that is little Calvin when he was ten years old," shuffle shuffle, "And here he was before that, in kindergarten," shuffle shuffle, "And this is his wife, Katy May, who has always been a little sickly, and oh, here is my Merl again; you see, here are all the five generations in this picture, Merl and Spike and Jonny D. and.... "

So it went, until Junee attempted to come up for air, deciding she must whether it was rude or not. "I noticed that you have many medications in your bag. I hope you aren't battling a difficult condition?"

Betty wished that she did have such a "difficult" condition just because of the elegant way in which the newcomer phrased the question, but unfortunately she must answer no. "Oh, no, Ms. Bailey. I always carried these pills for Merl. I was careful never to leave home without them. I took good care of him, you know."

The perky brunette with the fluorescent smile said, "And that you did, Betty. You must have loved him very much to still be carrying his medicine after all these years."

Junee decided that no doubt Betty had heard that praise often before.

Patting her purse, Betty said, "Oh, I did. I loved him so much!" Her eyes had reddened and she sniffled, then extracted a wad of tissues from her purse and another handful of photos. It was Maureen who saved the day.

Overriding the murmur of one-on-one conversation, she announced, "Ladies, it is time to begin. First, I will have to tell our newcomer all about our rules. We have very few rules, Ms. Bailey. (Junee interjected once more with 'just call me Junee,' which was once more ignored.) Very few rules, but we are very strict about them. The most important is that you must be a widow to belong. The idea is that what we are going through is different from what anyone else in the world has gone through, and it hurts so bad, and that by sharing with each other, we can make it easier."

Looking around at the somber faces, Junee was not convinced; her loss of Ethan was private and she wasn't anxious to talk about it with this strange bunch of strangers. Gritty spoke up. "Junee, it might help to know that we have turned down some people. Abby Senderson wanted to join us when she lost her twin brother in a street confrontation in Chicago, and Kitty Latham asked to join because even though it was her choice never to marry, she was lonely, just the same. We like both these women very much, and it was difficult to do it, but we got up our courage and turned them down."

Carol Haddon shifted uncomfortably in her seat. " Even yet, I'm not sure we did the right thing," she said in a small voice. "I feel badly that those women were sad and lonely and we didn't take them in."

Gritty and others seemed to concur, but Maureen said briskly, "No, widowhood is special. There are other clubs for lonely people in this area. It would be like someone who ate too much trying to join Alcoholics Anonymous instead of Weight Watchers.

"Which brings me to our next rule. This is just like for A.A.; we go around the room, and each of us is required to say her name and say that her husband is dead, and that she is very sad. If she wants, she can also say a few words about him. That is the only other strict rule, and I will lead off and show how it is done."

Junee felt her eyes cross. This was dreadful! How had she gotten roped into this? Some of these women must have been doing this for years — hadn't they had enough, already? She tried to listen, but it looked as if she were going to be last, as they were progressing in order around the circle of chairs, which meant she also had to keep in mind what she would say about Ethan. It would be the minimum, she would guarantee them that.

As promised, Maureen led with the "I am Maureen, and my husband is dead," requirement. She then launched into a detailed account of his being drug to death by his horse until he bled and bled and finally died, back broke, tangled in his rope, and covered with bruises, and he had loved that horse.... Apparently Junee was the only one horrified. It had happened eight years ago, so for the others, she realized, it had become old news. The details of this account were clearly directed at her, the newbie, and intended to impress.

Junee noted that each said how long they had been a widow, and that none said her last name. This was interesting, especially if you viewed this gathering from a scientific perspective. Ah, that could help. More focused, she endured as Betty sang Merl's praises once more and circulated worn photos of him. "Gone five years now, and he still visits me from the great heavenly beyond."

This caused Deb Smith to produce sheets of moisture from deeply reddened eyes, and Letitia Dash to snort into a big, dark blue, western hanky, the type that some use as a bandana. Looking more closely at the big blond woman, Junee realized that the snort was a disguised gesture of derision at the idea of Merl Oglehozer's ghostly visits. Herself suppressing an inappropriate jolly upturn of her own lips, Junee focused with renewed interest on the next to speak, Gritty Anderson, who had managed to wrench the floor from Betty.

Gritty's comments were no-nonsense, just the required declaration of widowhood and a statement that Mel had been a wonderful man. "He's been gone over a year, now, and I still miss him very much every day." Junee joined in the nods; she decided she might be able to say something like that about Ethan. Then she realized that Gritty was adding something. "He suffered so much at the end, you know. I was glad to see him go."

Letitia's big bottle-blond head bobbed in agreement, the age wrinkles patterned across her face that had been deepened by wind and sun seeming to shadow stories that might never see the light. Her heavy hands, the skin work-broken and cracked at the nails, were wringing in her lap as she, once more, declared her husband dead. Then she said, "I hear ya' when you talk about sufferin', Gritty. I always figured he'd end up sudden, buried by a big slab of coal in the mine, but he never did. He made 'er through to retirement, all right, but the mine got him anyhow. Black lung. Never drew a pain-free breath, not for years." She lowered her head and growled, "Fucking coal mines."

This language, not typical for Letitia, sent a shudder through the group, and Maureen, sitting beside her, took one of the awkward hands and held it. It was clearly Carol Haddon's turn now, but she appeared to have lost the thread of the meeting. Her gaze, far in the distance, was glazed. Eileen spoke sweetly. "Carol, dear, your turn."

Jerking back toward the room, Carol gasped out, "I'm Carol, and my husband is... Will is... Billy is... Oh! I am sa... s... s... Oh, I cannot go on living without him!" This sent the grief accumulating in the room past the boiling point. Everyone jumped up, churning around Carol, all tumultuous with consternation, sympathy, and concern. Carol winced and shrank back into a little fat wad in her kaftan, compressing herself to escape the clustered women. Junee was dismayed. She must stand to avoid appearing heartless, but she hung back thinking that now maybe the meeting would be over and she wouldn't have to make her own statement after all.

No such luck. Things settled down. Carol shook her head at repeated offers of support, shaking it with especially intense vigor to refuse the offers of those who would spend the night with her. The storm of grief having abated, everyone sat back down and Deb Smith declared efficiently, "I'm next." She had never stopped weeping, so the required statement of widowhood didn't visibly bring an increased intensity of emotion for her. "You know, I'm like Carol," she wept. "Lester has barely been gone ten months, and I'm not seein' how I can live without him." There were murmurs of sympathy, but she continued, "You know, I begged him not to hire out to Arnold Clenting last fall. I have never thought of that Clenting as a reliable outfitter. He'll take anybody on a hunt; the only requirement seems to be that they have to want to kill something and bag a big trophy. He don't care whether they like nature or can shoot safe or not, so long as they can pay him. Arnold wants that money. And I guess

Lester did, too, because that's what he told me. He said, 'Deb, we need that money, and I know how to guide. It's this or the mines, isn't it?"

Deb's tears had miraculously stopped. She sighed. "You know what I miss the most? It's strange, I guess, but I wish I could ask him what really happened. Was it really a hunting accident, or did somebody get mad, maybe shoot him on purpose? Nobody ever really checked. I'm not accusing any-body, but I think I remember that Arnold Clenting was a sharp shooter in the army. But why would... why would anybody shoot Lester? Lester had a hot temper, but anybody knew him would know he had a kind heart. That's what I yearn for. I want to know how he really died."

It was a heavy speculation. They avoided each other's eyes, and finally somebody mumbled, "Can't blame you, Deb." Junee felt drained. Only she and the perky woman who was not Latino, but who would have been the right age to be the woman she was searching for, were left. Well, maybe Miss Top-Knot could be the one, but probably not. Junee sat forward to listen with muted curiosity, then lost even that little interest when she discovered that no real information would be forthcoming. "I'm Eileen," said the perky lady, "as you all know. There has been so much emotion here tonight, I'll just keep this short. All I will say is that my husband has been gone seven years now, and I still miss him terribly."

Junee's head went up. Seven years? Well, that fit. Maybe she needed to get past her preconceptions. Maureen was saying, "Ms. Bailey, it is your turn. We will all be so grateful for what-ever you share."

Automatically, Junee said, "Oh, don't call me Ms. Bailey. To you, I can be Junee." No response, and she took a deep breath, keeping her gaze on Eileen. Would there be a reaction? "So. I am Junee Bailey, and my Ethan is dead, and I am very sad." No reaction so far. She kept watching Eileen. "He was killed seven years ago in a helicopter crash over the Persian Gulf." Was there a flicker of the eyes as she said that? She couldn't be sure. "I was pregnant at the time, and he never got to see his child. I miss him very much, but I am glad I have at least something left that was so much a part of him, our dear child, Sophia. His own child."

Watching Eileen, for a moment Junee was sure. There had

been a marked reaction. Behind the great lenses, Eileen's eyes dropped; her lip trembled; she swallowed. It was only when she looked at the others in the room that Junee realized her mistake. All the women had been touched by her story, not just Eileen. Betty dabbed her eyes with tissues; Deb nodded gently behind her permanent mask of tears; even Gritty looked across at her with a smile of quiet compassion. They all, not just Eileen, shared her sorrow. It made her want to howl like a wounded she-wolf, to howl like she had never permitted herself to howl, not even on the day they had delivered word of Ethan's death. She couldn't howl here, either, but she could not suppress a groan and a massive sound, a sob, released like a burp.

As she struggled for control, she realized something was prying at her subconscious. She sought for it amid the murmurs of understanding and sympathy, all with Maureen now standing to say kind, summarizing words about the meeting, and Letitia, the hostess, disappearing into the kitchen to fetch dessert. Everyone seemed relaxed; their grief, like deposit in a toilet that needed flushed, had been cleared for a time, and they were ready to face the hours and days that must elapse before the next meeting.

The thought buried in Junee's mind pushed its way to the surface. With a start, she realized that when she had been looking for a reaction from Eileen, and all the women had simply appeared appropriately sympathetic, one of them had actually looked horrified, rather than sympathetic, and it had not been Eileen. It had been Carol Haddon. When Junee had scanned the room, Carol's eyes were wide and her hands were holding her stomach, as if it had been sucker punched. Carol. Not Eileen.

Junee looked over at Carol now, assessing. Everything seemed to have shifted back to normal; at this point she was eating cake and saying something to Gritty about her dogs. Deep in thought, Junee jumped when Eileen spoke at her elbow. "These meetings are a little odd, aren't they?" she sparkled, her floppy loose bun bouncing. "Sometimes I think we should call ourselves the Black Weirdos."

"Oh, well, I... " Junee began, seeking tact, but chuckling in spite of herself; the fluorescent smile engulfed her.

"No worries. We all understand. It sounds as if I lost my man at about the same time you lost yours, but we've both moved on with our lives, haven't we?"

Junee had no idea whether Eileen had moved on with her life, but she knew she herself had, in most ways, so she said, "Well, one must, I suppose."

"How are you and little Sophia faring so far at the Peaseford Clinic?"

"Well, so far things are going well. Dr. Clary is a... a helpful... uh, mentor. And Sophia loves his friends, the old guys." Junee was warming to her subject. "They tease her, you know. They call her Soapy and... "

Maureen had leaned into their conversation. Disingenuously, she asked, "And how do you like Annabelle?"

Taken aback, Junee said, "Well, I... well, I haven't met Annabelle. Yet."

Satisfied, Maureen leaned back. "And you probably won't. Not yet, or ever. That is one woman who is cold as a stone. She secludes herself in that house and is beyond the reach of humanity. Some of us wonder why Doc sticks with her. It can't be because he likes her."

"Really, Maureen," Eileen chided.

"Well, it's true. She'd never make a Widder, heaven forbid that Doc should die. Not enough kindness in that black heart of hers."

"Really, Maureen," Eileen repeated. Then, before Maureen could interrupt and continue dissing Annabelle, she turned to Junee and said, "Won't you come to our next meeting? We'd love to have you come back. It's at my house, and we'll have music and games. I try to set the right tone, and sometimes the women will talk about their interests and their work. Letty can tell you everything about farming, and Maureen, here, can give great tips on reporting if you get her started."

Another of these meetings? Junee looked around at the little group of sad, kindly, misplaced women and shocked herself by saying, "Yes. Yes, I think I would like that. Thank you, Eileen. I will come."

11

A LINE OF TAMARISK AND RUSSIAN OLIVE straggled down a series of draws that collected waste water from the irrigation activities taking place in the fields above them. The invasive pests tapered out at the rise of land that preceded Highway 46, where Sheriff Pat Garrett and Deputy Leigh McCracken had parked and locked. They had used the line of brush as a guide to make their way to the gully indicated by the complainant, Arnold Clenting, which was marked by some cattails and a smattering of hopeful cottonwoods. Clenting was accusing his neighbor, Bennie Senderson, of encroachment, and had called the sheriff in a fury, insisting he meet him here and arrest Senderson.

Garrett now stood scowling, chewing at his cud of minty, tobacco-free chew, spitting frequently, accurately, and vehemently, and cursing inwardly. Among the mandatory responsibilities of a sheriff was the one which required him to keep the peace, and when it involved a scene like this, it was his least favorite duty. In fact, it made him cranky. He wondered if this kind of stuff was what the boys in the big office had in mind when they wrote up job descriptions for sheriffs.

There were six people here, two of them arguing loudly and irrationally, two others inserting inflammatory comments, and at least five packing guns. Garrett and McCracken, of course, had the usual firearms that went with their sheriffing business. Arnold Clenting had some kind of fancy hunting rifle, looked foreign made; Senderson was carrying a humbler .22 rifle. Billy Ray was carrying a little pistol which she kept pointing around to emphasize her statements, until McCracken put a heavy, admonishing hand on her wrist and gave her a stern look. No gun was evident on Gump, but Garrett figured it was there, all right, concealed for use as necessary. The guns didn't bother Garrett much; it was how people dress in this area. He knew that McCracken had a steady eye on the situation, and would pounce like a muscular cougar if anything here got dicy. What bothered him was this pointless nitpicking over property boundaries and fences in an area where twenty feet of dry dobie dirt either way wouldn't mean squat.

Clenting and Senderson were at the middle of the dispute, and Garrett assumed Billy Ray was here because she had some kind of property interest in the old Clenting place that had devolved to her from the divorce settlement. Fair enough, but what the hell was Gump doing here? Was he here just because, as the only other candidate for county commissioner in this district, he felt he had some kind of right to know? And how had he found out about the place and time of this meeting, anyhow? This had to be an extreme example of how everyone in this area knew everyone else's business. As it was, the sheriff stood to one side and watched as Arnold and Bennie carried on their heated argument and Billy Ray gestured with her pistol. Gump's whitish-blond wig-like comb-over flopped heavily to one side, as usual, and his ponderous face expressed what could only be described as a knowing smirk.

As for the principles, they were directing their arguments at Garrett, each focused on trying to get his attention away from the other. Clenting was pushing papers in front of the sheriff's face. Neither was hearing the other, nor developing a reasonable statement. Clenting shouted, "I know Colorado is a 'fence out' state. I know that. That isn't the point here. Livestock have had free range since the 1800s, no matter how much damage they do to your neighbor's property. Property like mine. Can't fight that. This old bastard, Bennie, he can let his sheep wander scot free wherever they please and I can't get 'em stopped from messin' with my crops or eatin' all they want of my good cow pasture. Eatin' for free. Bottom line, it's theft, plain and simple."

Senderson, who glowed red when he was worked up, yelled, "But I tell you, they don't. You can't show me a one of my sheep on your damned fields." Then, as afterthought, "Fields you ain't got any irrigation competence to have, anyhow."

Shoving a paper at Garrett, Clenting growled, "Just read

this, sheriff. You think if I obey the law to the letter, that it will protect me one bit from this jerk's woolly hoards?" Garrett pushed back at the paper, and Clenting huffed, " Okay! Okay! You won't read it? Well, I'll read it to you. All of you, you all will listen."

Dramatically he held the paper and said, "This is from Colorado Revised statutes, Title 35, Section III, about livestock, Article 46." Looking up, he added his own emphasis. "See, this is Colorado law. This is what Colorado law is, just like all the other big government shit; it don't help nobody at all. I'm supposed to put up a fence to protect my property from these so-called free range animals, but let me read this now, about what is a lawful fence." He held a shaking, angry finger on the paper to mark his place and Garrett sighed, resigned. Clenting read, "A lawful fence is a well-constructed three barbed wire fence with substantial posts set at a distance of approximately twenty feet apart, and sufficient to turn ordinary horses and cattle, with all gates equally as good as the fence, or any other fence of like efficiency." Clenting looked up, shaking the paper toward Garrett, and said, "You see how this is? You think how much this would cost me? You think any damn bureaucrat ever tried to think this through? I get all done, spend all that money, and get that fence up, and those sheep will just sneak right under it. A fence that is lawful, me obeying the law to the best of my ability, and that kind of fence ain't gonna hold out his man's sheep for even five minutes. They'll crawl under, and if the crazy bastard decides to go for goats, too, they'll go under it and over it, too."

Bennie said, "I tell you, I don't let my sheep free range," while McCracken mumbled, "Well, it does say something about making any other fence of like efficiency. You could make a sheep proof fence, if you wanted to."

His mouth turned down, as always, and his face arrogant, Gump said, "I don't see how you could free range your animals, Senderson. Your free range sheep could get on the highway from here and cause a hell of an accident."

Shaking his fist, Bennie said, emphasizing each word, "Listen to me. I am always with my sheep. My dogs and I are with them. Whenever they are out of the sheepfold, I am with them."

Eyeing McCracken, Clenting snarled, "Yeah, sure, a sheep

safe fence. You think of what a simple fence, for horses and all, what that would cost? Well, a goddamn sheep proof fence would bankrupt me."

Appearing thoughtful, Gump said, "You know, I read somewhere about some livestock owners driving their animals onto the highway at night, then when some poor, unsuspecting commuter makes his way from the mines after the graveyard shift, he's tired, he can't see them, and runs into the whole mess. The owner then files for damages and collects more insurance money than the animals were originally worth. And the poor miner's rates go up."

Senderson was livid. "Jesus Christ!"

Still harping on the fence, Clenting said, "If I put in a fence, it will mess with migratory patterns of the wildlife around here. I'm a goddamn hunting guide, and I pay attention to wildlife, and what does the goddamn government give a shit about little people like me?"

Whirling on him, Senderson roared, "*You* care about wildlife!! *You* care about wildlife!! I am an *agent* of the Department of Wildlife. That's all I *do!* I worry about wildlife."

Gump mumbled, "Well, that pushed a button."

Clenting said, "See what I tell you? D.O.W. — government. More government, but doesn't care about migration. And Senderson here just bought a dozen more of those little woolly bastards. Talk about overgrazing! What's left for wildlife after your four-legged mowing machines get done with it?"

"Well, it *could* stress the land," murmured Gump.

Senderson growled, "You got no goddamn business how many sheep I have, you little snoop." He started to walk toward Clenting, purposeful strides, and McCracken stiffened, watchful.

"You see that, sheriff? He's comin' for me! You better get him stopped." Clenting stumbled backwards. "He's out to kill me, always has been!"

Billy Ray said, "Oh, for God's sake, Arnold. That's just breath from your own bad attitude blowing back in your face."

Clenting twisted and screamed, "Shut up your own bitching face, you cunt! This isn't your business!"

Garrett's scowl deepened, and McCracken took a step toward where Senderson was approaching Clenting. Clenting was still backing away, but the old man pushed past him and walked up the short rise behind him. "You see this?" he shouted, gesturing. "I want you to see this, sheriff. That's Clenting's land, that to my right, and this is mine. You see what his fields look like? They haven't had any loving care since Hector was a pup, and you see what mine... " Senderson stopped short, leaned over, and kicked at the ground. "My land. My land starts right here, but somebody has dug up the pin! Somebody has dug up the survey pin!" Flushed crimson, he jogged back to the group. "Sheriff, the official survey pin is gone. Been there for years, but somebody has dug it up."

The group, temporarily distracted from the main dispute, was moving toward the hill where Senderson had made the discovery when Gump bent down and said helpfully, "Wait! Here's your pin, Bennie." He brushed detritus from around the metal marker. "I think you were just looking on the wrong hill. Probably forgot where it was, Bennie—kind of thing happens to everyone when they age."

His mouth working with rage, Senderson said, "I know where my pin was, Gump. I take care of this land, and I know where the survey markers are. Were." He rounded on Clenting. "I'm damned if you didn't move my goddamn survey pin! You move it like that, thirty feet, and multiply that thirty-foot move down the length of the property line, and you've added dozens of acres of my good land to your useless shit. You dirty, sniveling, cross-eyed side-winder."

Garrett was examining the pin, its current location and its purported correct location. He said tersely, "It's been moved, all right."

His expression one of righteous shock, Gump said, "Why, Arnold! Why would you do that?"

"But I didn't do that!"

Garrett glanced at McCracken. She'd caught it, too—there was genuine surprise in Clenting's voice. Billy Ray, looking critically at Arnold, said, "Well, who else would have done it?"

Before Clenting could explode with another misogynistic rant, Garrett said in a tone that brooked no interruption, "Look, you all got some difficult issues here. Both parties. It's time to go over them."

McCracken adored her sheriff, and she was especially awed by him when he took command like this. Her hand resting on her gun, she stepped back to listen appreciatively. Garrett said, "First, you, Mr. Clenting. If you are truly fearful of Mr. Senderson, and can show good cause, then you need to file in court for a restraining order. Once the court grants it, then we will have some legal basis to keep an eye on him here."

"But..." Clenting started to object when out of the corner of his eye he caught a subtle move by McCracken. Casting her a resentful look, he shut his mouth.

"Second," Garrett continued, "And again this applies to your concerns, Mr. Clenting. There is some new law concerning open range livestock coming out of a case that originated in Archuleta County, down south of us here, and is now making its way through the Colorado courts. It seems there's a real pretty subdivision down there, lots of houses dotting the lush, green, rural landscape, no fences marking the property lines to ruin the view. The subdivision also includes kind of a park, or commons, if you will. That part is tax-funded by the metropolitan district.

"Now, one of the landowners has sheep, lots of sheep, maybe three times what Bennie here owns, and he has traditionally let them graze across all the land in that subdivision. He claims the right to do that, based on Colorado's fence out laws. Some of the people in the subdivision love to see the sheep drifting peacefully across the land, but others see them as a nuisance.

"Long story short, the metropolitan district sued to keep the sheep off the commons, and they won in the lower court because they had expressly forbidden grazing in those open areas without written permission.

"So, to repeat, long story short, Mr. Clenting. Keep your eye on it. It's still in the courts, but you might have a case against Mr. Senderson's sheep sometime down the road. Meanwhile, I suggest you go hire a lawyer, see if you can get papers drawn up that expressly prohibit unwanted grazing on your property. Just in case."

"But lawyers!" Clenting squeaked. "Half of them crooked! All cost a bundle!" McCracken shuffled her feet, and he subsided.

"Now, Mr. Senderson. You know, I don't see any evidence of your sheep encroaching on Mr. Clenting's property. He'd have to show us that they are actually going on his property before he could even consider an encroachment case.

"Now, unfortunately, this brings me to the next problem, which also requires proof. It is clear to me that your survey marker has been moved. What is not clear is who moved it, and until that is established, my hands are tied. It is a misdemeanor in any state to remove a survey pin, but while tampering with your pin was clearly illegal, you have to be able to prove who did it to get relief in this. You need a confession, or a videotape of the act, or a witness willing to testify. Something like that. You also need papers on the original survey, or possibly a new survey... which, as Mr. Clenting would be quick to point out, would cost more money.

"Now, if you can get evidence that shows who did it, you can take that person to civil court, and once it is shown that he did it, he'll have to pay survey costs, court costs, fines, and so-on. But evidence is crucial, Mr. Senderson and Mr. Clenting. For both of you."

Garrett spat skillfully past Gump's feet. "Now, my deputy and I have some important work we have to get to, so we'll leave you people to discuss your issues, if you still think that's necessary."

Moving back down the draw past the tamarisk and olive, toward the highway, the sheriff waited until they'd gotten out of hearing range of the contentious neighbors, then leaned and said quietly into his deputy's ear, "I'd say we might be able to find some important work at the Cowpath. I heard their burgers and fries have gotten out of hand, and that they are waiting for the law to deal with them. What do you say, Mac?"

12

JUNEE HAD DONE SURGERY in her flip-flops. That would never have happened during her internship at Angell Animal Center. Angell was a classy place, and the staff dressed professionally. And after Angell, of course no flip-flops. You needed muck boots for the dairies. Sitting with her feet up in the clinic waiting room, sipping a post-surgery soda, she was trying to figure out how she felt about all this. This little clinic was so damn relaxed. In Boston she'd felt selected, important, on a mission. Memorial was so overt about doing surgery right and saving animals from pain. Everything from their surgical tables to their web pages was organized and sparkling. Doc Clary's approach, in contrast, seemed almost accidental. He spent a lot of time poking around on the animals (Oh, well, be fair. He palpated them.), raising legs, looking into mouths, mumbling to himself. He also spent a lot of time talking to owners. Often what he said didn't make a lot of sense to Junee, but the owners received his advice with understanding and relief. His bills were shockingly low, but for the most part his patients seemed to heal and thrive. If she were a statistically inclined person, she suspected that she could compare his success rate with far better equipped urban clinics, and the comparison would come out in Doc's favor.

There was the small private issue that she had to deal with here in Colorado, then she had planned to go back to Boston, be near her family, and work in a first-class clinic. She had not taken into account the unexpected warm feeling she was starting to associate with this humble medical shack, situated at the edge of acres of dry dobie dirt, nor was she prepared to deal with the other complications that were arising. Sophia was taking to this place like a...well, like a cliché: like a fish to water. Worse, Doc and his buddies seemed to have taken to Sophia in equal measure. If she made up her mind to return east, it was going to be the devil's own dilemma as to how to peacefully dislodge her kid at this point.

Right now was a perfect example of how the problem was shaping up. Doc Clary and Sophia were bent over her iPhone, and she was explaining her game to him in intricate detail. Any other old rural man would have said, "Uh huh, uh huh, real nice," and left eons ago, but both Doc and Sophia seemed enthralled. He had started by asking her what she had been doing while he and her mother were doing surgery, and she answered importantly, "Right now, Doctor, I am playing 'Clash of the Clans.' It is a strategy game, with defensive and offensive sides. Our clans fight wars."

"Ah." Doc sat down beside her. "What clan are you in?"

"We call ourselves the Beastly Beauties. There are lots of clans and clan names, but I got in this one because I wanted to be in the same one as my friend, Cricket."

Junee, sipping her soda, thought, "Hmm. I didn't know that. I thought we had left sneaky little Cricket behind us."

"So Cricket's a real person?" Doc asked, taking the iPhone to examine the game.

"Yeah, she was my best friend from where Mom worked last."

Doc appeared fascinated. "So. Are you telling me you play this game with real people, people you know?"

"Some I know, some I don't, but yeah, real people." Then she looked at Doc anxiously, making sure he understood. "The stuff there on the screen, that's not real. That stuff, it's kind of like, well, kind of like, you know what I mean if I say chess pieces, right, Dr. Clary?" She pointed at the screen. "That stuff, the stuff in the town, we can move it around according to the rules. You know. The players."

"But you can play this game with real people, from any-where in the country?"

"Yeah, kind of. I mean, all over the country, but all over the world, too, I guess. You know."

Doc said, "Wow." He actually was impressed — technology was trampling him.

Sophia said proudly, "Yeah, I'm already at level six. At level seven I can get new barracks and an army."

"And do you have weapons for the army?"

"Oh, yeah! I can really defend. I got mortars and cannons and air defense, and of course I got air sweepers, and here's an archery tower, and here's the clan castle, with troops, and they have air bombs and spring traps, and giant bombs to get at the giants, and I got two wizard towers, and... "

Junee interrupted. "But Sophia! The last I knew you were into Minecraft. Isn't that more of a constructive game than a... I mean, it wasn't violent, was it? It didn't have all this war and fighting?"

Glancing at her mother, Sophia shrugged. "Oh, yeah, I do Minecraft sometimes. But this is fun to do with Cricket."

"How do the game players get all the stuff, like you just named. Do they have to win a war or draw the right card or what?" Doc asked.

"Oh, we have mines. We have mines for gold and elixirs. When we get enough gold and elixirs, we can get dragons and healers, too. And see this? This is the laboratory. We make potions here."

Doc shook his head. "Well, Soapy, I don't know how you keep it all straight."

Regarding her daughter anxiously, Junee said, "I'm not sure she should be keeping it all straight. That is one violent game."

Sensing trouble, Sophia ran to the door. "I think I'll go play now, Mom. You know, explore in the real world, like you always say."

"Stay where you can hear me call," Junee exclaimed to the closing door.

The phone rang, and as Doc walked over to pick it up, he said to Junee, "You know, I wouldn't worry too much. It's just a game; when you think about it, the old ones are violent, too. Monopoly and chess. Most games are about competing and fighting to win. And just think how her brain cells are growing to keep ahead of this kind of stuff and keep up with her generation."

Before Junee could respond, he picked up the phone and growled into the receiver, "Now what the hell do you want, you damned old sonuvabitch?"

The first time she had heard him do this, Junee had been appalled. It took her a few phone calls before she realized that Doc was skillful with caller I.D., and that this particular greeting was reserved for some of his favorite clients. Putting aside her worries about Sophia's game, she sat back to listen to Doc's end of the conversation. She had found that how he discussed cases with clients was not only entertaining, but also educational.

"So what the hell you doin' calvin' in August? Too damn lazy to get your fences fixed?" A pause. "Nah, you probably did the right thing, John. If the little devil's too big, you should give 'er a little time before you try to pull. If it's small, probably got a problem and you need to get it on out. And thing is, how you gonna know? You ain't gonna fool mother nature." A pause. "So tell me about the blood you're seein' by its tail. Real red and runny or thick and black or what?" Pause. "Bright red, not much? That's okay, probably got a little external tear. She'll heal, but you watch 'er; get to seein' dark, you got trouble further up." Pause, and then in a rough, comforting tone, "Nah, John, you probably didn't wait too long. If that calf's not the old yellow color of baby shit, you didn't wait too long. It better be gettin' that colostrum down pretty soon, though. It been up yet?" Pause. "All right, you get it nursin' now in a couple hours, or you come by and get a bag of colostrum. Hell, ain't every polack knows enough to calve in August like you do. Now you got no troubles with the snow and the wet like the other dumb bastards got back in March." He was chuckling as he hung up.

The phone rang again, and Junee, slipping back into her flip-flops, wondered, "What is it with animal owners and dinner time, anyhow?"

This time it was, "Hello there, Jack, what d'ya' know?" The pause, then, "Well, bring 'im on in. We'll see what we can do." To Junee, "Well, you may as well hang around. Sounds like old Toughy was takin' a little nap on the engine of their pickup when Jack and Betty decided to head to the Cowpath for supper. Seems he did a couple rounds with the fan belt."

Jack and Betty were one of those couples who talk at the same time. Jack described the incredible resilience of the cat, and assured them that Toughy had once taken on a coyote and lived to tell about it, and further assured them that "I would've just shot the stupid old s.o.b. in the head, but he's Betty's cat and she insisted on bringin' 'im in," while Betty, a little breathless with the drama of it all, described the thunking and squealing sounds made by the cat as they started the engine and assured them that Toughy had always been Jack's cat and she couldn't imagine how he could get by without that cat being around to follow him everywhere. "Just like a dog. Yup, that cat loves Jack just like a dog, and he loves 'im back."

Doc and Junee set the battered and offended old gray cat on the exam table. It took persuasion to get Jack and Betty to leave the cat and go on down to the Cowpath, Doc explaining that Toughy would probably live, but that it would take him and Junee time to check for damage, broken bones and so-on, and Toughy would have to stay overnight no matter what, just to be observed. At last the couple exited, Jack looking back to say, "Don't let the old devil give ya' any trouble, Doc. He gets to yowlin' too loud, just knock 'im in the head."

Broken bones he had, and by the time he was anesthetized, tended and settled into a cage, Junee had developed a nagging worry about Sophia's whereabouts. Hadn't she been gone an unusually long time? Had she come into their apartment from the back? She checked her watch. What time had it been when Doc and Sophia were discussing the game? She couldn't remember, and Doc was hunched over the exam table, doing paperwork, pre-occupied. Slipping back to her apartment, she encountered Sneaker, who did the bounce-and-run-everywhere routine that meant she was a dog who had been left alone in the house, so she had assumed you were never coming back, and now that you had amazingly resurrected into her presence, she simply did not have enough muscles in her entire body to express her overwhelming joy. Junee picked her up to allow the wiggled chin licks. Why wasn't she with Sophia? Knowing it to be pointless, she checked Sophia's room. Empty, of course. Messy, but empty.

Stepping into the back yard, she looked up to see a mango sunset, a sunset of mango and raspberry sherbet melting down into the distant mesa. But no Sophia. Increasingly alarmed, she set the dog back in the house and stepped out of the yard. It was really getting late. Putting her hand above her eyes, she peered in every direction, into the dobies, past the sheds, everywhere.

Nothing. Finally, hating to raise a ruckus, she gave a rather soft, "Halloooo? Sophia?" Nothing. She upped her courage and filled her lungs. "Sophia! You are supposed to be where I can call! Where are you? Sophia!" Turning back toward the house, her mind was whirling—what should she do first? Did they have adequate 911 here? Should she tell Doc? What…?

A distant voice. Looking everywhere, trying to pin the direction, and now it came again, and not from where it should have been. "I'm right here, Mom." Sophia was coming down the lane that led to the Clary house. What in the world was she doing up there? She had never been expressly forbidden to go there, but shouldn't she know? Hadn't she overheard the talk about Annabelle?

Kicking aside a tumbleweed that rested in the path, Junee rushed up the steep lane toward her child, who was obviously not only all right, but quite perky, and carefully carrying something, a dish. Before she could close the gap between them to a comfortable hearing distance, Sophia began to talk. "You and Doc were busy, and I've seen all that stuff around the clinic, so I thought I'd just go across the road a ways, see if I could see a coyote or a rabbit or something. I planned to stay where you could call. I was going to look into that little gully, that one right there." She used the word 'gully' proudly, since it had not been part of her vocabulary back East. Junee, going uphill in haste, had reached her, but was too out of breath to respond. Instead, she was trying to decide whether to hug her or shake her, and Sophia, a kid with a lot to say, continued.

"So, anyhow, I happened to look up and there was this lady that looked like a witch, only not really, just flyee gray hair. And she was gesturing to me like this." Sophia illustrated a beckoning motion. "So I knew you wouldn't care if I went to see her, because you were busy and it was Mrs. Clary, not a stranger or anything."

Junee neither hugged nor shook. She just knelt and looked into her daughter's face and said, "Oh, honey…!" Sophia kept talking.

"So I went on up, and she took me to see her horses, in that pretty green pasture out behind her house. They are really beautiful, Mom. They all have names like Miss Fancy and Gracious Lady and stuff, and they are different colors, tannish and reddish.

Then we went in the house after we'd petted them a lot, and then, Mom, I met her cats. She has four, all real fat and purry. Their names are Tony, Tassel, Teaser, and Tinkerbell. Tony is the only Siamese. Tassel is… " Junee interrupted.

"You went into her house?" For some dreadful reason, she visualized her child nibbling on the house that wasn't really bricks, but candy, and ending up locked in a cage watching the oven get fired up while the blind old witch felt her arm to see if she was fat enough yet. Sophia's next words didn't exactly set her mind at ease.

"Oh, yes ma'am. I not only went in and petted the cats and all, but she served me tea and crumpets. Only not really crumpets. It is banana bread. She just baked it today and said she had plenty, so she sent this for our dinner." Sophia held out the plate she'd been carrying and, with a flourish, removed the napkin that covered it to reveal several fragrant slices of banana bread. "Have a piece now. It is delicious. And she also said for me to tell you 'welcome to Peaseford.'"

Junee was stunned. What had happened to the cold, distant Annabelle described by the community? Was this the same person? Taking a piece — if it was poison, she reasoned, at least she and Sophia could die together — she took a bite. Damn, she was hungry and it was good! All she could think to say to Sophia was, "It's good, honey. Well, I… well, we better get on down home. It's getting dark."

"Oh, I've got my phone light," Sophia said helpfully. "Anyhow, I want to tell you, she is so nice, and I think she really would like Sneaker. She likes all those other animals, and Sneaker isn't much of a dog. Kind of the size of a cat, really."

Sneaker? Who was to say. Maybe what people said…. Junee thought better of it. "Honey, I don't think you should take Sneaker around her. Sneaker's still a dog, and everyone says Mrs. Clary hates dogs. Maybe… maybe she'd hurt her or something." There, the threat of Sneaker being hurt might slow Sophia down. She wouldn't want her dog hurt. They had reached the main road and Junee could see Doc closing up the clinic, switching off lights, pulling the door shut. Suddenly, she didn't want to get into a discussion with him about Sophia's afternoon adventures. The whole thing made her feel funny. Waving across the yard at Doc and taking Sophia's arm to steer her firmly to the path toward the back, she said, "Sophia, I left the gate open into our yard. Let's go in that way. Sneaker's really anxious to see you."

"Okay, but she's a nice lady. I don't think she'd hurt my dog. They even have chickens, Mom. And also, she showed me the old trail where the Ute Indians used to cross this land. It goes right behind their place and off into the trees, over there. She says that sometimes she looks out and can see them, those Indians, walking there. You know, like ghosts."

13

THE COWPATH WAS BUSY. When the Lucky Lantern went under, the bank sold it to a business man who decided he could do better with a gas station and convenience store, so what little restaurant traffic the bankrupt café had entertained now made its way across the road, adding to the regular dinnertime bustle enjoyed by the humbler, but homier, Cowpath. As Garrett and McCracken grabbed a table, Jenny hurried over and set down water and menus. Leaning in, she whispered, "Look, I've got your table. It might take me a few minutes to get to you, but you don't want Shalene today. Her twins took off for their first year of college, and she likes to play it tough. She doesn't want to admit how much she's gonna miss 'em, so she's taking it out on the customers. Cranky as a bear."

"I thought you'd be getting off."

"Hope so. Maybe in about ten minutes. Cherish is running late; her donkeys got out, but she's on her way. Here, save me this chair, and you can buy me a burger when she shows up. Coffee?"

Garrett and McCracken both nodded, then studied their menus. They knew them by heart, and knew what they would order, but examining the menu was what you do at a restaurant, so they followed through while taking in the flow of talk surrounding them. A stary-eyed woman and three beefy, thick-necked, heavy-bellied men were sitting at a table to their left. The woman was picking at a plate of fries, and the men were cramming down platters of barbecued pork ribs with beans, buns, and slaw.

Garrett liked to classify tables with patrons of the Cowpath as either business, technical, or social. Social was always louder,

and this one was definitely social. There was the usual boister-
ous clap on the shoulder by men entering the restaurant and
passing the table, the diners reacting with something like, "Hey,
Hank, the old lady finally get ya' outta bed so she could get some
food down ya'?"

In this case, Hank, rail thin, and the woman with him both
chuckled conspiratorially as he responded, "Looks like nobody
needed to worry about gettin' you boys to the trough on time,"
after which, and after more merriment of the same type, the couple
rambled on toward the back. Now the loud conversation at the
table ranged from hunting stories: that buck musta been goin' 65
miles an hour and right at old Lenny. I guess it didn't see 'im,
and old Len, his eyes bulgin' out, he raised his rifle and nailed
'im right between the eyes — to cussing the government. "I
always did say that Obama is a foreigner. Just look how he sucks
up to them A-rabs. Doesn't care shit about the poor damned
unemployed Americans."

Garrett sighed and turned his attention to the table to their
right. It was clearly technical. Two men in jeans and duck-billed
hats were hunkered over a large paper, dragging on coffee and
making worried comments about PSI and water efficiency in the
old pump as compared to the pressure in the new one. They
were done eating, just exchanging scrawls on the paper, and
every few minutes Shalene would stomp by their table, cast
down an evil eye, and snap, "You guys still here? Well, I suppose
you gotta have more coffee." Half ignoring her, one covered his
cup with his palm while the other nodded absently and pushed
his cup toward her. Coffee hit the cup with an angry slosh, sending splatters across the blueprint, which he brushed at absently
as he brought the cup to his mouth.

A business table was forming toward the back. At first, a
small fellow, tidy and out of place in blue slacks and a white
shirt, entered alone, his eyes puzzled as they roamed around the
room. Jenny, dropping coffee off for McCracken and Garrett,
stepped over to the little guy and gestured toward an empty
table. He smiled courteously, nodded, spoke to her briefly, then
went back. Soon after, two women entered, one solid as a rock
and carrying a laptop case, the other teetering slenderly on high
heels and telling someone on her cell that she'd "be happy to
show you that property at 3:00 tomorrow..." Garrett was grateful

that their voices were no longer audible as they took the rear table, the little businessman standing to pull out the women's chairs.

At the table to their left, the socializers were leaving, to Garrett's relief. The woman was saying, "Well, if the government's gonna pay for that shit, we may as well take it." A beefy hand fell on Garrett's shoulder as they passed and its owner said, "Well, sheriff, you old fart. You been lockin' up any criminals lately?"

"Sure as hell ain't been lockin' up enough. Looks like you're still on the loose."

As they moved along, Gritty Anderson rolled in, alone. Looking around, Garrett saw that there weren't any tables open that could accommodate her chair, so he caught her eye, raised his eyebrows, and pointed to the opening at his and Mac's table. She smiled and came over.

A new social group was arriving at the table that had just been abandoned. This time, it was a middle-aged couple and a younger couple, all in some variation of camouflage: hats, tees, full coveralls. The young guy was muscly, big as a bull moose. The banter started again as a passerby clapped the older man on the shoulder. The older man said, "Well, hey, Gene, how ya' doin'?" which was answered with, "Hangin' in there. Just hangin' in there. That's all a guy can do these days," and, after receiving an affirmative "Yup, ain't that the truth," Gene dragged morosely past among the tables, headed toward the back and being comforted at several stops along the way.

The tech table was discussing the implications of an 80 pound pipe being hit with 85 pounds of pressure. Shalene, meanwhile, was leaning over Jack and Betty, who had settled near the front, asking, "You two still workin' on that? Ya' want some pie?" The younger woman at the social table was complaining, "Well, here we are eatin' out on the one day I planned ahead and put somethin' to cook in the pot." The older woman commiserated, but the massive young guy ignored them. "What do ya' think, Dad? I been lookin' at them figures from last spring, and it looks to me like them Saler bulls test a halluva lot better than either the Angus or the Simmentals. Good semen, that breed."

Shalene had reached their table. "Ya'all need a menu?"

The big guy cast her a flirty look. "Maybe. Ya' got one with pictures?"

This amused everyone at the table and at a couple of the tables nearby, but Shalene snorted and jammed menus down onto a blob of spilled catsup in the middle of their table, then whipped out her order pad. "Whadda ya'all wanna drink?"

Another table hopper passed and slapped the older guy on the shoulder. "Bill. Damn, ya' still workin'?"

"Too damn poor to quit."

"Yeah, can't quit. Had too much fun when I was young. If I'd'a knew then I was gonna live this damn long, I'd'a takin' a lot better care of myself back then."

Garrett sipped his coffee and questioned his categories. Over to their right, a group of two men and a woman that seemed half social and half technical was taking a table. To the fascination of those around them, the woman stood and was shrugging out of her shirt to expose strong, tanned muscles and who knew what else might appear. It turned out to be a spaghetti-strap tank top, a small stamp of cloth that still left a few things to the imagination. As she pulled at the shirt, causing wiggles that were pleasant to view, she was saying, "Hot son-a-bitch, ain't it." The men with her nodded in agreement, then continued the conversation they'd been involved in earlier. "Here's the deal. You're cleanin' an irrigation ditch with that excavator, you don't want it deeper. You just want that grass pulled out from the side, so you're better off workin' from the side."

Cherish appeared, fresh from the donkey chase, feeling friendly and bringing water. "Where ya'all workin' today, Shane?"

"Ah, up on Tiffany Gallenas' place. She's got a busted cistern pipe to that old dump used to be Hallie Flute's, and we got the cistern turned on right now, tryin' to get the water to bubble up to show where her pipe needs fixed."

"Bless her heart," said Cherish, moving along, and the tank-top woman said, "I had a pipe broke once up at my place by the county road, and damned if I could take time to call the gas lines and phone lines and power lines and all that stuff. I just parked the machinery and grabbed my shovel."

The second guy said, "Yeah, best way to do it. You can spend the day on hold, tryin' to get through to the government."

He leaned his chair back, taking aim at the other social table. "Bill. Ain't seen ya' in a while. Whatcha up to?"

"Tell you what I used to be up to. Used to kick the shit out of this kid every day when he was young, tryin' to teach him somethin'." He indicated the bull-moose sized man across the table from him. "That's why he's so damn puny."

Amid generalized chuckles, Shane at the excavator table interjected, "So just one question. You tried any of that kickin' stuff lately?" This brought down the house, except for Shalene, who, still scowling, pushed past with plates of food for the big guy and his family. Garrett and McCracken were also still grinning as Jenny appeared.

She had forgotten to ask them what they wanted to eat; she was bringing them what they always ordered, and now that she realized her presumption, she felt flustered. "Oh! Oh, damn, Leigh—I just brought you the potato soup and salad. And you two—Patrick, double cheeseburger; Gritty, Croissant croissant. I forgot to ask!" She set down the food. "I'll go back."

McCracken was tickled pink She accepted the fact that her sheriff was now in a serious relationship with Jenny, but that didn't keep her from feeling a little jealous, even so. She was pleased that Jenny had shown herself to be less than perfect. Plus, she had wanted her regular soup and salad, anyhow. "I'm good, Jenny."

Gritty was chuckling. "I didn't realize I was such a creature of habit."

Garrett had Jenny's hand. "You did good. Don't go back."

"Gotta go back." Slipping free, she planted a kiss on his bald head. "Cherish is here, so I'm done. I'll grab a burger and be right back."

The dinnertime rush hour was almost over, and most of the tables had been served. Like a barn full of clamoring blackbirds that had suddenly found the cattle's fodder, the restaurant quieted and private conversations among diners at each table could go forward. To his everlasting joy, Jenny placed a hand on Garrett's knee, patted, and asked, "Well, Patrick, what have you and Leigh been up to this afternoon?"

With professional restraint, he said, "Oh, we were dealing with a boundary dispute and some encroachment issues."

With less than professional restraint, McCracken added,

"Somebody moved Bennie Senderson's survey pin."

Her eyes twinkling, Gritty said, "Uh huh. Senderson and Clenting. Now that's an old feud—goes back generations, I suppose."

Thoughtful, Garrett said, "You're right, of course. It was Senderson and Clenting. Gump showed up, too. Don't ask me why."

"Honestly, Chief, I felt like there was something fakey about the whole thing."

"Politics, probably," Jenny said. "It's quite an election this year. That whole bunch is going at it hammer and tongs."

"But it's just a county commissioner race!" McCracken objected.

Garrett agreed. "That's what I'm asking myself. What's really at stake here? It can't be just a few feet of dobie dirt, or that a couple of sheep walked across somebody's place. What's so valuable about the commissioner position? And how does fighting about this trivial stuff help anybody? Are they just trouble-makers, or what?"

"Well, I can talk about it a little," Gritty said, setting down her fork. "I've known the Clentings and Sendersons all my life, and Gump's relatively new, been here just a few years, but there's community scuttlebutt about him. Bottom line is this. Gump is devious, and Arnold Clenting prides himself on fighting anything he perceives as an affront to his dignity. Billy Ray, she's ambitious."

"So...?"

"I doubt that Billy Ray and Arnold are in cahoots. They hate each other. One of the dozens of things they fought over was that pit bull pup, Killer. It's from the same litter as Gump's pup, Cuddles. Well, they made that dog a bone of contention—no joke intended—but Arnold was awarded custody of Killer. He won that round, but when the dust settled from the divorce, Billy Ray ended up with half interest in the old Clenting place itself. This infuriated Arnold. He couldn't conceive of the old family homestead going to someone whom he now considered to be outside the family. Way outside! Billy Ray had left some of her stuff in the house, and one thing they said Arnold would do is, he'd take something of hers, have Killer smell it, then bury it with some fresh bones with meat on them and try to train Killer to find them and dig them up. I don't know if that was successful, but he made icky, half-threatening comments that if Billy Ray ever *accidentally* disappeared, Killer would be trained to find her."

This prompted a generalized "Eeeeooo" reaction from around the table, and a gap of thoughtful silence, then McCracken said, "So what about Bennie? Does he do gross stuff like that?"

"Bennie Senderson? Nah, he's an old stump. He's been here forever, got roots that go down to bedrock, and fresh hopeful green sprouts coming from the top. He wouldn't intentionally hurt a flea, but he's set in his ways, and he likes his own ideas."

"So he's running for commissioner because he wants to act on his ideas?"

"I'd say so. There's money involved. The salary is over $60,000, which is big bucks in this area, not to be sneezed at. But I don't quite see any of those candidates making such a fuss just for the money. And of course, Arnold himself isn't a candidate, so the only way I can see him being involved is that he might want to give Billy Ray trouble."

Garrett had finished eating and was tugging at his mustache. "So what about Gump? What would he gain from winning this race?"

Shaking her head, Gritty said, "Honestly, I don't know. I don't think I've helped you much."

Speaking at once, Garrett said, "No, it helps to get some background," while McCracken said, "Money or power. It's always about money or power."

Jenny said, "Or revenge. Gump has some kind of issues with that settlement down south of him. Rumor has it that it was, of course, an expensive property, pinyon-juniper forest, the spring, and all, and when the Critchelows put it up for sale, Gump was scrambling to get his assets together to buy it, and he was just ready to make a bid when the people there now scooped it right out from under him. I guess he was furious."

Garrett grunted. "How does being county commissioner help him?"

"Well, back to power. The commissioners have power. They set policies and deal with budgets and hiring. They have their fingers on land use planning. There's stuff like eminent domain, you know, where the government can take your land toward the greater public good. Gritty just said Gump is devious. Maybe he's got a plan to mess with the settlement people."

There were tired grunts of "Mmmph," and "Beats me." The restaurant was emptying out, and Gritty turned to Jenny with a teasing grin. "I'm still not seeing you at the Black Widder meetings."

"Nah, I don't feel much like a Widder anymore, now that I've got Patrick." Garrett blushed.

"Understood." Gritty beamed at the two of them, pleased with their happiness.

Garrett said, "I just met those Widders for the first time when we were at Carol Haddon's place that night, about her dog and the possible hit and run. Have you heard any more about that?"

"Not really." Gritty was digging into her purse, finding cash for her supper. "But you know, that Carol Haddon's another funny one. She was really withdrawn the other night, kind of in another world. I get the sense that she used to be full of smiles she couldn't contain, maybe a sparkling glow that faded when her husband died, and that her widowhood seriously bruised her, like it does everybody. But it's like there's more to it. She seems so jumpy. She's really anxious about something."

McCracken mumbled, "I think she looks like Arnold Clenting."

This got everyone's attention. "What?!"

Garrett said, "Have I got the right woman? The Ms. Haddon I saw had dark hair, was kind of a beauty. What I see of Arnold is short, stocky, blond, commonplace..."

"Yeah, Chief. I know. I can't put my finger on it. Just a funny take, I guess. Shouldn't have said anything."

14

MAARIKA HAUNTED HER. Will's supposedly legal wife, who was not dead enough, well, she assured herself, she meant not dead enough to be a ghost—she still haunted her. Carol hadn't slept a full night since Sassy had been hit. And that was the problem. By 3:00 every morning, Carol had reasoned it all out and each time concluded that the object hadn't been to hit her, but to hit the dog. She was sure it was Maarika, but Maarika would be crafty. If she had hit Carol, the law would have found her, one way or the other. As it was, what the sheriff had was only a probable accident, a dog that had run in front of a car, no more. He had no context, no sense of the problems nagging away beneath the surface of Carol's life. That's what hurt—Maarika had planned it so the law couldn't help and Carol's hands would be tied. Carol was getting pale and haggard, dark circles formed around the striking green eyes. As the heavy August sun shouldered its way across the mountains to the east, her head drooped tiredly over her mug of tea. She rested her hand on her stomach; the baby fluttered inside. Coffee was brewing for Bennie and Patch, who should be here soon. "I'm just paranoid," she chided herself, and then her uncontrollable mind circled back to trundle down the same worn path once more: Sassy, Maarika, Will, the baby....

That woman knew that it would hurt her terribly to hurt one of her dogs. How could she? How could she hurt a dog to get at its owner? It wasn't just the feelings of the innocent dog, although that was bad enough. It was that Carol's dogs were an elemental part of her Self. When they herded at the trials, they brought into existence a wondrous form of beauty, beauty that was a gateway to the soul; they were rhythm and movement, purpose, skill and grace. Now her joy in the herding competitions was sapping away. Maarika had set her up. Every day she must worry about the safety of her dogs, how to protect them. Whenever they were out, she must look anxiously about, fearful of what that woman might have planned next.

This was why Patch and Bennie had insisted on the new routine. She and Bennie had been taking their dogs out to train with the sheep twice a week. Bennie had high hopes of bringing young Cupcake along at the nursery level, and Carol was focused on teaching her novice, May. Patch always joined them, bringing Buddy, just to help and watch. Normally, before the damage done to Sassy, Carol would just unpen the sheep when it was time and allow Sassy and Sic'em to do their job, taking the flock to the pasture across the road, working like the professionals they were. As they did, she would work with dear May, which mainly meant helping her to contain her joy and excitement, and to resist bursting past the sheep to get through the gate.

After Sassy was hit, her two old friends understood her anxiety as being an owner's normal protective reaction for her dogs and sheep. They decided to help her by arriving at her house shortly after daybreak on training days. After coffee, they would all set up the mock trial field across the road from Patch's house, then Patch and Bennie would each take a stand on the road above and below the crossing, ready to signal cars coming out of the hollow below, or topping the hill above, to warn them to slow down for the livestock on the highway. They were to watch and signal, and Carol and her sheep were to cross. This plan did little to settle Carol's nerves. Maarika, she assumed, would ignore the waving men and gun her engines toward the animals. There was nothing Carol could do; she couldn't tell the men about her suspicions concerning Maarika. She must accept their plan, which was, after all, so well-intended.

The coffee filtering into the pot gave a conclusive burp, meaning the guys would be here soon. She was eager to get into the field, but they would want to talk. With those two, the drinking of coffee and eating of cinnamon rolls and talking of gossip were a favorite part of the day, and could go on for quite a while before they actually stood up to take the orange traffic cones across to get the mock-trial field set up. She sighed, closed her eyes, and waited, rolling her dog whistles in her palm.

One was ordinary, but one was special and beautiful. It gave her peace. Sheep dogs were taught to respond to whistles right away, individual sounds that meant such things as "stop," "slow down," or "look back." Whistles were necessary; they were a sound dogs could distinguish over other noise, particularly wind. Carol smiled. She remembered one trial that was held in Laramie, at the grounds of the Wyoming State Prison. That time, the dogs couldn't hear even the whistles. The prison was along the interstate, with cars and trucks roaring by, and when the trials started a howling, sheep-scattering wind had come up. Nobody could hear anything, and the competition had to be canceled.

Some handlers could whistle through their fingers, but Carol had tried and couldn't make it work. A friend of hers, a Basque shepherd, solved her problem with a DIMA whistle he had brought from Spain. It melted her heart. He had hand engraved it. One side had her name, and the other showed a Border collie and the words, "Leap of Faith." Waiting now, she passed the whistle from hand to hand, letting it soothe her. Then Bennie's old truck rattled into the driveway and as she stood to greet him, the whistle dropped and bounced. She made a frantic dive and retrieved it. "Damn, Carol," she chided herself, "If you want to stay in the dumps, just lose your whistle."

It was as she knew it would be: coffee, cinnamon rolls, and talk. As if these guys didn't talk enough over at Doc's. At any rate, she loved them both and was able to relax into it. First, the bad news. Bennie was missing a lamb. The problem was, he said, that he didn't see evidence of coyotes, mountain lions, or a dog pack. No tracks, no blood. He told them about Arnold Clenting moving the survey pin—he was certain it was Arnold—and said that it would be odd, but he wouldn't put it past Clenting to steal a lamb, just to harass him.

Patch rumbled, "Do them hippies out back of us have dogs?"

Bennie and Carol said they didn't know, and Patch grunted. "Huh. You know that 'know your neighbor' policy that Gump keeps yapping about? Idea is if you might think someone's a terrorist or foreigner, you turn 'em in and the sheriff's office has to investigate. You know about that, right?"

Carol drew a sharp breath. "Did somebody report them?

Those… uh, those hippies?"

Patch giggled, a strange and toxic sound. "Nah. Somebody reported me. Said I was part Indian, which I am, and that I was plottin' trouble for the government. Which I might be."

Carol was chagrined. She could never tell when Patch was serious or when he was leading her on. Senderson growled, "Don't worry, Carol, Gump ain't in any office and he never will be if I can help it, so we don't need to worry about him and his mean-spirited ideas."

Shuffling to the coffee pot, Patch refreshed everyone's cup and doused his with the half'n'half and sugar Carol had provided. Bennie went for another cinnamon roll, and, wiping his hands on his coveralls, said, "Speaking of politics…"

"…About all you ever speak of," grumped Patch.

"Yeah, well, anyhow. Yesterday Abby was at an AAUW meeting, and they'd invited Billy Ray in as a guest speaker."

"AAUW?"

"You know, Patch. The club for old women that graduated from universities. I guess that group is sexist; I'd like to be a guest speaker, but I haven't heard them clamoring for my good words. I suppose they don't want to hear from a real man. I'd sure give them an earful."

Offended, Carol began, "Oh, Bennie, I'm sure they aren't sexist. Just ask them, they'll invite you…" then she realized she'd been had again. Of course Bennie was teasing. He knew all about the AAUW; Abbie was a long-time member, for Pete's sake. The men both grinned at her.

Bennie said, "Probably not. Why, in fact, Abby told me that Billy Ray tried to lead everyone in a pep cheer for women's rights. Yup. Sexist."

Carol opened her mouth to speak again, but Bennie continued. "Seems the women saw it as a political move, a kind of 'vote for me because all us women are in it together' kind of thing. Abbie said it went over like a lead balloon."

Playing devil's advocate, Carol said, "But Billy Ray's had a lot of experience. She's been in local politics forever, working and volunteering. This would be her second term as county commissioner, so she should know what she's doing."

Patch mumbled, "I bet she does," and Bennie said, "Ptah. This is a woman who says she wants to protect mines, claims there's lots of coal and oil reserves, and that they are clean energy now, cleaner extraction, clean use."

"Well, isn't it? After all, people need those jobs."

"Carol, she's leading people down a primrose path, givin' 'em false hopes. The mine closures will continue, because they're being driven by the economy. Alternate energies are boomin'. Figures in the billions. It's like Billy Ray ignoring the auto industry and promising that the horse and buggy would come back real soon."

Well, did she disagree with him? She wasn't sure. She did like to see the ardor with which he expressed his views, so she gave it another shot. "So, what would you do, Bennie?"

"I'd find ways to give those unemployed miners a hand up into the saddle. They need work, and they need it around here, where they made their homes, and if they can't get something right away, they need some support until they can. Then try to get stuff going in this area."

It was Carol's turn to say "Ptah," but Patch broke in. "That Billy Ray's probably just like her husband. You know, old Arnie was accused of embezzling from the Peaseford town funds when he was on city council."

"Seriously, Patch, not funny. It was never proven, and Billy Ray hates the man."

Bennie was grinning at Patch, who said, "Oh, you never know."

That did it. Carol stood, saying, "Whatever, you two," but as they all shambled out the door, she knew that despite her impatience, while she had been fending off their teasing, she had not been fretting about her own troubles.

She had a dozen ewes and two wethers, one named Roy, the other named Rogers. She regretted that she would have to break up the Roy-Rogers duo, as Rogers had become obnoxious and would be going to the auction soon. For today, though, the sheep trotted happily into the training area. Sic'em was doing okay without Sassy. Carol was relieved. May was explosive with excitement, but she looked back at Carol and agreed to restrain herself. Bennie went to bring his sheep up from his place. Carol especially needed his flock in the field; it would help May learn to ignore distractions.

There were four training levels: Novice, Nursery (for dogs

under three years), Pro-novice (also called Open Ranch), and Open. Sassy and Sic'em had reached the top of the training pyramid and were both at the Open level, but May was still a Novice. Carol was hoping to advance with her to Pro-novice and attend some of the more prestigious dog trials with her. She was currently hoping for Soldier Hollow, in Utah — wow, if she and May could pull that off! She would work with May today and Sic'em could wait politely beside her.

Patch and Bennie had taken their positions as "Setters," the people and dogs who kept the flocks up field and served as the kinds of distractions May was supposed to ignore. They were also keeping an eye on Carol's work with May, awarding her mock points for each step of the exercise. This would give her some idea of how she might do with May in the real trials.

Carol took her position at the handler's post, a position she couldn't leave until her dog had completed the Drive and was ready to Shed the sheep. She formally stated her name and her dog's name, then said, "Come by" and May correctly took a clockwise direction to move behind the sheep. She was steady now, and Carol smiled. May was going to do great.

Once May was behind the sheep, she had to Lift them, which meant that she had to get them started toward Carol. Roy and Rogers had balked. They had stopped dead and were staring with interest at the dog. She could not bite or grab — big point loss, possible expulsion from the competition. Carol held her breath. May considered briefly, then flattened herself in front of the two trouble makers, giving them the Border collie's version of the evil eye. She stared them down. As Carol sighed with relief, the two turned to join the flock, and it began to move. Now May had to do the Fetch, meaning to bring the flock calmly and directly to Carol. It went without a hitch.

Buddy, sitting by Patch, was eyeing some big old sturdy willows that were growing in a swampy area where irrigation water drained from the smaller ditches above it. He shifted on his butt and gave an imploring look up at Patch, accompanied by a quiet whine. Patch said, "Hold on, Buddy." Carol's flock had reached the most difficult part of the sequence and the one with the most points possible, the Drive. At the end of the Fetch, Carol had extended her right arm, signaling May that she was to bring the sheep to the right. Now the sheep had a right hand turn to begin the drive. The little dog must take the sheep away from her handler and drive them in a specific pattern through the orange cones. Patch stepped up, watching this operation closely. Buddy jigged at his heels, restless, tortured by thoughts of what might be in those willows below them. Could it be? It was surely possible — squirrels. Yes, squirrels.

May finished the Drive and Carol and the two men caught each other's eyes with wide grins. The dog had done superbly. The next step in the sequence was the Shed. This was counter-intuitive for the collie, whose breeding required her to keep the sheep together. At this step, she must Shed one or more sheep from the main flock and keep them separate until she was told to let them return. At this point, Carol was allowed to leave her post and approach the sheep. Giving the signal, the two went to work.

It was then that the squirrel did the unthinkable. It shot directly past Buddy, dived frantically under the bellies of several sheep, and achieved the willows. Now, Buddy saw his sole purpose in life as being to conquer squirrels. With two wild yips, he shot after the varmint. The sheep scattered and May, ever susceptible to unexpected doggy excitement, abandoned her careful work and tore after Buddy to see what was going on. Sensing that something wonderful might be happening that they must not miss, the other dogs dashed after the first two, casting backward glances filled with varying degrees of guilt and apology.

Buddy had already climbed into the lower branches of the old willow and was now busily backing up after the wildly scolding squirrel. The handlers, left alone by the sheep, were whistling and calling between curses. Finally realizing the extent to which they should be ashamed of themselves, heads and tails drooping, the more mature dogs, Sic'em and Bennie's Little Belle and Corky, all made their way back to their humans. Cupcake, half pup, and May the Novice stayed by the far more interesting willow, sniffing around, poking under the leaves by the ditch.

Patch left the flocks and hitched himself down toward the willow, prepared to command his wayward dog to get out of the tree, but as he got there, he felt something was not as it should be. May looked up at him, grinning past a size extra-large wiener that was half swallowed and hanging from her mouth. Cupcake, a couple of feet from her, was eating voraciously. "Something wrong here!" Patch rumbled, then used his big bass voice to yell up the hill for Carol and Bennie.

He had the meat away from the dogs by the time the two reached him. "This ain't right," he said, holding out one of the wieners for them to see. "Somebody's put a whole bunch of these wienies here, and they been stuffed with something. I think we better get these dogs on up to Doc, and fast."

15

A WARM BREEZE COMING OFF THE DOBIES was inadequate relief from the dry August heat. When Garrett and McCracken reached Clarys', they found the front door of the vet clinic propped wide open with a large rock, which let in the breeze, but when they stepped inside, no one was in the exam/waiting area. Voices could be heard from the back, and following the sound, they found the back door also propped open. Doc, Junee, Bennie, and Patch were sitting in lawn chairs in a yard area with a variety of untrimmed shrubs, tufts of pasture grasses that had been mowed at one time, an old, gnarled juniper, and a couple of table-sized rocks that had no doubt been there eons before the present building had been conceived. More or less in the center, its legs perched precariously on the uneven turf, was a folding table, the top of which sported a large jar of iced tea, some tall glasses, and a platter of oatmeal cookies. Seeing the law officers, Doc said "Come on out and get you some tea and cookies. We're just tryin' to get a breath of air out here."

Bennie hopped up and pulled out more chairs. Once the sheriff and Mac were seated with their drinks and cookies, he said, "Well, maybe coincidence, but we were just talkin' about all the lawlessness around here lately, and here comes the law itself. What brings you all up?"

"Hmmmph." Garrett, his long frame draped half out of the wobbly chair, finished chewing a cookie. "Kinda wanted to see how those dogs were doing that enjoyed those hot dogs so much."

"Doin' okay," Doc said. "Me and Doc Bailey got a little peroxide down 'em. Got their stomachs cleared out."

"Good thing, then," Garrett said, reaching for another cookie.

"We got the lab report this morning. Basic chemical in that wienie stuffing was chloraphacinone. Trade name *Rozol*."

"Poison," rumbled Patch. "Bad poison."

Senderson had gone red. "Of course. We knew that. Arnold's harassing me, tryin' to kill my dogs."

"We just came from Mr. Clenting's," McCracken said mildly. "He pointed out that *Rozol* is a poison formulated to kill prairie dogs. He suggested that someone had put it out to help with the prairie dog problem. He didn't name names."

Bennie snorted. "I'll bet he didn't. That's not how you use *Rozol* on prairie dogs, and that's not where you'd use it. Not down in an irrigation drainage, and not in wienies. You go into the dobies where the prairie dogs actually are and stick it down the hole, no food additives. It's like rat poison — they'll eat it."

Garrett said thoughtfully, "You sound as if you know."

"Oh, yeah, I know all right. They don't want that stuff just kickin' around anywhere. It's a restricted-use pesticide, and you're supposed to have a license to put it out. It is prairie dog bait. It does target black tail prairie dogs, and I've had a license for years. Almost never use it, though, because I never like to kill what I don't have to."

"Do you think Mr. Clenting has a license?"

Again Senderson snorted. "He probably don't need one. The licensed neighbors around here will loan that stuff out because there's a lot of people in this neck of the woods that got no use for prairie dogs in any way, shape, or form. And I'm tellin' you, it was Clenting put that stuff out. He's been out to get me for years."

McCracken set down her empty glass near her chair legs. "The thing is, he has some hunting dogs there in kennels, and he's got a pit bull that he seems to think the world of. He calls it 'Killer,' and he claims that Killer is such a good dog that he can just let it run free. He said he didn't think Killer would stray, but, in his words, he 'might get curious once in a while.' The point he was making is that he would never put out poison, because Killer might get to it."

"Mmmph — I doubt he'd let that stop him."

Junee said, "Well, whoever did it got Sassy and May, too. Maybe somebody's targeting Carol Haddon and not you, Bennie."

"I don't see it. Too bad, though. Carol knows she can call me if she has predator problems, or if she is aware of poachers, and now I guess she's going to have to worry about Clenting, too. Even if he doesn't have any reason to target her dogs."

"See, that's what we're trying to puzzle out. What dogs would be down there where they could even spot those wieners—that is, what dogs would fairly routinely be near that willow?" Garrett pulled his mustache. He was baiting them a little, trying to get them to think outside the box. "What about Buddy? Was that a regular climbin' tree for him? Or maybe somebody just wanted to get at predators, maybe coyotes, and figured they could get them there."

Patch, offended, declared, "Buddy, he sticks with me. He don't roam around like that damn Killer does."

Senderson was stirred up. Standing, he gripped the back of his chair and said, "Here's the deal, sheriff. That's right near where that survey pin got moved. Clenting knows I walk my property line pretty often, just to keep tabs, and my dogs like to go with me. He also knows that Carol enjoys taking her dogs out for runs when they don't have to work, and she gets out in that direction sometimes. None of that is regular. What *is* regular is that we train our dogs same time, same day, twice a week. It didn't cost Arnold anything to take a gamble, put out some poison. Maybe one of the dogs would slip away and find it after the sheep were penned or something, maybe not, but he figured it was worth the try, and he lucked out. I suppose he's plotting to get me off the track and clear the path for Billy Ray's bid for office."

Garrett's eyebrows went up and he shot a glance at McCracken. This wasn't what they had heard about the relationship between the divorced Clentings.

Before he could say anything, Sophia wandered out the door, her face bent over her iPhone, Sneaker snuffling along at her heels. Buddy was thrilled. He jumped up from Patch's side and went over to set his nose on the little dog's back. He loved this thing that was half dog and half squirrel. He hadn't decided what to do with her yet, but he did know he liked to be wherever she was. Doc said, "Well, hello there, Soapy. What are you two up to?"

Looking up from her game, Sophia said pleasantly, "And

we might ask the same of you, Dr. Clary."

Pressing her temples, Junee snapped. "Sophia! Don't be rude!" but at the same time Doc responded, "Well, I asked first, lady, and I got the full weight of the law here to back me up. So spill the beans."

Without missing a beat, Sophia said, "I ain't no stool pigeon, copper. Me and my sidekick, we got our stories straight." She had stuffed the phone in her pocket, her eyes sparkling. Even her little knees were braced, ready to parry the next teasing comment.

This was the first time McCracken had encountered Sophia, but she cottoned to her at once, and had caught on to the game. Gesturing with her thumb toward Garrett, she said, "Looka here, kid, bad cop's over there. He'll play rough. You better deal with me before he gets to you. Wanta cookie?"

Sophia began with, "You ain't gonna... " then her eyes went around the yard. "Uh oh! Where's Sneaker?" Her tone had changed, causing the adults to straighten and look about. It only took a moment to spot a well-fed canine bottom, enchanted waving tail attached, protruding from a tangle of buck brush ordering the yard. This was Buddy, and at his forward end was a scuffle of dark fur rooting industriously among the early leaf fall. Burrowing after her, Sophia scolded, "Come on, damn it, Sneaker! Damn you, come out of there."

At this, Junee gathered herself. "Watch your language, Sophia." Then, to the men, "My daughter spends way too much time around you foul-mouthed old codgers," and then, back to Sophia, who had gotten the dog in hand, "Where is her leash, Sophia? You are going to lose her for real one of these days."

"Mom, she doesn't like to be tied on her leash. She wants to run free and hunt."

Properly chastised, the old guy contingent jumped in to support Junee. Patch rumbled gently, "Ah, Soapy. Your poor little Sneaker has the heart of a lion, but the body of a chicken. When she goes huntin', there's gonna be lots of stuff huntin' for her, instead."

Bennie added, Yeah, she'll get out in that p-j and a lion'll get her."

Confused, Sophia asked, "P-J's? Pajamas?"

"No, honey, p-j, pinyon and juniper. Over there south of

us," Benny pointed, "You can see that big thick stand of pinyon and juniper, big forest that goes on over past the spring. There's all sorts of things in there that would like to eat your little Sneaker—owls and coyotes and lions..."

Her eyes wide, Sophia stared where he had pointed. "Like a jungle? It's got real elephants and lions and stuff?"

"Well, not quite that kind of jungle. More an American forest. No elephants, and the lions are cougars; they're mountain lions, but they'd eat Sneaker, just the same. And you, too."

Seeing her daughter's worried face, Junee pulled her onto her lap. Partially just to bait Bennie, Doc said, "I figured old Clenting would have those cougar all hunted out by now."

Bennie looked disgusted. "Take a better hunter than that..." he swallowed the word, looked at Sophia, "...than that son-of-a-gun. Plus the Critchelow heirs weren't around here, so they didn't care. Now that cult's moved in over there. I think they're tree huggers or something. They don't like people in there. Really ticks off guys like old Arnold Clenting."

"Would of been different if Gump had got it," Doc speculated. "He sure did want it. I figure once he had it developed, and had the water in the spring cornered, he'd be lettin' hunters in there by the dozens. Maybe not Arnie, though." Doc grinned.

Garrett caught Mac's eye and pointed at his watch. As they stood to take their leave, an officious voice intruded from the exam room, "Anyone here?"

Gump appeared in the back door and took in the scene in the yard. He was leading a pit bull that McCracken immediately assumed was Killer, Arnold Clenting's dog. While she tried to put the pieces together, Gump was saying, "Well, hello everyone. Having a little picnic?" It could have been a joke, but he didn't smile. His mouth was turned down, his eyes assessing. Doc stood up.

"What can we do for you, Ron?"

"First, you don't go yet, sheriff. I saw your car go by, and I have information I want to give you. Since I'm also concerned about a growth Cuddles has under her left eye, I thought it would be a good time to bring her along. I always keep her with me, you know."

McCracken looked again. Oh, Cuddles. The dog that was the litter mate to the one she and Garrett had seen at Clenting's earlier. Killer, he had told them, was a good dog and was thus allowed to roam. He could have gotten into the poison, but his sister, Cuddles, was always kept on a short leash. And indeed she was. She was straining against it, looking with great interest at Buddy, who had attained the lower branches of the juniper, but Gump had her well in hand. She didn't even appear aware of Sneaker, who had taken cover inside Sophia's shirt.

Garrett didn't like to be pushed. He said shortly, "Well, Mr. Gump, you have information?"

As if saddened to have to say it, Gump waggled his head. "Just this. I'm afraid you may have overlooked the role that the terrorists over the hill may have played in these issues that are arising on the Clenting and Senderson land. They are trouble-makers, and their plotting is elaborate. It is no doubt those people — they are Russian, you know. Tools of Putin. Or perhaps not. Perhaps Chechnian Muslim rebels. At any rate, they no doubt left the poisoned meat out to bait local dogs, like dear Cuddles, here. If this kind of thing continues, none of us will feel safe living here. We'll all have to sell out."

For a moment, Garrett just stared at him, speechless, but McCracken found her tongue. "Uhh, why in the world would they do that, I mean, poison dogs?"

Gump looked down his nose at her as if her remark had been made by a babbling idiot. "Why, they are practicing what tools to use to thwart bomb-sniffing dogs, of course." Now it was McCracken's turn to be speechless, at which point Gump looked her up and down. "Haven't you gained a lot of weight, deputy? I suppose it's not just fat, but muscle growth from all the work-outs you find it necessary to do to keep your job. Still, it's quite obvious, isn't it — all that bulk?"

Now Garrett had his voice. "Time to leave, Mac. Thank you for the hospitality, Dr. Clary and Dr. Bailey." He started to brush past when another old fellow, leaning on a cane, came to the door behind Gump. Seeing him, Doc called out, "Hey, Lew, good to see you. Come on down." The tension broke.

"Where ya' been, Lew?" Patch asked.

"A little under the weather. Rheumatiz, I guess. Left knee. Come on, Lucky."

Lew hobbled into the yard, and Sophia's mouth fell open. "Mom, it's the invisible dog! Can I pet him, please, Mr. Lew?"

She jumped off Junee's lap and approached the limping old man. Cuddles' eyes followed her and the dog grumbled, deep in the throat.

Dr. Clary said, "Come on, Ron. Let's have a look at that growth you see near her eye." Junee followed them into the exam room; Garrett and McCracken followed, also, on their way out.

Kneeling by Lew Harris' knee, Sophia said, "Wow, this dog is rad! I can't see it at all!" Patch and Bennie looked at each other, not sure what to say. In the adult world, Lucky was tolerated as being a figment of Lew's elderly imagination, not really there, but good, since it was a comfort to Lew. They had no idea what the nonexistent dog might be to Sophia, but she was saying, "Look, Mr. Harris. Have you tried taking this dog up to visit Mrs. Clary? She thinks she hates dogs, but I bet she wouldn't hate Lucky, 'cause she wouldn't realize he is even there."

Garrett and McCracken had been held up on their way out by the activities involved in getting Cuddles into the exam room and lifted onto the table. Neither wanted to be anywhere near Gump, so they made a wide circle to the door.

Once in the car, Garrett asked, "Well, what did you catch in all that?"

"Meaning besides the fact that Ronald Gump is a creeper?"

"Yeah, besides that."

"Well, for one thing, he said he saw the sheriff's car go by and that's why he came up, but he didn't. He couldn't have. We didn't even come in that way or pass his place. We came from Peaseford."

"So, he's a liar. Well, I'm not surprised. My turn. One thing for me: Sophia reminded me that we might have another suspect here."

"Seriously, Chief? Who?"

"Doc Clary's wife. Remember? Annabelle Clary is famous for being weird. Cold, stand-offish. *And* for hating dogs."

"Well, whadaya know." They were quiet for a few minutes, contemplating, then McCracken said, "Chief, do we even have a crime here? I feel like we are lacking something important, a *corpus delicti*. We don't actually have us a dead body or anything."

"I thought you'd never ask." He grinned. "We do have a

legal transgression, you might say. It's a little one, but it is a crime. You see, it is illegal to apply *Rozol* Prairie Dog Bait from March 16th through September 30th of any given year."

"Seriously?" McCracken looked at him in astonishment. "That's why we're up here—somebody put out prairie dog bait at the wrong time?"

"Seriously, Mac. I'm quoting you the letter of the law. And that's our excuse." He turned left, heading into, and soon out of, Peaseford. "The problem is, I just have a hell of an uneasy feeling about what's going on up here. We don't have a *corpus delicti* now, but I'm afraid that if we don't get ahead of it, we could have a real *corpus*, and sooner than we want."

"A gut feeling." She watched as the little town passed. She trusted her sheriff's gut feelings.

"In fact, Mac, get me a land line to Hobbs. I'm gonna see what our detective can do for us." Once on the line, Garrett said, "Asa, I got some things I need to know about people in this area. Got a pencil?"

There was a pause, as Asa reminded his old friend for the Nth time that with his kind of memory, he did not need a pencil. "Okay, then, here goes. See what you can find out about Carol Haddon, up along Old Grand Road. Then look into all of the candidates for county commissioner in this district, and you probably should check out Billy Ray Clenting's ex, while you're at it. Arnold Clenting. See if there's money for him somewhere if she wins the commissioner race. Then, last but not least, I'm kinda curious about that outfit that settled up in the p-j, by the Sunshine Spring, at the end of Forest Road. They came in as some kind of group. I'd like to know a little more about them."

16

MAUREEN MACKLENBURG referred to what she did as "crunching the numbers." That seemed like the appropriate modern term; when she crunched the numbers, it seemed clear to her that the only honest thing to be done was to report in her "Croissant Crumbs" that Gump was way ahead in the polls.

She conducted chit-chatty polls, which was why she was so pleased with herself to have spoken with twenty people this time. That was a lot! It had taken her almost two full days to make the calls. She loved to visit, but she was not always comfortable approaching strangers. Even so, she had her standards. She knew a good poll was not just about what your friends thought, so she did random calls, too, and did them first, to get them over. She set herself a certain number that she must make before she could move on to people she knew. This time, she forced herself to call ten, using her own criteria for making the calls random.

The way she did this was to close her eyes, open the phone book, and run her finger down the page without looking, then call the number where her finger stopped. Sometimes she didn't call the name at quite where her finger had stopped because itwas a difficult name to pronounce, or she had a bad feeling about it, or she knew someone with a similar name with whom she had once had a bad experience. In that case, she would look above or below the name until she found a name she was comfortable with, then make the call.

In the interest of good journalism, she always introduced herself and explained that she was doing a poll for the *Valley Views*. The newspaper had not commissioned her to conduct a poll, but saying this gave her a nice sense of how important this poll was, and she was sure her editor would be excited to receive it. She then told them that the paper wanted to know how people planned to vote in the upcoming District Two county commissioner election. Here was where it got interesting. She was thrilled with the variety of responses she got, everything from "Oh, how lovely, dear! What would you like to know?" to "I sure ain't got time for this shit," followed by a slammed receiver.

By far the most frequent response was, "Oh, I didn't know there was an election. Where's district two again? I'm probably not in it." This was also Maureen's favorite response, because it opened the door for her to show off her extensive knowledge. She could tell them about the districts and discuss the candidates, describing in detail what she knew about each. Once she and the person who had received the call began talking, it usually turned out that they did, after all, know one or more of the candidates, and they would exchange information with her about Ronald Gump's commendable efforts to keep terrorists from buying on American soil, or Billy Ray Clenting's issues with her husband, who remained a problem for her even after she divorced him.

After she dutifully completed her calls to strangers, she went to work on friends and neighbors. These were better, as she felt she already knew most of their views anyhow, so they didn't focus much on the election. In fact, a couple of times she forgot to ask the poll question, so she just put down what she knew they would have said. What they did do was exchange local news, and Maureen came away with a good deal of gossip to share all around.

She kept a careful tally, adding notes as appropriate. Four respondents said firmly they would vote for Senderson, conveying the idea that he was an old-timer whom they trusted ("I went to school with the guy") with good ideas for the county. Five would vote Clenting. Of the five, one expressed his appreciation of the fact that Clenting planned to bring in broadband, and the others just cited her experience. One woman said, "Well, Billy Ray's already served one term, and she didn't mess it up yet, so she may as well go for another."

Seven said Gump, clearly more than Senderson's four or Clenting's five, so in Maureen's book, he won. She supposed their reasons didn't matter. One noted that Gump was a developer and could make something out of "this ass hole of the world," and one liked his cowboy art collection. Maureen, whose husband had worked with cattle all his life, hated his art collection. She'd seen it, and it portrayed fake, romanticized, cowboy wannabe's, with oversize Stetsons, alligator hide boots, and dramatic dusters, but she was an honest pollster and wrote down their intended votes.

One of the respondents said that she might not make it to the polls, but if she did, she'd seen Gump's signs, so she'd probably vote Gump. Maureen wrote her down. Two were very excited about his Know Your Neighbor proposal, but for dramatically different reasons. The first liked it because it would hold down on foreigners, and the second liked it because she felt it was important to love your neighbor as yourself. That was what Jesus would want, she explained.

The two other respondents that Maureen marked for Gump actually just said they hated politics and Gump would shake it up around here, so he was as good as any.

There were four undecided. One of those she hadn't phoned: Eileen Garcia popped in with her joyous smile and a dozen fresh eggs for Maureen, who noted with interest that the spriggy black ponytail still bounced atop Eileen's head, but the fringe of hair in the layer below it, bordering her neck, was now a shining rusty red. The two visited a bit, then she asked Eileen her poll question. Eileen blew up. "Well, it won't be Gump, that xenophobic bastard." Maureen didn't know xenophobic, nor could she imagine how it might be spelled, but she leaned forward anyhow, anxious to gather in the full force of this passionate response. "Maureen, he hates people like me."

Maureen was even more baffled. "People like you?"

"You know. Me. People named Garcia. Mexicans. Brown people. He's using us to drum up support from people who think we take their jobs, who think they are something called white, and that to be really 'American', you have to be that. White."

Taken aback, Maureen said, "Oh."

"It is such a crock of shit. My husband died for this country, Maureen. I wouldn't vote for Gump if you threatened my... my... to cut off all my fingers."

After a moment of silence, Maureen said hesitantly, "So...

who do you plan to vote for?"

"I don't know yet. I'm undecided. Just not Gump."

Crunching the numbers later, Maureen worried. She was honest, and she would have to say in her column that Gump had won, because numbers don't lie, but the real bottom line was that while seven people had named him, ten were voting otherwise, and in some cases were strongly against him. She sighed. She admired statistics, but one just didn't always know how to deal with the truths they had to tell.

17

SOPHIA KNEW SHE PROBABLY SHOULDN'T be listening, but her mother had left her bedroom door ajar to catch more of the warm dobie breeze, and every word of this side of the conversation came through crystal clear. Well, crystal clear with a little effort on Sophia's part. She propped herself up against the wall near her own open door, unnecessarily shushed Sneaker, and was very quiet. After all, her mother hadn't told her not to listen, and she was bored, anyhow.

The first thing her mom said wasn't a game changer. "I just needed to talk. I have such a headache." Whatever. Her mom got migraines sometimes, and Sophia had tried to help, but there didn't seem to be anything she could do. It was her mother's next sentence that brought Sophia closer to the open door.

"Mom, I'm growing more and more convinced that this place isn't for Sophia and me. I told Sophie that I was just going to home school her for a few weeks until I could find time to look into the local schools, but the fact is, I simply don't want her to get attached here." Sophia stiffened and clutched Sneaker so hard that she gave a muffled yip.

"What kind of mother is she?" Sophia fumed inwardly. "She lied to me! What else hasn't she told me? What is Grandma saying about this?" In a moment, her mother's voice continued.

"Well, I did think it would be good for her and you, both, if she were closer."

Had her mother lost her mind? Grandma was always busy, attending meetings, writing papers. Busy, busy, busy. She wouldn't have time for Sophia if she... if she were glued under her armpit, that's what. Sophia paused to relish this extremely disgusting and negative image. Her mother was saying, "Well, yes, I know that she is already becoming attached here, too. She is awfully fond of those old geezers I told you about, and lord knows, with no father and now her own grandfather dead, she could use some men in her life." Her mother found the grit to chuckle past the headache. "Maybe just not that batch of wobbly old hooligans."

Sophia was still visualizing the ramifications of being "attached," in Croissant or in Boston, possibly by glue to an armpit, when she realized that her grandmother must have asked about why Junee was so unhappy here, because her mother was listing issues. "Mom, I know it sounds trite, but it is so damn hot and dry here right now. Almost scary. Everyone keeps wishing for rain, and they seem to think it will get better, but right now everything that moves kicks up dust. The irrigation water comes from the mountains, and it seems to be gone for this year. You can't see snow up there anymore. Where they have irrigated, there are cracks in the soil that are starting to be canyons, and my skin would be cracked into canyons, too, if it didn't suck up moisturizer by the bucket. My lips are chapped, my hair is stringy..."

Grandma must have interrupted, because her mother snapped, "Yes, I know, Mom. I do drink lots of water. That's not the cause of my headache—I had them in New York, too, remember?" There was silence, and Sophia assumed her mother was huffing, as she'd seen her do before. From what she had heard so far, she wasn't so sure Grandma was just jumping all over this "moving back in with you in Boston" thing. Maybe she should call Grandma herself; she might have an ally there. In fact, she had just successfully defended her clan castle using only one wizard and a healer. If Grandma was up for it, she could be the healer and Sophia would be the wizard. Maybe that way they could deal with that woman, as she liked to refer to her mother in moments like this.

Her mother was now saying, "Mom, it goes deeper. At least you are where you and dad lived, and where dad died. I miss Ethan so much, and I just feel so alienated here. Half the time all people talk about is the weather. And sometimes their values... well, they suck. Sometimes, at least. Doc and I went out a couple nights ago to a ranch, some big bruiser and his big bruiser son and a big ugly woman. It was another calving case that should not have been happening in August, but there it was. They reached Doc and he called me, and we staggered out of bed sucking microwave coffee, arriving at that place in just *minutes*, and you know what they did?"

Sophia tensed, waiting impatiently during the Grandma saying what-did-they-do? pause, and her mother said, "They couldn't wait just a few minutes. Not even that few minutes. After dragging us out at midnight, they just kept applying their caveman techniques. We could have gotten that calf, a little time, a little oxytocin, but those burly bastards pulled on it so hard they broke both its legs. After tearing it out, they looked at the damage they had done, pulled out a gun, and shot it. All we could do by the time we got there was try to help the poor old battered mother cow."

Grandma must have been saying something to try to be comforting. As for Sophia, she had curled into a small ball of fury. "I will stay here," she thought, "And when I am big enough, I will go punch those bastards out so bad they can never hurt another baby." Bastards. A very good word—Patch used it a lot.

Her mother was saying, "No, Mom, I can't just get away for a few days. Doc really does need me. Like they say, he's all stoved up. There's no relief from this place. There aren't other clinics in this whole valley. We're it—when people need help, day or night, it is just Doc and me. And when he does retire, it would just be me."

They probably talked more, but Sophia was no longer interested. She pulled Sneaker into her room, shut the door, and got on the bed, where she sat hunched over her feet, picking at the blisters and callouses that had formed from going barefoot all last month. She was angry—her mother had lied to her!—and she was still bored. The old geezers, as her mother had so rudely called them, wouldn't be here until evening. Not even Doc, who had gone into Riversmet for supplies. She was sick of the iPhone; she'd won big on that castle defense, and that was enough for now. They'd been to the library, but even there her mother betrayed her. The DVD's they got were kid stuff. She had wanted a book about zombies, but her mother nixed that. Instead, she got her some dumb thing about a secret garden, which she said they would read together. "I loved it when I was your age," her mom had said.

"The idea," said Sophia to herself, feeling rebellious, "Makes me want to puke. Secret garden? Yeah, right. Parent home-schooling propaganda." This cranky language added to her bad mood, and she went to the door. No more phone voice. Quietly, she peeked into her mother's room. Junee was lying sprawled flat on her back in just shorts and a bra, limp. She was snoring. "Come on, Sneaks," Sophia whispered to the dog. "We're gonna go do something exciting."

Going up the hill was not so bad. She had Sneaker on her leash, so her mother couldn't yell at her about that, anyhow. And once everyone realized how much Annabelle loved the little dog, they would quit warning her away. Besides, if her mother said anything, she could say, "Well, you lied to me, too, Mom. Like you always tell me, it's a matter of trust." Sophia rolled those words around in her mouth, appreciating the impact they would have, rephrasing them to associate how she imagined her mother's face would look. Sneaker tugged ahead, thrilled to be out. Sophia was distracted by the melting of the popsicles she had brought as a friendly offering. Hurrying, she made it at last to Clarys' door, and, sugary juice now dripping past her elbow, she rang the bell.

It wasn't what Mrs. Clary said that sent Sophia stumbling backward. It was her face. And then the rest. For a very brief moment, as she saw the child on the step, a welcoming smile flickered across her face. Then she saw the dog. She gasped and began to shake and wring her hands. Her face went all horrible and witchy. "No, I can't! No, you mustn't! Get away! Get away! You are a terrible child — terrible! Don't bring that, not that thing. Get it away from me! Oh, God, help me!" At that point she simply sank down into the doorway, covering her dreadful, transformed face with her hands, her sobbing hysterical.

Dragging the baffled dog like a dead weight behind her, Sophia ran.

ANNABELLE WEPT for a long time. It was too much. What had come over her? How could she treat that little child like that? Once more she had lost control, perhaps worse than she ever had, and she had no idea why or what she could do about it.

She didn't know who she was. Others seemed to know. Sometimes she got up her courage, went to get a few groceries, and people would greet her, "Hello, Mrs. Clary. Hello, Annabelle," and she would try to greet back in the right way, but who was it they were speaking to? Who was this Annabelle, this Mrs. Clary? She had no idea. She hadn't had any idea for years. Had she ever known?

Annabelle Clary was an empty thing; there was nothing there. She began to tremble. The child. Why had that empty thing spoken in that way to the child? Who was it that had done such a thing? She was getting worse, this she was sure of. Only Doc could reassure her, but he wouldn't be back for hours. Still trembling, she wondered what she must be to him. What did he see, when he looked at this empty thing, so dependent, always so frightened. Such a dreadful, dreadful burden. She had been nothing but a problem to him for… She couldn't clear her mind. For years. It had been years, hadn't it? Years that that good, kind man had spent trying to comfort this shell of a woman, a thing that was in the end not even a thing. A not-thing. Nothing.

He could be better off without her. Without this bitter onion that was all peeling, no seeds, no core. It was surely time to free him. She walked to the gun cabinet and took down her rifle. Hers, she thought, but she didn't know why, or from where, or when. But hers. She knew how to shoot it—it rested securely in her hand.

She left the house by the back door.

18

JUNEE AWOKE WITHOUT HER HEADACHE. Nothing else in her life was better. The sun was scorching its way under the mountains to the west, leaving behind air that was roasted and brittle. Looking in on Sophia, she found her to be cross and withdrawn. She was poking with what appeared to be great concentration at her iPhone, Sneaker lying morosely beside her. When Junee tried "What's up, Sugar Pup?" Sophia gave her a 'leave-me-alone' look and mumbled, "Nothin'." Grimly, she left her daughter and made her way into the clinic.

The geezers, of course, had begun to gather, although even they looked defeated by the heat, unshaven and sweaty. Doc was back; a rancher whom Junee recalled as being named Jerry Biskit had come by to pick up vaccine, but was ready to chat, and Doc pointed him into the shade in the back yard. Someone had brought cold beer, and this seemed to be rousing them from their lethargy. When Patch arrived, he gestured behind him. "Feel that sun?" He began to rumble pleasantly, "It's goin' down, down, down in a burnin' ring of fire..." and somebody cracked, "Okay, Johnny Cash. Shut up and have a beer."

Bennie handed Junee a beer and she popped the tab, feeling better as the icy bubbles hit her mouth. Sophia drug listlessly outside; she sat on the top step and studied Doc, as if she expected him to say something to her, but Doc and all the other geezers were involved in a discussion of someone's exceptional expertise with his cattle, so Junee sat down beside her daughter and put her arm around her shoulders. Sophia stiffened. Now Junee became concerned. "What's up, honey? Is something wrong?"

The little girl ducked her head. "I told you, nothing's wrong. I just... I just got a headache. Like you always do." She thought, "I will never tell her. Never."

Junee peered closely at her. Well, this confirmed her fears. This place was getting at her daughter, too, just like it was getting at her. "Are you thirsty, honey? You need to drink lots of water in this heat."

Sophia looked up, an oddly adult, assessing look. "I'm no thirstier than you are, Mom." Didn't her mother remember how she had told Grandma that she knew all about water and headaches? Well, so do I, thought Sophia.

Trying to think what might be a treat, Junee asked, "Do you want some soda? Everybody here has beer, so I don't see why you couldn't go get yourself a soda from Doc's fridge."

Her eyes down again, Sophia said passively, "Okay." Then, glancing once more at Doc, she added, "I think I'll just get a soda and head for bed. I'm tired."

Watching her go, Junee sighed. What had she done to deserve a teenager when the kid wasn't even eight yet? She tossed back the rest of her beer and went for another. The geezer stories were starting not to sound so bad to her. Lew cackled, "You know, that old boy, he really knows his herd. Got over 500 head by now, don't he?"

Doc said, "Seems like more than that, when I look out there in the corral and put on my sleeve to get ready to preg check 'em."

Lew continued, "And got every damn one named."

"At least got their numbers plumb straight," Doc said.

Jerry Biskit expanded. "Shit, he can tell you which cow pooped under which tree."

"Yesterday," added Patch.

Doc chortled. "Hell, ten years ago."

Junee remembered that Jerry's wife's name was Laura, and that she was supposed to have had eye surgery recently. Reaching for another beer, she asked, "Jerry, how is Laura's eye doing?"

Jerry shook his head, serious. "Not so good, not so good. Doctor says it ain't gonna be easy to fix. He says the retina's wrinkled."

This, and the beer, saddened Junee. "Oh, no! What can she do?"

"I dunno. Iron it, I guess. Or stretch it." He chuckled, pleased with himself.

By the time Junee caught up with that one, though, the exchange had moved along. Bennie said, "Speakin' of wives, Doc, we saw yours headin' out from the house a little bit ago. She was nippin' right along, considerin' the heat."

Doc shrugged. "Yeah, she gets tense sometimes; sometimes somethin' will upset her, and she won't want to talk about it, so she'll just get out and hike up that old Ute trail. She usually makes it as far as the spring, then comes on back. Seems to relieve her worries a little."

The men nodded the wise nods of those who really don't know, but probably should. Then Bennie added, "Does she hunt while she's walkin'? She was packin' a rifle."

"Nah," Doc said. "I've always asked her to carry a gun when she goes up that direction. She skirts Gump's place, but there's other varmints out there. She's a good shot if she gets in trouble."

Buddy whined, and apparently Lucky whined, too, as Lew patted the space beside him and said, "It's okay, boy, we'll get on home pretty soon."

"Us, too," rumbled Patch, using his sleeve to wipe the sweat off his face. "So what happened to Soapy, anyhow? She didn't stay long."

Junee had another beer and was feeling quite mellow about it all. "Just tired, I think. She went to bed; she'll probably be around tomorrow to give Buddy some reason to want to head up a tree."

Biskit, getting up to leave, said, "Yeah, ain't it right. Not many cow dogs can climb trees. Which reminds me, speakin' of that varmint, Gump. You know what he told me once?"

A dispassionate grunt came from the old men as they struggled to manage their beer-bedeviled legs and rise from the flimsy lawn chairs. Jerry continued, "Gump was watchin' Buddy, and he said, 'You know, Jerry, when you see a politician that's climbin' like that dog there, he's either after a pretty fat squirrel, or he's scared and runnin' from somethin' that he don't want to admit to what it is.'"

19

"MAARIKA'S THE ONE WHO'S DOING IT." Spoken with finality into the dark August night, the moon just a sliver.

"You're so obsessing. It isn't helping." Even in the deepening dusk, she could see that his whole body looked defeated; Will had dropped his head, resting his forehead against their tree. "It could've been Gump," he mumbled. "He'd do anything to get his hands on our property. Can you imagine what he'd do if he got it? How he'd destroy our trees?"

What could she say? Will, too, obsessed. He believed with all his being in the Anastasian prophecies of cosmic healing and the restoration of the radiant Vedic civilization. He lived it. It guided his thoughts and actions every minute of every hour. It was he who had submitted to his own vision, allowing himself to be brought to this very place. For him, a holy place. A place where the trees were already filling with cosmic light, preparing to bring forth the great transformation of his own country, his America. The trees would not be the cedars of the Russian taiga, but the beautiful pinyons of the West. Just as it was in Russia, when they were ready, they would ring, and when they rang out, telling everyone that it was time, they could be harvested, cut into pieces small enough to be worn as pendants, which would be distributed as far as Will and his friends could distribute them, because each piece of the body of the holy, ringing tree would bring its power to heal human bodies and souls, bringing harmony and light back to the world. He really believed it, and his belief made it powerful, and his belief drew Carol in. She believed it, too.

It hurt her incredibly to see him slumped, leaning against their tree. He was such a strong man. It was he who had gathered his friends and brought them here, the lot of them, intent on creating kin's domains in this forest. It was he who led the effort to raise the money, purchase the land, assure that all their holdings, including the Sunshine Spring, were legal. It was he who kept everyone on track, making sure they communed with all the plants, that they personally tried to know every individual plant, wild and domestic; it was he who gently urged each member of his group to always take personal responsibility for the restoration and re-balancing of Earth's natural systems. They were to own a piece of Earth, their planet, their home, and they were to care for it accordingly. They were to live within nature, not as exploiters, but as participants. His vision was noble.

She and Will had spent many hours under this tree, dreaming together about what this kin's domain, here by Croissant, would be like. She'd seen pictures of others, the idealized offspring of Russian *dachas*, and they were beautiful: beehives and gardens, fields and workshops, living hedges... Each was the unique domain of one family of kin, and the goal was for that family, on the 2.47 acres of land they were allotted, to become self-sufficient. The domains were all part of a larger community that provided everyone with a supportive network: a school, a meeting center, roads, and so-on. The community part must be built first, and that was what Will and his friends were working on now.

Carol often slipped through the trees, concealing herself on the point above the settlement, just where Forest Road dipped down, to watch them work. Right now it looked nothing like the beautiful pictures that she and Will admired. It looked dusty, disorganized, and as if there were a lot of problems appearing just from what their friend, Nature, could deal out. Still, Carol was confident it would eventually take form. Will's friends seemed to be as competent and dedicated as he was. Carol would watch them work and fantasize about being able to join them, of helping to form and stack dobie bricks, of pondering with them where they might locate the kitchen gardens, of bringing in her little band of sheep. But no, of course not. She couldn't go there. There was Maarika.

She sat by the tree, looked up at her love, and didn't speak, because she didn't know what to say. The silence weighed heavy. At last Will turned around and leaned his back against the tree.

"It doesn't ring."

"I know. I cannot hear it." Carol fought tears. Couldn't he think more practically, just for once, and address their problems with Maarika and the baby?

"It hasn't rung since I heard it on that first day."

Again, Carol was silent. He knew she knew. He said, "I think we are calling in the dark energy, Carol. You know about the great power of human thought. I think all our thoughts, our fussing about Maarika and the dogs and all, that is destroying the light that was being held by this tree."

Driven to distraction, Carol pushed her growing bulk off the ground to stand, facing him. She must speak. "Will, your brain is in the wrong place. You are thinking backwards! If anybody is bringing in dark energy, it is Maarika. She knows you don't love her, and never have. She knows you would do anything to make it right with her if she would only free you. She even knows I'm pregnant. She hasn't any reason to hold you except malice. Just get a divorce and get her away from this place."

"I know, I know. I'll try. But I fear her. She'll fight it. We've talked about this before—I don't know if we can get rid of her soon enough. Our baby... "

Carol gave a sharp, "Oh!" and did a surprised side step. Something heavy and furry had emerged from the dark and moved against her leg. Will said, "Wha... ?" and, following her eyes, looked down. They both saw him at once. Buddy, his dappled coat making him invisible in the dark, had taken a place at Carol's knee, and was looking up at her, his face plainly saying, "Well, what next?"

Roughing his fur lovingly, Carol said, "What are you doing here, Buddy?"

For the first time this night, Will gave Carol his old, happy grin. "I guess he just followed you out. I suspect you're a lot more interesting than old Patch at this time of night."

"I suppose. I talked to Patch when he got home earlier, and I think he was going right to bed after a beer drinking party at Doc's." They both laughed and petted the dog, then Carol said hopefully, "But you were going to say something about our baby?"

"Oh, just that I think Maarika will do everything she can to stop us, and she may be able to embroil us in legalities, since the marriage was in Russia. She'll make our baby a problem, call it an affair and all. As an errant foreign husband... well, what if they drag me back to Russia for marriage counseling or something? Drag me away from you and the domain and... They won't care about the American wife and kid. We need some way to get rid of her sooner. I need more time. I need to think this through."

"But you're right, my beloved. Time is what we don't have. Do you remember what I told you, that my mother says I have an inheritance somewhere in this area? She keeps a tight lid on it, but I guess it's for real. She says that before my father died, he set it up, and that I'll be notified when I'm 25. We have an awful lot to lose if Maarika forces me away, even if we win in the end." Will looked grim.

"You can't ride two horses at once, my love. The mysterious inheritance is just that. Mysterious. Who knows what your mother has up her sleeve? But let me say this. You think I never think about the baby. Well, you're wrong. She is almost everything I think about any more. I'm not waiting to love her. I love her now." His voice had become edgy. "I hate to say it, because I know you'll lose your temper and think all I think about is the domain, but part of what I worry about is getting you and that kid into the village so you can have a proper home birth, and so that our child can get the right education and step into her own Vedic role in bringing about the new civilization."

"I understand," Carol placated. "I agree. It's just that I think we can't put up with Maarika much longer. Time's passing. Now she's poisoning dogs. Maybe the next thing she'll do will be to poison me and the baby."

Before Will could respond, Buddy gave a low, throbbing growl. He was looking into the trees with a fixed stare, and they realized they could hear a stealthy movement in the underbrush, the crack of a twig. Alarmed, Will put his arm around Carol and pulled her into the dense, shadowy darkness surrounding a nearby serviceberry bush. From this retreat, they looked back. In the pale starlight, they could see that Buddy had achieved the lower branches of their pinyon and was climbing fast, leading, as always, with his hind end. Below him, looking up with great interest through narrow, frowny eyes, his bowed front legs set belligerently, was a big, heavy-set dog, a light brown pit bull with white markings. Its ears flattened close to its head, its tail stiff with its mission, it began to snuffle and dig at the base of the tree.

Holding Will's head so she could whisper into his ear, Carol said, "It's Killer." Will drew his head away and looked his question into her eyes. "Arnold Clenting's dog."

Buddy had flattened himself on a branch, and the dog below now ignored him. Carol took Will's head again, her little hissing whisper teasing at his ear. "It could be Cuddles, I guess. Killer's sister, same litter. Looks just like him, but she's Gump's dog."

Will nodded. He hadn't heard it all, but he really didn't care who the dog belonged to, anyhow. He was trying to figure out how they would get away from here. He took Carol's head. "Is it mean?"

"I don't know." A low sound came from the direction of Forest Road, a sound like a whispered whistle. The pit bull unfolded its pointy ears, sticking them up, and trotted off in the direction of the sound.

"I'll walk you home." This time, it was Will who was firm. Softly, they called Buddy, but he eyed them with scorn and wouldn't leave his branch.

Carol shrugged. "Look, he'll probably follow in a minute. Let's go on, then, before whoever that was comes back to ask what we're doing here."

20

PATCH HAD ON OLD, GRAYED winter underwear because, in Colorado, even in August, the nights could be damn cool, and his circulation wasn't so good anymore. Sometimes he found himself shivering just thinking about it. His old feet were bare, displaying the thick yellow toenails that he cut, not frequently enough, with his pocket knife. Gums that failed to show a full complement of teeth were set deep in the unshaven, grizzled stubble that had sprouted above the wild white beard that emerged around his chin. Static sent what little hair he had left toward the ceiling, and his eyes were bleared with the remains of sleep. "Ya stay sittin', Doc," he growled at his unexpected visitor. "Ya stay put. Coffee's comin'. Ya don't have to get it all out right off."

Doc, wheezing and sucking for oxygen, was bent over, clutching at his damaged knees. As bad as Patch looked, Doc looked far worse, and he couldn't have told his friend anything, even if it had been his intention to try. He was mud to his knees, beset by twigs and leaves, deathly pale, and now his hands had begun to tremble. The coffee heating, Patch sat down at the table and studied him. "Ya need me to call an ambulance? Ya don't look so good."

Shaking his head, Doc said, "No. No, damnit, gimme a minute."

Bringing the coffee, Patch pushed the mug along the table. "Drink this. It'll warm ya. His wrinkled, bald head slick with sweat, Doc didn't look as if he needed warmed, but he gathered himself, gripped the mug, and obeyed.

Still pulling for air, he spoke between intakes and said, "Patch. Thought I wouldn't make 'er here. Came down Forest

Road. Needed to reach you, but damn near didn't get here."

"See that, Doc."

"It's Annabelle. She never showed all night."

Now Patch was rubbing his stubble, getting stirred up. "All night? Not since everybody left, Lew and Jerry and me and all?"

"Before that. You saw her headin' up the Ute trail earlier than that." Done trembling, his color improved, Doc pushed the mug toward Patch for a refill. "I waited awhile, figured she'd come back when she got it walked out, but it got to be too long." He dumped sugar in his coffee and stirred. "Got me my spotlight. I could pick up her tracks as far as the spring, then I lost 'em. She mighta gone on, but that trail gets more overgrown, farther you get. I couldn't find anything past the spring."

Doc had begun to tremble again. When he set the cup down, it bounced against the table. Patch ran a hand over his electric hair, thinking. "And you looked good right at the spring? No sign of her?"

"Did my best with the spotlight. Willows and brush thick as shit. Dark as the devil, but I couldn't pick up any tracks in that mud around the spring." He looked at his watch. "Almost six. It'll be full daylight soon. I gotta get back out there."

Patch grunted. "You ain't in any great shape. We better call search and rescue."

"You know Annabelle would hate that." His eyes haunted, Doc looked directly at his friend. "Either way."

Receiving the look, Patch nodded. "All right then, Doc. We'll do 'er different. I'll call Lew and Bennie and scramble up some eggs. Need that. Won't take 'em long to get here. We can use our four-wheelers, Bennie's and mine, and get in as far as we can up by the settlement before we start to walk."

21

IT HAD GOTTEN TO BE A HABIT. As the cool morning breeze escorted the sun up, getting it ready to pass over the eastern mountains, Sophia, half asleep and shivering, would reach for the duvet and Sneaker. Snuggling them both close, she would curl in for those last soothing minutes of sleep.

This morning it didn't happen. Something was amiss. Patting around on the quilt, the fact took full form in her waking brain. No Sneaker. Where was Sneaker? Not yet alarmed, her bare feet found the floor and she puttered about, calling, looking under the bed, looking in unlikely places. Lower bookshelf? Laundry basket? No dog. Well, this was odd!

Her mom, cursing the lack of air conditioning, always left doors open to catch cool air at night. Her bare feet pattering, Sophia passed through the living area and into their little private back yard. Sneaker would have to be there. Where else could she be? Fussing at the dog for not coming when called, she poked under bushes and flowers and even looked into the tree, thinking that perhaps Buddy had taught Sneaker to climb. Then she saw the gate.

She'd been scolded before for waking her mother. Veterinarians worked dreadful hours, and had to get sleep when they could. Junee didn't take kindly to being awakened just to hear about Sophia's latest gaming triumph. This time, Sophia didn't care. This was different. She ran back into the apartment and burst into her mother's bedroom, shouting, "Mom! That damned Annabelle wants my dog dead! She hates Sneaker. She came down and opened our gate!" Then, "Mom? Mom?"

No one was there.

Swallowing tears, Sophia straggled back into the living

116

area, where she finally saw the large, hastily scrawled note on the table. "Sophia. Horse with colic. Can't reach Doc. Cole should be here to do clinic chores soon. Stay with him. Be back soon. Mom"

Oh. Sophia sat down hard on a kitchen chair, then popped back up. After all, she didn't have to think. She knew what she had to do. Scurrying back to her room and dressing in hiking clothes, she gathered up her fanny pack. Water, yes. Breakfast bar, yes. Package of gum from her mother's desk drawer, yes. Phone? No. There wouldn't be reception where she was going, or at least that is what they said. She dropped it onto her bed so she wouldn't lose it.

Next, she flipped her mother's note to the blank side and carefully printed, "Mom Sneaker gone. Went to find her. Be back soon." Tapping the pencil on the paper, she scowled in thought, then added, "Just be carful. Anabel is realy a wich. She opened our gate wile we were asleep."

22

BENNIE HATED LIKE HELL TO BRING IT UP, but he knew he couldn't get out of it. He chewed for a while on Patch's rubbery eggs, listening to the others lay out search plans and trying to think how to put it to avoid hitting Doc too hard. Lew, who was quite a talker, was all wound up with excitement and worry, and it took Bennie some effort to get a word in edgewise. Finally he just said it. "Abby took a call from Carol Haddon just as I was leavin' to come up here."

This being out of context, they all looked at him blankly, so he took a deep breath and continued. "You know, I told Carol some time ago if she heard poachers on her land, or had any more trouble with somebody trying to hurt her dogs, to let me know, and I'd look into it."

Now he had their attention. "So, why'd she call?"

"Well, I didn't talk to her. I was in a hurry to get over here, so I just waved it off, you know," he demonstrated with a dismissing motion of his hand, "And Abby told her I'd already gone out, but that she'd tell me and she was sure I'd look into it."

"Look into what?" Patch was scowling, his rumble annoyed, impatient to get to the point.

"I guess, according to Abby, Carol was out of breath. She told Abby that she just thought she'd take her dogs for a little morning run up Forest Road, because she was having trouble sleeping, but as she got toward the top of the grade, she heard a shot. She thought someone was shooting at her or at her dogs, so she ran all the way home."

A deathly silence fell. Bennie finished lamely, "She told Abby it could be poachers. That's why she called me."

It didn't fly. Nobody thought it was poachers. The implications of the shot were clear to everyone at the table. Doc, scraping his chair back, said, "That's enough. I gotta go."

There was jostling as they reached the door. Patch called Buddy, and Lew let out several sharp whistles for Lucky. Neither the climbing dog nor the invisible dog came. Looking up into the tree that bordered Carol's yard, Patch growled. "Son of a bitch. Now where'd he go? Never knew him to stay away unless he thought he was playin' a trick on me."

Bennie was starting up his ATV, and Lew, climbing up behind, said helpfully, "We gotta get goin'. We're gonna have to leave 'em for now, Patch."

Doc was chafing at the bit beside Patch's four-wheeler, so he went on over, worrying at it. "Damn dog. He ain't even got his breakfast yet."

MEANWHILE, BUDDY had gotten deeply involved with the one thing that could have kept him from returning home to Patch. It had been a wonderful night, more rich in adventure than any he had spent for a long time. First, there had been the hike out into the forest following his old friend, Carol. Then there had been lots of time to explore the vicinity of the tryst tree while the humans talked nearby. He had been somewhat frightened by the pit bull, who had never acted like a pal no matter where Buddy had encountered him, but he trusted Carol and the other human to deal with the problem. Climbing the tree? Well, that was just a precaution. Then that dog left, and the humans left, and he got down to follow them home, but there were just so many things to smell and do! A rabbit in the brush; a trace of squirrel; other dogs, perhaps. He actually lost track of Carol, and by the time he realized what was happening, he had sniffed his way across Forest Road and entered the dense section of pinyon, juniper, chaparral, and buck brush south of Gump's place.

It was then that he saw her, the weird little squirrel-dog. Now here was good fortune! She, too, was out hunting. Curious and pleased, his tail wagging, his nose to the ground, he trotted along, following closely behind the fascinating creature as she busied herself beside the logs and in the underbrush.

23

GARRETT USED McCRACKIN'S PRIVATE LINE. It might help a little, but he figured that no matter what he did, it wouldn't take that bunch of people up there long to spread this sheriff business all over the community. They were like a bunch of ants; even when they didn't seem to be doing anything, they were communicating.

She answered groggily, and he said, "Hey, Mac. Sorry. Time to suit up. We got a 911 up in Croissant."

"Croissant? WTF. It's barely daylight—what did they do now? Somebody run into a black cow with his truck?"

"Not this time. Besides, it's almost 6:30, Deputy. I figured you'd been up for hours, liftin' weights and tonin' up them big muscles of yours. Now I am shocked to find out you're sleepin' in."

"Let me get my coffee," she groused.

"Yeah, bring me some more, too. I'm on my way in right now; meet me at the office?"

"Urgent, then?"

"Dispatch said the caller kept cutting out, one of those bad mountain connections, but she got that there is a woman down. Shot, she thinks. People kind of spooked, anxious to get somebody there to secure the scene."

She was on speaker, and had shrugged into her uniform while she talked. It was last night's coffee, but she could nuke it. She grabbed two cups, still talking. "I'm out the door. Dispatch give us an address?"

"Old Grand Road. 2350." He slid the car smoothly into his parking slot; Riversmet was quiet as a stone at this hour. "Isn't that where the dirt road takes off Old Grand and heads up to that outfit by the spring? Those survivalists or whatever they are? Maybe I'd better pick us up a couple rifles while I'm here.... Or wait, was that where those widows with the dog were meeting last month?"

"No, I think you're right—it's that turn on up into the forest. Not the Widders." She'd made it to the car, phone shouldered at her ear. Maneuvering the coffee into the holders under the dash, she laughed. "Maybe a Bundy stand off, huh?" She couldn't conceal her excitement.

Less pleased, Garrett said, "Maybe. I'm thinking of calling for backup." Then, just to be ornery, he added, "So, any idea where I might locate Red?"

24

CHILDREN LEARN EARLY ON that there are small 'd' dangers and big 'D' dangers. They can tell by the tone of voice of the adult giving out the warning. "Wash your hands after you poo or you'll get sick": very small 'd'. "Quit trying to do wheelies on that hill—you're going to break your neck": medium 'd'. But "Don't talk to strangers?" Junee always made that one big 'D', but Sophia felt confident in her own judgment about this, and preferred to decide according to the individual circumstance that arose. She figured she could tell a dangerous stranger if she saw one.

In this case, when she saw the stranger, she was standing next to a large sage bush that was growing by Forest Road. He didn't see her. She felt as if she'd been hunting Sneaker forever, and she was discouraged, weepy, and a little frightened. She had lived all her young life near people, on streets, near parks, always in urban areas. Searching for Sneaker, she found that everywhere she looked there were only trees, thorny bushes, dust, and sky. She was starting to wish powerfully that she had someone to talk to about her lost dog, someone to commiserate with. She had wandered across rough country for almost an hour, and now she worried that she was lost. She wasn't sure how to find her way back.

She stood very, very still by the sage, watching the stranger, debating, but as he drew closer, she knew. The man looked distracted, upset, maybe angry, but it was the dog that clinched it. It was a large, slavering pit bull that seemed to push the air in front of its heavy chest as it stalked behind its master. Sophia cringed, then slipped to the ground and made herself small, as silent as a frightened rabbit. The man, pre-occupied, passed, the dog trotting purposefully behind him.

Forcing herself to remain still, Sophia hunkered by the sage root and worried. That man looked mean, but so did the dog. What if it had found Sneaker and hurt, or even killed, her? It could have done that. Anxious now on behalf of her dog, she could hold herself quiet no longer.

The man had been walking down a road. Roads lead places, and a road would be easier than the bushwhacking she had been engaged in. Slipping from the shelter of the sage with renewed determination, she set off in the direction opposite the man, scurrying up the road. She was afraid to call her dog now, for fear the man would come back, so she struggled to see, forcing her eyes to examine first one side of the road, then the other. Thus engaged, she failed to notice that a woman was approaching until she was almost upon her.

Annabelle Clary was limping directly toward her, her rifle heavy, barely held up as it swung at her side. Annabelle was not in good shape; she had spent the night with death. Her original intention, on leaving the house, had been simply to find a quiet place, a lovely place, and shoot herself. She took medications for pain, which Doc said were part of her problem, and she had tried to quit them before, but this time she brought them all with her. This time they were not for pain. They were for courage.

She could no longer live with whatever it was that she was. She knew she had had a dreadful reaction to that little girl and her dog, but she didn't know why. This kind of thing had happened before, and she was totally unable to understand who that person was, the person who screamed at children and shrank from dogs, even small dogs. Doc had tried to explain it many times, but she never believed he told her all. As for herself, she remembered nothing of what had caused her to be like this. Even now, things happened, and she couldn't remember. As she walked from the house, she focused on remembering that the child was innocent, and that she, Annabelle, was helping no one by remaining alive on this earth. She believed herself dangerous.

As she walked, her conviction was beset by ghosts, the Ute who had walked this trail, who had loved this earth, who had loved this very place and lost it. They were all around her, murmuring, fussing, asking how she could think of giving this up, these trees, these mountains, when they, a whole people, had fought so bitterly to keep it?

Their sorrow and loss began to drive her mad. She left the path. Working her way through the untraveled forest, breathing in the night air, listening to the soft sounds of darkness, the whisper of trees, the call of an owl, she found herself high above the settlement. Tired of climbing over fallen logs, pushing aside bushes, she rejoined the trail. There were spruce here now, and she found a bed of needles under one. Utterly exhausted, she slept.

She awoke chilled and shivering. She had dreamed, and the dream was about her husband. She knew this, although there were no images, no sounds, no wrinkled old forehead, no shuffling limp. At first nothing with a name came to her dream, but instead a feeling of power, of shielding and enfolding, of protection. And within that strength, the empty shell, the thing that had no being, the pointless thing that made her shudder. Then she did see him, her husband, the old man, picking and hammering, engaged in a disturbing prying and knocking that it seemed had gone on for a thousand years.

Something fluttered inside the shell, frightened, frantic. What if he succeeded? What was it, that fluttering thing? Could it hurt him? Wasn't it just a restless ghost that should have been long gone? It flattened to the wall, trying to hide in the shell as he pried and pried and pried, endlessly persistent.

It was a dream, and this time, the shell cracked. Was it she who had broken? No, she was not the shell. She was inside. Try as she might, she could not see what it was, the thing inside. Instead, she saw her husband's face. The shell was evaporating, falling away, and it was not empty. What he was watching was a caged thing freed, and as she watched his face, she knew that the thing was not a ghost. It was real. It went to him, and his face was suffused with joy. He opened his arms and she felt herself within them, real, a person, no longer lost. "Annabelle Clary," he said, "Here you are. Here you are at last." She felt his relief. She felt his completion.

It was a dream. A dream only. She struggled from the needles, her bones old and aching, and began to walk down the trail. It was a long way back, but it was almost dawn, and the ghosts who walked beside her were gentle now. Pulling the pain medications from her pocket, she threw them into the trees, scattering them as she walked.

By daylight, Annabelle was so tired. She couldn't even recall passing the settlement, but now she found herself on Forest Road, and she was glad of that. It would be easier to walk down the road than deal with the overgrown path she had just left. She trudged along, keeping herself moving, needing her home. Then she looked up, and there she was. Sophia. She was appalled. They both stopped in their tracks.

Sophia, too, was dismayed and frightened, but before she could think what she must do, her focus was torn from Annabelle. She had spotted her quarry. Just in the bushes to her right was the pleasant, mottled body of Buddy, busily making its way through the brush, tail all awag and ears cocked with pleasure. In front of him, much smaller but now visible, was Sneaker. Sophia didn't think. She simply broke into a run, screaming, "Oh, it's Sneaker. Help me! Please, Mrs. Clary, help me! Help me get her!" Sneaker, ambushed and astonished, ran.

Annabelle's tired old body went rigid. She stared after the child who was fighting her way through the underbrush, and a great war exploded within her. Briefly, she raised the rifle, thinking she must shoot the dog. Something held her. Something told her it wouldn't be right. But what must she do? She began to work her way toward Sophia. She was weeping.

They had reached a tall pinyon with cranky bark when Sophia, scolding, finally got the attention of the rebellious dog. At last Sneaker stopped and crouched in submission, flattening herself under the tree. Her mistress pounced, snatching her up, kissing and scolding at once. Annabelle had caught up, confused and struggling with her devils, when Buddy shot past, leapt over the relieved child, achieved the lower branching of the tree, then began to scrabble upward. He was whining as he climbed. Annabelle looked behind them, following the climbing dog's worried gaze. Emerging from the trees was a large, light brown pit bull, his mouth sufficiently agape to show the strong teeth, his enthusiastic slobbers dripping across his bowed front legs as he trotted toward them. He stopped to regard them with interest and his neck ruff rose. He gave a low growl.

They say a crisis can bring out superhuman strength. In this case, Annabelle dropped her rifle, ignored her aged and aching joints, grabbed Sophia, who was clutching Sneaker, and simply pitched them into the lower fork of the tree. Shinnying up behind them, she gasped, "Climb, Sophia. Get on up. Get away from that dog!"

Here was the big 'D' danger. Sophia climbed.

25

THE LITTLE MESAS WITH THE SHADOWS going down their wrinkled skirts moved past, but they didn't go by fast enough for Garrett. He fought the temptation to hit the lights, even the siren. Riversmet was on the opposite side of the county from Croissant, which wasn't usually a problem unless trouble came up. Then, the distance could feel like light years. Driving too fast into the rising sun southeast of them, he glanced over at McCracken's pleased face. She loved speed. "Maybe better get me Hobbs on the land line. Put 'er on speaker and we'll both listen."

The detective opened with, "Hey, I was gonna call, but I had sense enough to wait until a decent hour. I'm kinda civilized, you know. Didn't want to disturb the rest of you high class folks."

Garrett grinned. "Yeah, yeah, so you say. Listen, it's after seven. All the folks that ain't just plain lazy been up and at it for hours." As if to confirm that statement, two pickups passed going west. Like overloaded burros, their beds were stacked so high with hay that the bales bulged over the sides and top, obscuring the fenders and covering the back window of the cab. No visibility. Could have been Garrett's issue. Not today.

"So, Sheriff, what's on your mind that's so important you have to wake a man at the crack of dawn?"

"Mmmph," Garrett said. "Maybe just psychic. You said you were gonna call me, right?"

"All righty, then, so it's down to business. I've been pokin' around in those areas where you wanted me to poke. So far, nothing new on the commissioner contenders. Nothing you can't read in the paper. Maybe you should hire that woman,

Macklenburg, to do some detectin'."

Garrett sent McCracken a puzzled scowl and she decoded. "Maureen Macklenburg's one of the Widders, Chief. She writes a gossip column for *Valley Views*. Right now, she's been all over the commissioner race."

Hobbs said, "That's true. She can be pretty funny, but I'm never sure if she intends to be or not. I think that she actually takes her work seriously."

"Huh. Got it. So what else you got?"

"The settlement up Forest Road is kind of an eco-religious group. They're called Vedrussians, but what little I could find out about this particular group, and by the way, there's only half a dozen of them or so here so far, but anyhow, I've been doing some tracing, and I don't think most of them are Russian. They seem to be Americans who for some reason have taken Russian names."

Now it was McCracken's turn to scowl. "So why would they do that? Are they terrorists or something?"

Hobbs cleared his throat. "Well, in this day and age, that's always the first thing we think of, isn't it." He was silent, perhaps thinking, then continued, "Honestly, Mac, so far that's not the vibe I've gotten. I guess it pays to be cautious, but I've done some general background work on the Vedrussian movement, and they don't seem like that kind of folk."

Garrett asked, "How so?"

"Their big deal is gardening, treasuring plant life, and so-on. The real religious ones, I guess you'd call 'em the orthodox ones, believe that good cosmic energy is collected by cedars in the Russian taiga, and when the cedars are filled with cosmic light, they ring. Some Russian guy named Megré had an affair with this mythically gorgeous blond up in Siberia. She put him onto this whole cosmology, and got him started writing books about it."

"Mythically gorgeous blond? Sure you're sufficiently awake, Hobbs?"

"I kid you not. Her name is Anastasia, and she's bent on leading the world into a whole new, trouble-free, future. Megré's written about nine books so far about it, and they sell like hot-cakes. Not just in Russia. Everywhere. So who knows his motive, money or a vision? Anyhow, I can tell you more about the

Vedrussians when I see you."

Garrett sighed. "Well, I hate to say it, but you'd probably better see me sooner rather than later. Mac and I are headed up to Croissant on a 911, woman down is all we got, bad reception. But I don't have a good feeling about this. I think you better pack up and come on up."

Hobbs groaned. "You couldn't resist, could you? Here I was, just plannin' out my peaceful day of paperwork and donuts. Well, before you let me know the details about just where I'm headed, I do have one more little piece of information you might be interested in."

"And that would be... ?"

"The person you know as Carol Haddon has a couple other monikers. She was born Halabi, then got into some kind of illegitimate marriage with somebody named Yelets. She called herself Carol Yelets for some time, then switched to Carol Haddon when she moved to Croissant. I don't think Haddon is a legal name. From what I can dig up, she made that one up."

This drew a serious "mmmph" from Garrett, squinting hard now into the rising sun, having to slow for glinting objects reflecting along the roadside. Concluding his conversation with Hobbs, he said to Mac, "Make sure the crime scene unit is on their way up, then it won't hurt to get Louie and your Red to head up this way, too. Damn long drive, and I'm still not sure we won't need backup."

26

THE DOG WAS HAVING SERIOUS DOUBTS as to whether it was doing the right thing. It stopped in the center of the road and watched its master's retreating back. It looked like the boss was headed on back to the house, totally unaware of his dog's existence. It was interesting here, dog smells, people smells, wild game smells, and sounds coming from deeper in the forest that seemed to signal some kind of excitement. The dog wanted to stay. It gave its tail a conclusive wag and turned around, trotting back up the road. It didn't feel it was being disloyal. After all, the boss had left it a task here that it knew it was expected to complete. It was a good dog. It would tend to it, dig it all up, just like it had been taught to do.

ESTABLISHING THEMSELVES in the branches, Buddy above them, Sneaker held close to Sophia's chest, Annabelle and Sophia took stock of their situation. They were both scratched and bruised from the hurried climb, and neither were prepared to challenge the pit bull below. Peering anxiously down into the trees and bushes, Sophia exclaimed, "Oh, no, Mrs. Clary! Look! Now there are two of them!"

27

IF IT HADN'T BEEN FOR THE BALE-BUCKING muscles, Cole could have been described as a gangling kid. Meek, pimply, his duckbill worn backwards, he was the kind of kid you felt might benefit from a reassuring hug, but as to this you should think twice, because he was also the kind of kid with quick country reflexes, and he might slug you before he was clear as to your kindly intent. When Junee got back from treating the colicky mare, he was in the front yard giving two post-surgical pups a welcome morning spin. Junee greeted him with, "Hey, Cole, how're things?"

"Pretty good." The friendly, Croissant grin.

"I don't see Sophia out yet. Hasn't she been helping you?"

"Soapy? Nah. I ain't seen her around this morning."

Junee frowned. It was getting on 7:30. Sophia liked that little extra snooze, but she was usually out by now. Worried that her daughter's mood from the previous evening had carried over, she went on into the clinic and washed off the horse hair and sweat, then went to the apartment. She didn't make it to the bedrooms; Sophia's note was prominent on the table. It shifted Junee's universe. "Mom, Sneaker gone. Went to find her. Be back soon. Just be carful. Anabel is really a wich. She opened our gate while we were asleep."

Snatching up the note, Junee hurried to the back yard door. Crap. The gate was open, all right, but it was she, herself, who had left it open. She recalled that clearly now. The hangover that still burbled at her belly had been even more distracting at four in the morning when that call came in, and her primary thought at the time had been whether she should wake up Doc or just go tend to the colicky mare herself. She had rushed out the gate, looked up at Clarys' house, trying to think, decided that Doc was probably as hung over as she was and that she should do one for the Gipper this time, hurried back in the house to scribble the note to Sophia, and left. No, it wasn't the "wich" Annabelle who had left the gate open. Maybe, Junee scolded herself, it was the wich Junee.

The headache was returning. Still carrying the note, she found Cole getting ready to leave. "Has Doc been by yet this morning?"

"Nah. It's a little early yet. You got somethin' wrong? You look mighty stirred up. Anything I can do?"

"Yeah, I... no, I... well, I've got a question for Doc." She saw the concern on Cole's face, and said, "No, it's okay. No worries. I'll just run on up and see if he's up yet."

She knocked lightly, politely, but something bothered her about the place. It felt empty. Casting caution to the wind, she pounded, then opened the door and shouted. She felt it all around her; something here was very much not right. Scowling, she returned to the clinic and dialed 911.

Garrett and McCracken were approaching Peaseford when their radio crackled and the crisp voice came through. "SO-1, SO-1. Croissant. Please call dispatch on their land line."

Garrett exhaled a mild curse, and Mac picked up the phone. "Croissant, SO-1. Copy."

Someone else also issued a mild curse. When Maureen Macklenburg brushed her teeth, it was as if she were sending her mouth through a car wash. This was why she kept her 800 on high while she did her morning ablutions. She had just gotten everything thoroughly sudsed up and was preparing to enter the rinse cycle when dispatch came on, but now they were going to a land line and she wouldn't be able to get the rest of the call. Damn. She resented it, even though she knew that the whole point of the land line was professional, to protect the privacy of those about whom the call was being made. "Seriously," she thought, "If they would keep me in the loop, at least, I could do so much." She felt entitled.

Meanwhile, Mac was telling Garrett that a mother was reporting a missing child, and that the child might have wandered off in search of her dog. Finishing, Mac said, "Shit, Chief. Soapy?"

Worried, Garrett grabbed for the 800 line. "Dispatch, this is SO-1. Please clarify last known location with R.P."

Leaning toward the radio, Maureen waited, breathless. This one she would hear. A few moments passed, then dispatch came back on. "Reporting party gives the last known sighting of the missing person as being about 8:30 last night, at 2200 Old Grand Road."

Mac and Garrett groaned. It had to be Soapy, and now she was out there wandering around near the area of the shooting. As for Maureen, she had a wall map of the area pinned above the phone, and she was running a quick index finger along Old Grand road. Ah, there it was, just as she suspected. 2200, the Clarys' place.

The sheriff's radio was on again. "SO-1, this is SO-2."

"SO-2. Go ahead."

"We copied that traffic direct. Would you like us to go investigate with R. P.?"

"Affirmative. Please switch to RSO-OPS 2."

Maureen tapped her foot She was being cut out again, but she had gotten all of it so far, the communications between the patrol cars. Now she was sure of it. Something serious was coming down, as she liked to say. She needed to do something, that much was for sure.

In the sheriff's car, they were getting the standard, "This is SO-2 on OPS 2. Go ahead."

"Good. SO-2, we are en route to a shooting at 2350 Old Grand Road. As you know, we may need backup. Persons of interest at this time include the missing child as well as a party nearby going by the name 'Carol Haddon.' Request that you proceed to location of reporting party, then keep open for instructions."

"10-4, SO-1. We copy."

With a little grunt of her own, Mac hit dial on her iPhone and did the half-joking thing. "Red. You and Louie be careful, okay? It's a jungle out there." She and Garrett were passing Clary's, both tense, their eyes combing the buildings and the countryside that now rushed by too rapidly as they continued to the address of the reported shooting.

Maureen, too, knew what she must do. Opening her list of names and numbers, she began to spread the news. Within minutes she had organized a telephone tree, mobilizing the community for a search for the missing person. So far, she didn't know who it was, but she would find out. She told them all to meet at Clarys'.

28

FOREST ROAD WAS A DIRT ROAD wide enough for two cars to pass each other, one going up, one down. Once it left Old Grand, it gained elevation rapidly, and there had been sketchy attempts to gravel particularly challenging places along its rise, but the road commonly defeated unprepared traffic once winter set in. It often came precipitously close to one or another of the eroded ravines common to the area, causing passengers not mountainously inclined to gasp and clutch for the dash board. About a half mile before the Vedrussian settlement, the road widened and flattened, allowing a place where four or more vehicles could pull off the main track. That pull-out was crossed by the Ute trail, which in its turn went past the small lake formed by Sunshine Spring to the west, and to the east and south traveled on into the mountains. After the pull-out, Forest Road regained its purpose and lifted sharply uphill until it crested, then dropped down into the settlement below.

Doc, Lew, Patch, and Bennie were at the pull-out, standing by their four-wheelers. They had already followed the trail for some fifty yards toward Sunshine Spring, but they had found no trace of Annabelle, nor had Patch and Lew been able to call in Buddy and Lucky. Friends though they were, they were still reaching a level of irritation with each other. Each had a different idea as to how this search should be conducted, and the consensus they were working toward involved splitting up. The issue they had to conquer was which direction each man should take. Aware of Doc's fatigue, there was an ill-fated attempt to persuade him to stay with the ATVs and rest. This being unsuccessful, they took up the idea of who should go on up the trail. Bennie considered himself to be younger and spryer, and before they could argue further, he announced, "Well, I'll walk on up," and took off. Looking sick, Doc said, "I suppose we need to go talk to those people in the settlement."

Lew, ever ready to meet people, volunteered, but this had Patch and Doc exchanging glances. If Lew went, he would do all the talking, and he wasn't noted these days for being all that firmly anchored in reality. They were pretty sure he might not get the information needed. Patch, forestalling him, rumbled, "Maybe before we tip that bunch off about the problem, we oughta give the spring another going over, this time in daylight. Might pick up some tracks."

Doc, even whiter, crumpled against the ATV seat. "Yeah," he said. "Yeah, I suppose we better." Then they heard the approaching vehicle.

Garrett and McCracken pulled up next to the ATVs and cut the engine. The presence of these old men was unsettling. So far, no one had been able to discern who it was that had been shot, and Garrett didn't like the look of Doc Clary. The officers got out of their car, and Patch stepped forward. "Howdy, Sheriff. How'd you get here so fast?"

Catching Mac's eye, Garrett gave her a warning look. Something was askew here. Carefully, he responded, "Somebody called in."

Doc, straightening, said, "Who the hell would call in? We're the only ones know she's missing."

Studying him, Garrett said, "We don't know who called, either. Phone service is bad up here. But now we got here, and we're gonna find out."

Bennie emerged onto the pull-out from the trail, holding something in his hand. "Doc, I found... ," then he realized they had company. "How the hell you people find out about Annabelle?" He turned to look over his companions. "One of you call in?"

There was general head shaking, but Doc had once more sunk against the ATV. His voice strained, he said, "Ben, what did you find?"

"A lot of these. I just picked up a few." Stepping over to Doc, he held out his hand. In it were a dozen white pills. "You recognize these? I figured you'd have an idea what they are, bein' you're a medical man and all."

Taking one with his stubby fingers, turning it over to inspect it, Doc said, "Annabelle's pain pills."

Bennie lowered his head. "So she went up that way."

Seizing the opportunity, Garrett said, "Look, you boys go follow that lead, and Mac and I will drop on over into the settlement, see what we can find out." Then, trying to reassure Doc, "We'll find her, Dr. Clary."

Patch's eyes had narrowed, assessing the law officers, but he rumbled, "Good enough." Mac and Garrett got into their car, and as their dust retreated up the hill, Lew eyed the Ute trail from which Bennie had just emerged with a measure of dread. He wasn't so sure he wanted to find what might be beyond those pills, but looking at Doc's strained face, he steeled himself. "Well, I guess we better get on up that trail and quit wastin' time."

Patch and Bennie weren't looking up the trail. Their eyes were watching the sheriff's car as it disappeared over the rise. "You thinkin' what I'm thinkin'?" Patch rumbled.

"Those two know somethin' they ain't tellin'."

"Yeah." Patch licked where his teeth should have been, thoughtful. "I wonder if we'd maybe be smart to get on over to that settlement. What your vibes tellin' ya, Doc?"

Lew was looking from the trail to the hill to his friends' faces, and he saw the adrenaline bring color back into Doc's cheeks. "Yeah," Doc said, standing. "Yeah, that trail ain't gonna go nowhere. Been there a long time. Let's go see what the Law is up to."

Bennie smiled to himself. Another of Doc's hunches. He'd known Doc a long time, and the man might not always be logical, but he was almost always right.

29

THEY SETTLED INTO THE BRANCHES in what might have been the companionable silence of good friends who just happened to have decided to climb a tree together, except for the fact that below them were two heavy-set pit bulls that seemed bent on keeping them up there. Never one to leave silence reign for long, Sophia spoke first. "Well, now what do we do, Mrs. Clary?"

"I don't know, Sophia." Annabelle stared down at the dogs. They seemed to have started some sort of project, working with a companionship of their own. The project involved digging a hole next to the tree, and they took turns. First one would dig with great vigor, sending sprays of dirt and detritus out behind it, pushing Annabelle's rifle around during the endeavor, while the other sat nearby, watching its sibling like a kibitzing construction worker, frequently looking up into the tree, its toothy mouth partly open, its stubby face projecting an eager scowl that seemed to Annabelle to be an assessment of what it defined as the fresh meat directly above it. After a few minutes of concentrated digging, they exchanged places. In an effort to lighten the mood, Annabelle added, "I hope they don't dig up this whole tree."

"Me, neither." Sophia's voice had the skinny, piping quality of a worried seven-year-old, and Annabelle could tell she was evincing more bravado than confidence.

Reaching for her hand, Annabelle comforted, "It's going to be okay, Sophia. We'll get home pretty soon. We just need to think about this a little." The phrase, 'think about this,' rattled around in her brain, in the empty shell of a brain, but the hammering from her dream could be heard coming toward it, a thunderous sound, increasing, increasing, threatening to burst the heavy shell asunder. Her head was trying to burst! Sophia's little voice came from far away.

"Mrs. Clary, you're not afraid any more, are you? You can see Sneaker right here; she won't hurt you. And Buddy wouldn't hurt a flea." Then she chuckled. "But a squirrel. He would hurt a squirrel."

Annabelle knew her eyes had gone wide. She looked up at Buddy above them in the tree, not threatening to any rational person, and at Sneaker clinging to the fat branch where Sophia had set her, and was shocked to realize that Sophia was right. They did not frighten her at all. The dogs below, though. That was a different story. And yes, rational.

Sophia had been poking and pinching matter of factly at the scratches and bruises on her arms and legs. "We got pretty banged up getting up here, didn't we? Let me see your arms, Mrs. Clary." She extended her left arm to Sophia, who identified a sharp scratch below the elbow and, to Annabelle's astonishment, kissed it. "There. That'll help. Now the other arm."

Annabelle balked. The right arm was not to be seen. Even in summer, if she thought someone might see her, she covered it with long sleeves. It was bare now. She was not supposed to have been around anyone today. Teetering on the branch, she clutched it to her chest. The child was insistent. "Man, you must have some owie, Mrs. Clary. Don't worry, I won't hurt it. Let me see." The hand Sophia held out would not retreat, and reluctantly, Annabelle extended her right arm.

Taking it into her hand with a professional attitude she must have gathered from her mother, Sophia examined the arm. The examination sent a shiver of ice down Annabelle's spine. Sophia's little fingers traced down from the elbow and around the wrist, then she met Annabelle's frightened gaze. "That's not a today owie, Mrs. Clary. That's a very long ago owie. A great big one. What happened? Did they take you to the hospital?"

The disintegrating shell made her shrink, trying to hide within it, but cracks were everywhere. Annabelle fought to bring forward a voice. "That's the problem, Sophia. I don't know what happened. I can't remember."

"Oh, I see." Sophia nodded matter of factly and smiled with clear comprehension. "That's called amnesia, Mrs. Clary. Once

Sponge Bob hit Patrick on the head and it made him have that, amnesia. Patrick didn't even know who he was, not either him or Sponge Bob, and then he was at Crabby Patties and something hit him again on the head and he was cured, just like that. Did something hit you on the head?"

Annabelle was speechless. She withdrew her arm, and Sophia said, "Oh, that's right. I guess you wouldn't remember." This struck her quite funny, and she didn't mean to be rude, but she giggled uncontrollably at the irony of her statement. No one had ever laughed at Annabelle's affliction before, least of all herself. Her hand went to her mouth, an unconscious motion of concealment, but her lips had already turned up into a real smile that went all the way up to her eyes.

"You're right. I don't remember. Edgar... well, that's Doc, to you... Edgar tells me things, and he told me I fell out of a tree and hurt my head, so I know I did, but I don't remember it at all."

Sophia was utterly fascinated. They had both forgotten their current dilemma. "I'm trying to imagine it," Sophia said. "It is just weird to know up in your brain about something that happened to you, but the you who you really are don't really know it. You must feel like two people."

Annabelle looked at the child with relief. She understood. "You're right. I do. And the thing is, Sophia, the one person can't control the other person or understand it. I also have to deal with something called P.T.S.D. That's when... "

"Oh, I know what that is, Mrs. Clary. It's when you kind of go crazy sometimes because you were once in a dangerous battle."

"Well, yes, I... "

"That's what you did when I brought Sneaker to see you. You went nuts. I hope you don't do that again, but it explains a lot. At least you aren't a witch."

No longer taken aback, Annabelle let the fear fall away. "No, I don't mean to be a witch. And I hope I never do that again; I am so going to do something... I will try never to do it again." Gritting her teeth, she carefully put out her hand and touched Sneaker, who continued to look unhappy about her own precarious position. A touch. Enough for now.

"Good." Sophia sighed and looked down at their current

problem. "That old owie on your arm? I think a dog bit you is why. I think that's why you hate dogs. Did Doc say anything about that?"

"Well, yes, he did. What he told me, Sophia, is that I tried to stop some dogs from fighting, and I couldn't get them stopped. I was in the middle of it, and they were biting me, too, and so I climbed a tree to get away, but I fell, and hit badly on my head. I was in a coma for a while."

This time, it was Sophia who was at a loss for words. "Wow!" she said.

"And you see, I don't remember any of it, and I'm not sure Edgar has told me everything. That other me, the different me we talked about earlier? That other me thinks something worse happened, that I did something bad. Edgar won't say I did, and I can't remember, but that piece of lost memory is still there somewhere, nagging at me. I am very afraid of it. I don't want it to come out."

"Like a booger in the night," Sophia said philosophically.

Annabelle shot her a questioning look, but the child was serious, so she said, "You're right, Sophia. Like a booger in the night." And for the second time that day, Annabelle found herself smiling, in a tree.

30

THE 911 DISPATCHER had told Junee to stay put, and that was driving her crazy. She could see why the sheriff would want to talk to her when he got there, but meanwhile she needed to search, and she was anchored. She checked Clarys' again—no one there. She circled the place as widely as she could and still keep an eye out for the sheriff, calling Sophia, even whistling, but the hot, oppressive morning was utterly still, immovable. There weren't even any clients showing up. She went back inside and paced by the cages, swallowing a cup of bitter, unnecessary coffee.

Hearing a car, she hurried to the door, hoping for the sheriff. No, it was... it was... now, the whole parking area was filling up, and people were pulling up along the roadside. What the hell? Standing in the open door of the clinic, she gaped as Maureen Macklenburg scuttled up the walkway toward her, followed by a whole community as they arrived and disembarked from their cars. The appearance of this mob sent her heart into overdrive. Had someone found Sophia? Was she hurt? Closing her mouth, she said, "Maureen, what is going on? What are you doing here?"

"We've come to find Annabelle. We heard she is missing."

Without thinking, Junee burst out, "But it's Sophia who's missing!" Then she added lamely, "But I guess Annabelle might be missing, too. I've been up there, and no one is around."

"Oh, my god!" Maureen exclaimed. "She must have taken Sophia!" This had never occurred to Junee, but before she could say more, Maureen took command of the step and turned to face the gathering crowd. "People! You must listen!" she shouted. "Both Annabelle and Sophia are missing. That poor child has been kidnapped by that deranged woman! We must organize, and quickly!"

She continued to shout, issuing commands, ordering certain people toward the north and into the dobies, others toward the forest, some to Peaseford. A buzz went among the crowd as newcomers arrived and were informed. Junee tried to say, "But Sneaker. Sophia went..." No one heard her. No one cared about Sneaker's role in the disappearance. She was not a woman with a weak constitution, but now Junee felt her knees turn to jello and the shouts of Maureen begin to fade into darkness. Before she fell, a strong arm was around her, supporting her. Two green eyes were peering at her through oversize glasses, and the sprigs from a wobbly top tail were bent toward her, tickling at her cheeks. "Come on, Junee. It's going to be all right. Sophia is going to be all right." Eileen was guiding her backwards, into the clinic. "Sit here and put your head between your knees. I'll get you water." Firmly closing the door on the shouting Maureen, Eileen pulled cold water from the fridge, then sat next to Junee.

"What happened?"

Color was returning to Junee's face. "I was out on a call, a colicky mare, and I left Sophia... you know, because she was asleep, and I knew Cole would be here to tend the animals before long, so I thought it was okay to leave her... but when I got back I found this." Junee pulled the crumpled note from her pocket, and Eileen read it carefully, then turned it over and read the other side. Pulling on her lip, she looked through the window at the chaotic group milling outside.

"Okay. So where do you think she went? What's your gut instinct?"

"Well, people kept telling her not to let Sneaker loose or she would go to the forest and be eaten by lions or coyotes, so I think she would have headed for the forest, up there south of us."

Eileen stood and flashed Junee her perky smile. "Okay, then. Let's go to the forest and find her. Is there another way out of this clinic?"

Standing to return Eileen's smile with a weaker one of her own, Junee said, "We can go through the apartment and out the back gate. That might let us escape." She was so relieved to be taking action that she completely forgot the sheriff's injunction to stay at the clinic. Instead, watching for their opportunity, Eileen and Junee slipped unnoticed out the back door, crossed the road, circled past the Gump property, and made their way up into the thicker pinyon and juniper to the south. Once they were away from the dispersing searchers, they began to call.

THE TREES, BRUSH AND LOW BRANCHES were unrelenting. They had persisted for nearly an hour with no results when, tired and scratched, they sat on one of the difficult logs in their path to reconnoiter and scrub at their sweaty cheeks with their shirt tails. "I wish I'd brought us water," Junee said.

"Well, if I have my directions right, we're getting closer to the spring. Maybe we can drink there." Restless, Junee prepared to go again, but Eileen placed her hand quietly on her arm. "Dr. Bailey, I've been trying to think how to say this, or whether to say it at all, but I think you need to know. I know who you are."

"Oh!" Junee looked at Eileen searchingly. "But your name is Garcia."

"Yes, it is. Partly. I guess you could say I was modern when I married Jesus, so I kept the name as Garcia-Lopez, then it was... losing him was so awful, and I was trying to find my way into something that took me forward, not just left me as a weeping, hopeless blob of a widow. I knew I was young, you know, and should try to have a life again. I dropped the Lopez. I'm not sure it helped."

Junee was frowning. "So you are the woman I've been searching for. You are the widow of Jesus Lopez."

"Yes, I am."

Junee shifted on the miserable, knotty log and faced her. "But how did you know who I am? My name is Bailey, not Cartwright."

"Well, you know how it is around here." Eileen tried to wave off a persistent swarm of gnats. "It didn't take long to learn that you came from the Boston area, and remember? That night at the Widders? You said your husband was killed over the Persian Gulf about six years ago, and of course, that tipped me off. Then the fact that Sophia is Black, like her father — it was all too much to be coincidence."

"So you were sure about me. I wasn't sure about you. It feels strange to me that you knew even then, that you were the only one at that Widders meeting who knew I didn't belong there."

"No, that's right. You never got the chance to marry him. I am so sorry. It must make the pain even worse."

Junee was picking needles off the nearby branches and crushing them in her fingers. "There was a long time I didn't think anything could make the pain any worse. Having Sophia helped me get through, and I feel like I've almost healed now, as far as such healing is possible. I'm not sure I should be picking the scab open again."

"It's okay. I know why you came. You think it is Jesus' fault that Ethan died. Maybe if it all comes out, if the wound drains, then real healing can happen." Eileen sighed. Her usual cheerful face was sober, her large lenses steamed.

Holding her head in her hands, Junee said, "They were such good friends. Why did they fight?"

"What did Ethan tell you?"

"The last I ever heard from him was a text. He said he didn't want to fly out with Jesus the next day because they'd both been drinking and they'd had a fight, and he didn't think they'd make a good team. Then he texted that he'd let me know more after it was all settled. That's all I ever heard. That's all I've ever known. Why did he go out, anyhow, if he felt like that?"

"Well, Junee, it's not rocket science." Eileen sighed. "If you look at it one way, it *was* Jesus' fault that Ethan went out. He wrote me the night of the fight, paper letter, snail mail. I have it if you want to read it. He did that sometimes when things worried him, wrote things all out to share with me. I guess it helped him vent, helped him think. He told me about the fight. He felt bad, and he said, and I quote, 'I hope to hell I can get Ethan to let it go and go on out with me tomorrow. In all honesty, I know he's right and I need to apologize. And these flights are dangerous; if we get into Iranian airspace by accident, they aren't above shooting. I don't trust anybody's judgment when it comes to navigating like I trust Ethan's."

Junee was gnawing her knuckles. "So Jesus must have just talked him into it."

"Must have. As you know, they were both up there. It was their 'copter that got too far northeast, somehow, and it did get into Iranian territory. Iranian guns took them down. It's the kind of thing you don't hear much about in the news—routine military loss. Nobody wants to mess up the big diplomatic picture."

"Shit." After a long pause, Junee looked up. "Did Jesus say what they fought about?"

"The news. That Black kid the police shot in L.A. Remember that? He was just a kid, about 16, and Jesus and Ethan were drinking. I guess Ethan was awful stirred up about it, talking about racism and the fear every Black person is born into in this country, an inescapable fear, so that not even a kid can feel safe, and not even a kid can count on protection from the cops. Well, Jesus made some kind of crack about how he'd hate to be a cop in that part of L.A., that that was pretty dangerous, too, and that set Ethan off. Anyhow, I guess you never met Jesus. He liked to kid around, laughed a lot. That's one of the things I miss most about him." She swallowed, then went on. "So he tried to kid Ethan out of it, and Ethan was taking it heavy, and pretty soon Ethan took a swing at Jesus, told him not to joke about what other people had to put up with, told him he had no idea about bigotry."

"But of course he did." Junee's voice was thick with understanding. "And the next morning Ethan must have let it go, and they made up. That's why they went out together."

"Well, I think about that fight. I think Ethan was especially worried because you two had just found out you were pregnant. He was thinking about how he was going to be able to keep his kid safe in America, the way it is now."

"You're right. That probably didn't help, from what I knew of Ethan." Junee took a deep breath. "Eileen, I'm sorry. You've been through everything I have. I am so sorry that I somehow got it into my head that Jesus was the bad guy in this. They both went, but Ethan was the navigator. I'm so sorry."

"It's okay. You were hurtin', girl. Sometimes what we need is somebody to blame." Eileen ducked her head, vigorously polishing at her glasses with her sweaty shirt tail. "Yeah. Yeah, it's okay." She raised her head and gave Junee a sad, twitchy version of the fluorescent smile. "We can move on now. So, let's go. We need to go find that kid that you and Ethan made."

31

THERE THEY WERE, at the Peaseford Vet Clinic, the location where they were supposed to meet the R.P., the reporting party, but there were absolutely zero people there. This wouldn't have been odd, except that there were almost two dozen vehicles parked in the lot and along the road. Louie and Red searched thoroughly. No one. Zilch. They contacted dispatch for instructions, and dispatch informed them that the reporting party was a close relative and had been very upset, so might have gone to search on her own. Louie rolled her eyes in disgust. "Duh," she commented to Red. "It's a mother whose kid is gone. Of course she's upset."

"You're a mother. You ought'a know." Louie had six kids and counting.

"Aw, shut up, Red. Don't say it."

"Whaaaat? " Dragging it out. "Say what?"

"You know what."

"Well, just since you asked. Just thought in your case one kid more or less wouldn't matter." This set Red chuckling heartily at his own joke, and Louie punched his arm, hard. "Ow!" he groused, pouting. "That hurt."

They were deliberating on what to do next, squinting into the hard, sun-bitten dobies, when the radio crackled again. "Go ahead."

"You might try the neighbors—R.P. may be searching there."

Louie gave Red what he called her monkey face. She thrust her head forward and showed all her teeth in a very wide, very fake grin. This was unique to her, and it meant something like, "Everyone around us is crazy as hell, so we may as well play along and do what we must." He twisted his nose at her, but he was pleased. "All righty, then. Off we go to the neighbors. Which ones? The ones back the way we came, or the ones on up the road?"

Chuckling, Louie said, "Well, we've already been the way we came, right?"

THE NEXT DRIVEWAY up the road was entered under an elaborately carved, heavy wooden arch. Deer, elk, bear, trout, mountain sheep, and every other imaginable Colorado game animal were carved into the pillars holding up the arch. Where the pillars met the overhead arch itself there hung large, multi-pronged antlers. Across the top, so big as to be unreadable except from a distance, were the letters G-U-M-P. Red stopped the car to stare at the contrivance, saying, "Well."

Louie responded, "Well," and then "Hope the damned thing don't fall on us." They went on up, winding along a wide, expensively graveled lane which was dramatically bordered by decorative river boulders, and ended at a circular drive near the house. The flagstone walkway from the drive led to a huge, modern, log affair set carefully at the top of the artificial hill that had been built to loom above the forest around it. Whoever was inside would have not only a magnificent view of the breathtaking mountains and lowlands in every direction, but also a clear outlook that could reveal most of the habitations of the Croissant-Peaseford valley. Red and Louie got out of their car, and before heading up the path to the door, they turned and took in the view. Louie grunted. "Wonder if he's got a telescope."

"Pair of binocs could probably get him into most of those bedrooms down there."

Feeling watched even now, they went on up the walk and had a go at the heavy iron door knocker. Gump opened the door at once and appeared surprised to see them, although his blondish comb-over was securely in place. He was wearing a dressing gown embossed with western designs: boots, saddles, and six-shooters, and he was carrying a cup of coffee. "Why, what can I do for you, officers?"

Louie leaned in, using an old proxemic trick she had learned over the years not only with suspects, but also with her kids' chatty teenaged friends. As she leaned, taking up the social space he had been rightly assigned by his culture, Gump stepped back, and she eased after him, subtly and gradually leaning again, edging him out of his comfort zone. Red followed, and they would have solved any problem of needing a formal invitation into the house, but they had only arrived into an entry hall with coat hooks and boot removers made from horse shoes, and whimsical cartoon pictures of rodeo clowns festooning the walls. They wanted at least a brief look inside, a chance to see if there might be a trace of Sophia there. It was Red's turn to try. His effort was overtly courteous.

"Mr. Gump, we are following up on a report of a missing child. Might we step on in for a minute?"

Gump's face flickered from fake concern to fake hospitable smile and settled in the middle. He said, "Please, be my guests," and stepped aside, gesturing for them to pass. They found themselves standing in a living area with immense wooden beams high above them. The entire room seemed open due to the great picture windows on all sides. They got no farther; Gump had collected himself, set down his coffee cup, and was now standing his ground, facing them with folded arms and an expression that excellently portrayed great solicitude. "A child, you say! That is dreadful. May I ask how old?"

Louie said, "It is your neighbor, Dr. Bailey's child, and I believe she is just seven." Meanwhile, Red was doing what he could with the position fate had given them, his eyes taking in sights, his ears mopping up sounds, and his nose working like a bloodhound to sort out scents. Somewhere far in the background he was sure he heard water running. A toilet? A shower? There were various scents, most overpowered by the coffee, but something... something... ah, he knew that scent! It was a fragrance Mac used. His lips tipped up slightly at the thought of Mac, but it took him only a second to retrieve the name of the fragrance. Patchouli. He didn't think men used patchouli.

Gump had just expressed his distress at the information that it was Sophia who was missing, and Louie was asking if he knew anything, had seen anything, or had any information that might be helpful.

"Why, no. No. I've just been having a leisurely morning here with Cuddles. A second cup, you know, to start the day."

Louie resisted making a wry face. A second cup in this

wonderfully air-conditioned, spacious room certainly would be lovely. A second cup in her own crowded home, roisterous with growing children, seldom proved restorative. Red was smiling conspiratorially at Gump. "Ah, Cuddles! Your wife."

Gump's return smile was smarmy; he was pleased. They were sharing a guy joke. "Oh, no, no, no. Not a woman. Cuddles is my dear dog. I live here alone, except for her, so she and I are very attached. She never leaves my side."

Both Red and Louie restrained themselves from looking at his side, where there was obviously no dog. Nothing more was to be gained here; they thanked him, encouraged him to call 911 if he observed anything that might be helpful, and sighed with relief once they had achieved the patrol car.

"Creepy guy," Louie said. Red was twisting to look where the graveled drive made its way behind the house. "You think he's got the kid caged up in a shed in back?"

"Nah. Just lookin' where his vehicles are parked. Near as I can tell, there's more than one back there. Could all be his, I guess. Maybe not. He wasn't alone in that house."

"Seriously? You just got a feeling, or what?"

"I heard water running. I smelled Patchouli."

"Wow. Literally, Patchouli?"

"I know it because Mac wears it."

Louie snickered. "Maybe Cuddles wears it. Maybe we interrupted Mr. Gump and his dog having playtime."

"Bleeeahh! I can't take that picture!" They made their way through the heavy, arched gate and then Louie snickered again.

"Maybe Mac was there."

"Oh, Jesus, Louie!" Red socked her arm and she snorted and pouted. "Ow, that hurt." They had reached Old Grand, and Red sprayed gravel, shooting the car to the right. Louie settled into the seat, watching the trees go sailing by.

"Okay, you're right, Red. Let's get on up there. I guarantee you, Mac'll be there with Garrett. And those two did say they might need back-up, didn't they?"

32

TOPPING THE RISE, Garrett drove cautiously, allowing himself and McCracken time to appraise the scene below them. Three field tents were anchoring the activities which had produced a variety of structures now taking root in a natural clearing among the pinyon and juniper. The constructions involved logs, adobe bricks, and even brushy limbs which had been woven together. Several patches of ground were being cultivated, and chickens were busy near a raised coop. Three small pickups nosed in next to the tents. In the center of this tableau lay a blanket. It covered a still form, and beside the blanket stood a woman who seemed to have been posted as sentry. Seeing their car approach, she had begun shouting, causing people to emerge from the various structures around the commons. McCracken, tense, hand on holster, counted five plus the sentry woman. They all ran toward the blanket, looking up at the sheriff's car and gesturing for their attention.

Garrett brought the car near the blanket. As he and McCracken stepped out, a worried murmuring ceased and the grouped people grew quiet. One young man stepped forward and held out his hand. "Thanks for coming, Sheriff. And Deputy. I'm Zhora." The others followed suit, speaking in muted voices. "Thanks. I'm Misha." "Marianna." "Luka." "Grisha." "Lada." This formality completed, they stepped back, confused, maybe shy, and fell silent.

Studying them, Garrett spoke. "So, what happened here? We received word of a shooting."

"Yes, there," pointing to the blanket. "Someone has killed Maarika."

Garrett knelt and pulled the blanket aside. Yup. She was

dead, all right. She'd taken a clean shot in the chest, thrown out her arms, and gone down like a rock. Seeing her again, the young people gave a collective gasp and took an involuntary step back. Pulling the blanket back over the dead woman, Garrett looked up at McCracken. "Crime scene unit?"

"Yeah. On their way. Maybe ten minutes."

The momentary silence was broken by two four-wheelers topping the hill and dropping into the clearing. The young people raised puzzled faces, but Garrett stood and walked to meet them, holding up his hand. "You boys need to stay back a little here. Doc, it ain't Annabelle. Turn off those machines and come over to reassure yourselves, then hang back some, okay?"

Continuing to scowl their suspicion, the young farmers looked askance at McCracken, who said shortly, "He thought it was his wife."

Once more Garrett pulled aside the blanket to reveal the dark-haired woman, at most in her twenties, who lay flat on her back, blood having seeped lazily from the wound in her chest and congealed across her smock. There was no question. Shaking their heads, the old men retreated, clustering near their vehicles, prepared to listen and confer.

"Okay, let's step on over here," Garrett indicated a space a few feet from the body. "The crime scene unit's on its way, and until it gets here I'd like a few words with you all. Who's the leader here?"

"We don't really have a leader. We live like lichen. We cooperate and interconnect and flourish as part of our natural environment." This was young Grisha, eyes wide and filled with idealism. The others appeared to ignore him.

"Mmmph." Garrett pulled his mustache. "Well, so, who saw this happen?"

"It's not exactly true. We kind of have a leader." Lada, petite, blond, and a little haggard, gnawing at a fingernail. "It was Will who gathered us up and helped us get this land. He did a lot of legwork, called old friends, and so-on."

"Okay, that works. Which one of you is Will?"

"He's not here." If possible, everyone looked even more worried, shifting from foot to foot.

McCracken had had enough. Sometimes the Chief's probing approach was annoying, too damn measured and patient.

"Look, you people. Somebody here needs to tell us what happened. Where is this 'Will'? Who heard something? Who saw something?"

Misha, a husky, brown man, sprouting tattoos around his sleeveless shirt, addressed the others. "Look, I know cops. Had my share in Cleveland. These aren't the same. These're okay, just tell them what we know, okay? And look, Zhora, this is America. This isn't the KGB, just the local sheriff. So you need to tell them."

Rolling his eyes, Zhora said, "Give up the Russian stereotypes, Bro," which caused Misha to snort.

As if speaking confidentially, Lada leaned in toward McCracken and said, "None of us are really Russian, you know, except Zhora and Luka. And Maarika. Was. The rest of us just took Russian names to show solidarity with the main Anastasia movement."

Speaking had opened them; they felt unstoppered, ready to release talk about the incident. Zhora, his accent mild, said, "Look, I think we were all up this morning early as usual, so we all heard the shot. I was the only one to see Maarika drop, and I looked up just in time to see a movement up there." He pointed to the top of the hill just before the road dropped into the settlement, and Garrett and McCracken, following his gesture, noted that the location he indicated would be consistent with the apparent line of fire. "The thing is, I didn't see anything else, just a movement, kind of a flurry of the brush."

"What time was this?"

"About six, I think." He looked to the others for confirmation and they nodded, but Marianna made a face.

"Oh, yeah. It was six, all right. I looked at my phone, because I heard Maarika rustling around outside. She likes to beat everyone awake in the morning. She was kind of a sneaky *suka*, that one. I had her figured out. She got up earlier than everyone else to steal one or two eggs every day, and when she got enough she'd drive into Peaseford and sell them, keep the money for herself. Other stuff we owned together, too. She took vegetables, potatoes... like that. She didn't fit in well here; I was getting ready to confront her. Too late for that, I guess." She shrugged. Zhora put an arm around her shoulder.

"Hey, don't speak bad of the dead, okay babe?" He made an

apologetic face toward the officers. "Marianna... well, I guess you can tell. She didn't think much of Will's wife."

McCracken picked it up. "Will's wife? Maarika was the wife of this guy you can't tell us where he went?"

There was an uncomfortable silence, then Zhora cleared his throat. "Uh, you see, well... you see, it's like this. Will Yelets and I have been friends forever. My family, they were *dachnikis*... "

"*Dachnikis?*" Garrett questioned.

"Well, see, back in the 1960's, millions of Russians became entitled to little plots of land. For free, they could get a couple of acres from the government. These are called *dachas*. Some are in forest, some in farmland, and so-on. So, like I say, millions of people took advantage of that, somewhere I read 70 percent of Russia's people. And a lot of them don't just visit their *dacha*, but they live on it and grow crops. Lots of potatoes. Ninety percent of Russia's potatoes come from *dachas*.

"So, my family were *dachnikis;* I lived a lot of my life on a *dacha*, and Will stayed with us when he was an exchange student. We ate fruit and vegetables that we grew ourselves. Delicious!" Zhora made a 'mmwa' gesture, fingers to lips and out.

He was smiling, but he had Garrett's attention. "So, you and Will Yelets, the husband of the dead lady here, you were close friends?"

Sobering, Zhora said, "Yes, that's true. Will is a good person."

McCracken's eyes had narrowed. "But Maarika, not so much?"

Everyone in the group nodded reluctantly, and Zhora, clearing his throat again, said, "Marianna's right. Maarika's a troublemaker. Was a troublemaker. She came from a pushy family, and Will blundered into marriage with her when he was just a teenager, but she followed him to America. She didn't love him, but she was pig-headed. She was determined to hold him to the marriage."

Marianna mumbled, "She didn't believe in any of what we are trying to do here. She just wanted to pry Will loose and force him to the city."

Misha had been watching Garrett and McCracken closely, and now he said, "You better not be jumpin' to conclusions, here, officers. That boy, Will, he wouldn't hurt a flea. He ain't the one we're scared of."

"You're afraid of someone?"

"There've been incidents, Sir." He looked at Luka, then said, "Just one example. Luka and me were checking out at the grocery store in Peaseford, and Mr. Gump gets in tight behind us. Not just in line, but pushed in close, real uncomfortable, and he starts making racist comments. He was talking low, pretending to talk to himself, but it was clear he intended us and the people around us to hear."

Garrett said, "This was Gump, alone?" as McCracken said, "What did he say?"

"Yeah, it was Gump, alone. He said stuff about how foreigners shouldn't be taking over America, and if he didn't succeed at anything else, he'd at least get the niggers out of the county, and stuff like that. Hard to repeat."

Grisha said meekly, "And he deliberately tripped me once in the hardware store. I actually started to say, 'excuse me,' but he growled at me and said, 'Just watch your step, boy. You and all them land thieves out there better watch your step. Your time's comin'.' It gave me the creeps."

Garrett's face had hardened, and McCracken looked grim. Lada took a deep breath and said, "Maarika was pretty, you know? She looked a little like that Carol Haddon over there, about the same size, dark curly hair, big eyes. She and I were out picking asparagus by the roadside last spring and Gump pulled up alongside us and said, 'Well, well, well. If it isn't the little cult girls. Or should I say cunt girls. I can see why your...'" Lada stopped, embarrassed, then took a deep breath and continued. "He said, 'I can see why those pussies you call men would want you to hide all that A-rab pretty under a veil. You tell 'em they better not let you wander around alone, or next time you might not be so pretty. Or do you little rag heads want to come home with me now?' Anyhow, Maarika was tough, and she spat at him and said, 'otvali, mudak,' which means... " Again, Lada hesitated, but Luka finished for her.

"It means: 'fuck off, asshole.'"

"Maarika gave him the finger, but I'm not so brave."

Garrett pulled a can of non-nicotine chew from his pocket and stuck a wad in his lip. He was contemplating the top of the rise where the shot had come from when a first cop car came over, followed by a second. The second, he knew, was Hobbs' special transportation, and he felt relieved. His detective's presence would help bring clarity to this mess.

McCracken, turning her eyes from the approaching cars back to the young people, said, "And where was it you said that Will Yelets went?"

She had persisted. Sighing in defeat, Zhora said, "He left about 5:30 this morning. He said he had... that he had some business to tend to. He'd stuffed a bag with some papers and cedar pendants he'd been polishing. Those pendants... well, that's another story. But he hoped to sell them, or at least distribute them."

"Thanks," McCracken said, keeping her eyes on his face. "And was he carrying a rifle?"

Zhora's lips went tight, but Misha said, "Of course. We didn't believe in guns when we came here, but now we are pretty well armed. I guess you can figure out why."

McCracken was calculating times: had he jumped into one of their vehicles, driven to the pull-out over the hill, gotten out, walked back to shoot Maarika, then gone on? And where? How had he been sure Maarika would be out there — maybe he was familiar enough with her behavioral patterns. Before she could think any further, a deep, troll-like rumble at her side made her jump. She hadn't seen Patch approach. He said, "We ain't got nothin' here that's helpin' us with Annabelle. Doc and me and the others, we think somebody better be organizin' a posse and get 'em to drag that spring."

33

SOPHIA WAS DANGLING UPSIDE DOWN less than two feet above the jaws of the pit bulls, who, in their turn, were standing on their hind legs, their front paws on the trunk of the tree, their mouths open and at the ready. Annabelle had Sophia's ankle, nothing else, and her perch was, at best, precarious.

The thing was, Annabelle was an old lady, and tired. She'd spent a long night alone on cold, hard ground; she'd been beset by confusing dreams, and she'd walked for miles. Now, inexplicably, she found herself trapped in a tree with two dogs and a child, and she simply couldn't get her foggy brain to wrap around any of it any more. It was a good-sized tree, and the branch on which she sat was heavy and dependable. She had just wanted to sit securely, lean against the trunk, and sleep. This might have worked, but the child was a talker.

She asked Annabelle whether, if they had the gun, they might be able to shoot so people would hear and come help. She talked about her mother and her grandmother and her grandfather, who had died, and her father, who also died when the helicopter crashed. She told Annabelle that she did not wish to be stuck in this tree and starve, thus also dying, which her mother wouldn't like. She talked about Doc and Patch, Bennie and Lew and the invisible dog, and she asked if Annabelle thought they might have started searching yet. She assured Annabelle that at least she knew her mother would be searching. She noted that Buddy was amazed to find Sneaker on the branch with him. She told Annabelle that the dogs below had gone to sleep, and she was pretty sure that they weren't really mean, anyhow.

Annabelle tried to make appropriate responses: yes, no, really?, oh, probably, uh huh... The child was driving her mad.

Her head throbbed, and she sought refuge from the nature of the tree. She studied it; she felt it, smelled it, tried to get it to devour her. She was surrounded by healthy, aromatic green needles which sprang two at a time from each node in each burgeoning branch. She turned her attention to the bark, a rich, satisfying brown drifting quietly into dusty gray in some places. Lichen, in shades of blue, green, and mustardy yellow, danced across its surface. Sap had slipped out, running like teardrops from within the long fissures that marked the bark's growth. There had been wounds—storm broken limbs, animal encounters—and these exposed a deeper wood, soft gray, healed, and as sturdy as good muscle. The bark was formed of chips that she could remove as the child talked, and Annabelle found the source of the sap just under the bark. Here was some sticky moisture, but also congealed form, and some bits as hard, glowing, and precious as jewels. She mined it. She picked at the scaly chips and the tree hummed peacefully, as if she were scratching an itch, and she wished herself to disappear within the deep seams formed by the protective bark. She barely heard Sophia say, "Well, all right then. It looks like they're both asleep. I'm going down and get that gun so we can shoot our way out of here."

Like all accidents, it happened so fast. One minute, Sophia was scuttling past Annabelle, on her way down the tree, and the next her fanny pack caught on a branch which then treacherously released it, sending her plunging headfirst toward the ground. She emitted a yip less of fear than of surprise, and reflexively, Annabelle grabbed her ankle.

They both stared down at the now fully alerted dogs, and Annabelle's first thought was, "But I'm old and weak. I can't hang on!" Sophia was trying to put her arms around the trunk of the tree. It was too large. Holding tight, near despair, Annabelle realized that the child's fall had jolted something inside her. Like the flash of lightning in a storm, the unexpected shock of the falling child had illuminated a part of her that had been buried over fifty years. There had been another person. Another tree. Dogs. Another fall. And another child—she even recalled his name. Zachary Marihew. A tiny thing, and he had run toward snarling dogs. She had screamed. She could feel the scream, even now, hear it pierce its way out of her, and she had tried... But this she couldn't remember. What had happened to little Zach?

The dogs? The scream? What happened to the child who shouldn't have been in the midst of the flesh-tearing, snarling mess, but who was there, even so, because of her. What had she done? Somehow she had been responsible for that child, and she had failed. She must not fail again. There must not be another fall.

Gripping the rough branch with her knees, she took Sophia's ankle in both hands and heaved, a superhuman heave. She was slipping backwards, but she disregarded that. Sophia scrabbled, caught at a branch, her weight lessening, and Annabelle, pinyon needles poking like knives at her cheeks and eyes, realized that she could free one hand and stabilize them both. Sneaker and Buddy, looking down at the crazy humans, were barking. Gaining purchase at last, Sophia said weakly, "Well, maybe barking will bring somebody to help."

Annabelle wanted to shake her. Instead, she said, "No, Sophia. It's my turn. I'm the grownup here. I'm going to get the gun." Sophia stared at her, but before she could object, Annabelle said, "I'm taller than you. I'm going to climb down— It's okay, child, I've climbed many trees in my life, and I can do this—I'll climb down, get the gun, and hand it to you. Now, pay attention. I will *hand it to you*, so that my hands are free to let me jump back up. So you be ready to grab that gun."

"But Mrs. Clary! Those dogs could hurt you! The bad dogs are down there and awake. You are afraid of them!"

Looking down at the toothy faces below them, Annabelle felt her stomach lurch. What she said, though, was, "Well, it's time I get over it, isn't it?" Then she said, "Look, child, have you ever shot a gun?"

Sophia's eyes had grown huge. "No, ma'am. I mean, only in games."

"Okay. Well, you look down there. See the gun? The brown part is called the stock; the long metal part is the barrel."

"You shoot the dogs, Mrs. Clary! I can't shoot. Not a real gun! I never even touched one before."

Annabelle put her hand to her forehead, needing to get through this. "Honey, I might not be... There are two dogs. I might not be fast enough... I... It is you that needs the gun."

"Oh, I get it. I will be safe in the tree, and I can shoot the dogs while you climb up."

She couldn't think too much about this. "Just look down at

the gun, Sophia. Listen to everything I say, and then repeat it back to me. This is a test, a very hard, very important test, okay?"

Meekly, Sophia whispered, "Okay."

"Now, the brown part is the stock, and the metally part is the barrel, and the end of the barrel is where the bullet comes out. The bullet comes out fast and it kills, you understand? The bullet kills, and it comes out the end of the barrel, so you must not point the end of that barrel at anything. This is not a game. It is real life, and if you shoot that gun, it can kill, understand? My gun, the gun down there against the tree, has bullets in it right now. It is loaded. So far, do you understand?" Sophia nodded. "Repeat what I have told you." Sophia repeated.

"Good. So, do you know which part is the trigger, the thing you pull to make the gun shoot?"

"I think so. There's the brown part, the stock, then a steely-looking part, and more brown part with the dangerous barrel coming along the top. On top of the steely thing that is not the barrel is a bunch of stuff, and underneath is kind of a handle, and in the... the circley part of the handle is a hangy-downy thing. Isn't that the trigger?"

Annabelle was pleased. No wonder Edgar loved being around this child. She was sharp. "That's right. Now, Sophia, you've seen movies, I think. You know, they hold the gun at the stock end, and they point the barrel at what they want to shoot, and they pull on the trigger, and you can do that with this gun. You are strong enough. It is a light little .22, but it won't shoot until you cock it, okay? When I hand it up to you, it will be kind of safe because it needs cocked before it will shoot. But still be careful, okay?"

"Okay. So how do I cock it?"

Annabelle hesitated. Did she really want the child to know how to cock the gun? But what good would it do her to know all the rest, if she couldn't cock it? How could she get help, or fire it for defense? There were predators. She plunged ahead. "Hold it so the barrel points safely; point it at the ground, understand? Then get hold of the handle, under the trigger, and pull it all the way down. All the way. Then pull it back. that will make the thing you see on top go back. That is called the hammer. It will go back, and the gun will be ready to shoot. You have to be so, so, so careful of where the barrel is pointing, okay? Because that gun can kill. It will shoot whatever you point it at."

"All right. I got it."

A shiver climbed Annabelle's spine. She couldn't reason this through. They could wait in the tree for help, but that didn't feel right to her. A wordless mass of necessity pushed her forward, and she put her hand on Sophia's arm. "Now tell me again, Sophia. Repeat to me everything I have told you."

Sophia nodded, pointed down at the gun, and began from the first to recite Annabelle's instructions.

34

THEY HAD FOUND THE BULLET. They were lucky, because it had gone through the woman's chest and exited behind her, where the angle of the shot sent it into the ground. Now, the crime scene unit was putting up tape. Red and Louie arrived, and Garrett set them to the task of watching the perimeter. It was possible that the shooter could still be out there, true, but he was more concerned that apparently the community had become aware of the problem up here. A thin trickle of ranchers and townspeople had begun to appear at the top of the hill. If it became a flood, it might take more than two deputies to keep them at bay in this wide open area. The tape at the top of the road wouldn't restrain them, but at least the next round of tape that marked off the body was providing an adequate boundary for the sheriff's officers to work privately.

Hobbs had a careful look at Maarika's inert form, then when a member of the crime scene unit pulled the bullet from the ground, he examined it thoughtfully, squinting down at it in the bright August light. Handing it over to Garrett and McCracken, he said, "Well, there it is."

As for the sheriff and deputy, they examined it briefly, then handed it back to Hobbs, grins of anticipation barely suppressed. Their chubby detective had an eidetic memory, an encyclopedic knowledge of firearms and ballistics, and he loved to expound. They couldn't wait to hear what he would have deduced from the one small object in his fingers. He turned it over again, looked up at the hilltop, and back at the body. McCracken shifted on her feet. "Well?" At last Hobbs grunted, resettled his waistline, and began.

"A good clean shot. Came from up there where the kid saw

the brush move." Garrett and McCracken waited. "Shooter maybe military or a hunter. Knew how to place a bullet. 7.62 mm caliber on that bullet."

Taking the bullet back into his hand, Garrett turned it over to examine it again. "So what kind of gun does this, Asa?"

"Well." A longer pause. Hobbs didn't want to make them suffer; he just wanted to make his statement accurate. "There's a gun known as the M39. Made in Finland, later in Russia, but the Finnish model is the one to collect. It's known as the best bolt-action battle rifle ever to see action. The Finns fought Russia with that gun for most of World War II. If the killer had one of those original guns, it would be a real beauty, the stock made of Arctic birch to withstand the Scandinavian climate, and excellent improvements and workmanship on the barrel, nose cap, and so-on. It had amazing accuracy, even with the original iron sights."

"Ahhh," Garrett handed the bullet to McCracken to admire while she imagined the gun. "You say it's an M39?"

"Of course the full name is the Mosin Nagant M39. Other possibilities are the Russian SKS and the AK-47, but my money is on the M39. I shot one myself once. It had a pretty hefty kick, but manageable. The cartridges slicked into the chamber like they were greased. If that was the gun—and we don't know yet if it was, just speculating—but if that was the gun, I think the shooter knew guns and was probably proud of the one that shot this."

Garrett pulled his mustache. "So, where do you think we might find this dandy gun?"

"Probably went with the killer. If he got too stirred up, he might have sacrificed it. So it might have ended up in the spring."

No one noticed that Bennie and Lew had slipped under the crime tape and were listening to the bullet discourse with avid interest. Now Bennie saw fit to interject. "For the love of God, Mr. Garrett. Look over there at old Doc. He's a basket case. Now you got the gun, so you got two good reasons to drag that spring. There could be a sniper out there with a helluva gun, and we oughta start movin' this search along, for Doc's sake. Get ahold of somebody with equipment that can deal with that spring."

Garrett looked over at Doc, then back at Bennie and Lew.

He spat non-nicotine chew thoughtfully, with fine accuracy, into some nearby brush, then said, "All right. We'll get it going. First, though, you two back right on outta this crime scene area. Get back under the tape before you mess everything up for the people who need to study it. I'll have some private words with Doc before we start messin' with the spring, so you other boys just go make friends with those kids and eat a carrot or something. And you, Mac. While I'm talkin' with Doc, you go on up and have a look around where everybody says the shot came from. See what you can see. And be easy — try not to drag this whole damn mob with you."

The "whole damn mob" did seem to be expanding, despite the yellow tape. It transpired that no one had realized there was a shooting. The community thought their purpose was to locate a lost woman and child, so when they looked down from the hill to see police tape and sheriff's vehicles, not to mention what was probably a body, they were filled not only with unease, but, more powerfully, with great curiosity. Inevitably they continued down into the settlement, gabbling like startled guinea hens. Some were edgy, watching the neighboring trees for the unidentified sniper. Others clustered, trying to sort out the information they had received so far and relate it to the original search, which they felt must continue. A few were enthralled with the settlement itself, since most community members had not seen it before. Those bent with Lada to discuss soils and vegetable varieties, or followed Grisha's gestures as he pointed out construction details. Ronald Gump arrived, his artificially tanned face sickly orange in the sunlight, and stood about with his hands behind his back. He, too, kept casting searching glances into the surrounding forest, but he also seemed unusually subdued. When someone spoke to him, he stressed that he always thought Annabelle Clary was a terrific person. Just terrific.

Zhora was moving anxiously around the compound, trying to assure that plantings didn't get trampled underfoot. Garrett had Doc in tow, and he caught Zhora mid-stride. Zhora nodded and gestured toward the larger of the three tents, so Garrett set off, Doc limping behind.

The tent was airless, hot, and reeking of cooking odors held captive past their prime. Large blue bottle flies were having a convention near the roof, their buzzing clamorous. Zhora had followed the men over, holding the door flap open in welcome, but if anything, he now looked even more anxious. "Will this do? I'm sorry. Our conditions here aren't so classy yet, I guess."

There was a log table with wooden benches on each side. Garrett said, "Thanks. This'll do fine. We just need a few minutes of privacy."

"Me, too," Zhora burst out. "This is all a mess." He seemed to be referring to the milling people outside. "You guys take all the time you need in here." He dropped the door flap, causing a swoosh of hot air to pass the two men, then settle around them.

"So, Doc," Garrett began. "Hated to bother you. Let's sit; this shouldn't take long. Just got a couple things." They sat; Doc's face was haggard, but the gaze he returned to the sheriff was steady.

"First of all, what did you boys find out there so far that might help us with Annabelle? Any clothing scraps? Tracks? I need to tap into some expertise here before the whole damn community obliterates anything that could be helpful."

"Yeah. Understood." Doc Clary nodded. "A lot of activity out there. Appreciate you showin' up. Thing is, I only got tracks as far as the spring last night, but this morning Bennie went on up the Ute trail over there and he found her pills. She took pills for anxiety and so-on, and he found 'em scattered all over loose in the brush up there."

"Well, that's where I'm tryin' to go with this discussion, Doc. Was she suicidal? Would she hide from searchers? About all I know about your wife is..."

Doc interrupted. "Let's cut to the chase, Pat." He cleared his throat. "I never talk about this, how it was, but now she's missing." He cleared his throat again, looked up at the ineffective vent near the roof flap. "Just give me a minute."

Garrett was silent, and after a time Doc said, "We were young. We were both really young, and we did stupid things, like all young people do." He sighed. He had it started now, and he would continue.

"We had a nice little mixed practice in Denver, dogs, cats, large animals, even exotics. This was over fifty years ago. Our folks gave us a loan for the building, and we had a good start paying them back. We worked together, Annabelle and I, and we hired one tech, and enjoyed the variety of clients and patients. Annabelle was happy then, bubbly, laughing, full of life. She was a song all by herself. She'd tease clients, and they loved her. Then one day I did the first of the stupid things I'm talking about. I let a client talk me into spaying his little blue heeler while she was in heat. You shouldn't do that; it isn't as safe, more risk of bleeding and so-on, but he just wanted to get it done, and so, with the bad judgment of youth, I did it.

"Annabelle and I were both responsible for the next mistake. Right behind the reception desk was a door leading into a little yard, and we used it for a dog run. We wanted our doggy patients to be comfortable, so if they were healing well, we'd let them out of their cages, thinking it must feel good to move around in the fresh air. Sometimes we'd put two or three in that yard. And to be honest, it saved us on some cage cleaning and walks, and until the day it happened, it seemed to work well for all concerned.

"On that day, though..." Doc shook his head, his face a study in ancient regret. "On that day, we stupidly put a big boxer out there. A young buck. He'd broken his leg, and it was firmly cast, so why not? His master was expected to pick him up in a few hours. Then we had another big dog, a mongrel, maybe some German shepherd, maybe some black lab. His owner bragged that he was part wolf, but the dog was a gentle soul, and people do that, so we didn't give the owner's statement much attention. That dog had had a nasty encounter with a pissed-off tom cat; he nearly lost an eye, and it had gotten infected, but it was healing well by that point. And, as I say, he seemed a gentle soul. The problem was that neither of those dogs had been castrated, and we added the little spayed heeler into the mix in the yard. What were we thinking?"

He stopped, and Garrett wasn't sure he would go on. After a time he said, "So. Well, anyhow. A young woman came into the waiting room with her little boy. Three years old, very, very cute. He had a roguish, round face, curly red hair, and the look of a tiny Irish imp. Kat, our tech, and I were in back, in the surgery. The woman was picking up her own animal, I think it was a cat we had neutered. She wanted to talk to me, so she sat down to wait and visited with Annabelle a while, then asked Annabelle if she would watch her little boy while she used the restroom, and Annabelle agreed."

Doc's tone had become defensive. "You know, Annabelle was an only child. She hadn't been around kids. She didn't know how fast they could move, or what they were capable of, so when she looked into the yard and saw the dogs fighting, she must have thought the little boy — Zach was his name, Zachary Marihew — she must have thought he would stay put. Those dogs were our patients, and the little female had just been spayed," Doc swallowed, "So she wasn't just still hormonal, but she was vulnerable. Annabelle's big heart and sense of responsibility sent her into that yard to separate them.

"Well, long story short. Annabelle got into the middle of the dog fight and they started to work her over with a vengeance. She still has scars. She struggled free and got up the one tree that was there, but the mother's trip to the bathroom took too long. Little Zachary, alone and curious, opened the door, went into the yard, and headed straight for the dog fight. We all heard Annabelle screaming, but before we could get there, the kid was under attack. I don't know what went through that dog's head, but when the wolf-dog mongrel saw the kid, he somehow saw a problem that he thought needed solved. I think the last thing Annabelle saw was that big dog tearing at the little boy's flesh. She didn't just climb down. She dived. I saw her. Kat and I were running from the surgery, and I saw her. She plummeted toward that dog and boy as if she were going into a swimming pool. But it wasn't, of course. It wasn't water. It was packed, cold, hard ground, and she hit it so hard she was in a coma for over three weeks."

Again, there was a long, silent hiatus, both men heads down, somber, the flies active above them, the old odors in the tent forgotten. Finally, Doc said, "When she woke up, she had total amnesia. She couldn't remember the incident; she couldn't remember any of her life before it happened. She didn't know who she was. She didn't know me. She didn't know her parents. She took our word for the state of things, and accepted us, and I think she learned to love me again, but she never remembered. We tried therapists, you know, and..." His voice tapered off, then he spoke again.

"The thing is, the little boy, he lived. He was in hospital awhile, and there was serious scarring that required some reconstructive surgery, but I kept up with him. We sold the Denver clinic and came here, and I set aside money for a college fund for him. He went to the University of Colorado. He's an engineer now. And a grandfather."

Garrett looked up, surprised, then did the math. It worked. "I'll be damned." He pondered. "Didn't the fact that he... that he got okay, didn't that help Annabelle face it?"

"She never saw him again. Something about it. The experts now are calling it a form of PTSD, but whatever it is, she won't accept what I tell her about the outcome. She... she goes out of her mind around dogs. When I tried to arrange for her to see Zach, she would... the best I can describe it is, she would leave reality. I finally gave up. She has completely buried that part of herself."

The atmosphere in the tent was oppressive. The flies buzzed heavy and persistent near the hot roof, occasionally dropping, kamikaze, to crash into the sticky table or one of the men. Finally, Garrett pushed on. He had to ask what he had to ask. "Doc, was she carrying a gun when she left the house?"

The veterinarian's face was grim. "The boys—you know, Patch and all—they told me that she was. They saw her leaving, and she does that, just hikes out sometimes to relieve tension. I assumed it was her own gun, her .22. I always asked her to take it for protection." He sighed, heavy and slumped. "Later, I've been scared to death that she planned suicide. She does. She gets headaches, and she can go into a helluva black depression."

"Could she have taken any other gun? Does she have access to other guns?"

"I got guns. I got a 30-30 from my dad, a couple of muzzle loaders I bought, a Sharps I couldn't resist. Client that knew I appreciated good guns gave me an SKS carbine... I never looked last night, Sheriff. I didn't think it was likely she'd take any of those."

Garrett hated it, but he had to keep going. Hadn't Hobbs mentioned the SKS as one of the guns that took a 7.62 caliber bullet? "But, Doc, say she was in a black mood, kind of in one of her other worlds.... Maybe she was planning to shoot a dog...?"

Doc met his eyes, his voice firm. "Look, Pat. I know you kinda gotta focus, have to put things together and figure out who killed that woman out there, so let's not mince words. It could have been Annabelle, but not the real Annabelle. If she did it, she wouldn't know she did it, and she probably wouldn't remember any of it when she was back in her right mind. You gotta understand something here; my own focus is finding Annabelle, hopefully alive. It might seem kinda strange to you, because it's been over fifty years and all, but I've never gave up hope. I love her the way she is now, but somewhere inside that woman is the woman I married. There is never a night when I don't go to bed hoping. Hoping that when we wake up in the morning she'll put her arms around me and say, 'Edgar, I remember. Edgar, I'm okay.' And I'll look into her eyes and see the real her, the sparkle. The song she used to be. I live that hope. If we find her destroyed, it will not be just her life, but my own that is gone. You go ahead now and hunt for a murderer. As for me, I gotta find Annabelle."

NORMALLY, THE HIGH, DRY mountain heat would sizzle against the vulnerable skin of their bald heads, but when the men stepped from the sultry tent, all they felt was the relief of free air and the tiny breeze that plucked at thin sunflowers near one of the half-finished adobe structures. The configurations of people had changed little. It looked as if the coroner had arrived. A few more community members had arrived, gathering with the curious groups already there. Doc limped his way back to his friends and their ATVs. McCracken had been watching the tent, and now she approached her boss. "Chief, I didn't see much up there; a few tracks, some disturbed detritus around the brush. Our people in the crime unit are on it. There was one thing, though. I caught the light glinting off this, and I picked it up. I thought it might interest you." In her hand was a metal object, shaped like a triangle, or maybe, more accurately, like a whale's tail. It was about an inch across or a little more, from either direction. There was a puzzling hole in the end. Garrett took it. On the one side it said, 'Leap of Faith,' with an engraving of a border collie. He turned it over. On the other side the words 'DIMA whistle' were engraved along the bottom. Across the top of the second side ran the words, 'Carol Halabi.'

Halabi. Haddon! Dog whistle! Garrett held the thing away from him as if it were a hot potato. "Aw, crap, Mac. Prints. We need to bag this."

A tall fellow from the crime unit had just produced the bag and started to kid with Garrett about contaminating evidence when they heard the shots. Everyone heard them. Two distinct shots, first one, then a pause, then a second. As one body, the crowd turned their faces toward the northwest, staring in the direction of the sounds.

35

THE FOREST DIDN'T STAND A CHANCE. Junee ignored the vigorous slaps of low branches, crawled through clinging underbrush, and scrambled over fallen logs, breaking whatever she could break if it stood in her way. Eileen did her best to keep up, her top tail pulled completely loose by the snatching shrubbery. Fortunately for their tender human skin, it wasn't too far. They had been making their way toward sounds that might have been dogs barking, although those barks ceased and occasionally crow caws, sounding deceptively similar to the barks, caused them to look anxiously skyward and doubt.

Their doubt was ill-founded. Following the barks had brought them closer, and when the shots went off, they were able to hone in directly on the tree. People in the settlement were not so fortunate. They had a direction, but no location. Mac got a nod from Garrett and set off on foot through the forest, running and jumping logs. Seeing that his deputies remained in charge of crowd control, Garrett ran to catch up with the ATVs. Hobbs, surprisingly spry for a stout guy, panted up behind him. The detective slid on behind Lew, facing backward and holding on for dear life as Bennie took off. The sheriff grabbed a perch on the Patch/Doc vehicle. Both ATVs struggled with the extra weight going up the hill out of the settlement, then sighed with relief as the road dropped down. They turned left on the old Ute trail, headed toward Sunshine Spring. The trail hadn't been maintained, so they had to stop twice to remove obstacles: logs, rocks, and undergrowth. Each time they cut the engines and listened. Patch gave sharp whistles through his teeth, then bellowed, "Buddy! Hey! Time to get home, Buddy!"

It was at the second stop that they heard Mac shouting just

north of them. "Over here, Chief. Here they are." The six searchers left the ATVs and plunged into the forest. Within seconds they were greeted by a very relieved Buddy, tail stub rotating violently, loll-tongued grin ecstatic. As the others moved toward Mac's voice, Garrett looked back. Patch was kneeling, cradling his dog, his old face crumpled and tears making their way through the wrinkled valleys toward the rumpled white beard below.

Reaching the tree, they were stopped short by the scene that greeted them. Junee hadn't wasted time waiting for anyone to climb down. She'd shot up the tree and seized her wayward daughter into a balance-defying, smothering hug, which in turn caused Sneaker, back in Sophia's clutches at this point, to let out a yip of protest. Annabelle sat elegantly on her chosen branch, queen of the forest, contemplating the activity below. Blood was running from her torn pant legs, dripping sedately onto her bare toes. She didn't seem to care. Her face had a quiet, indulgent smile. Her .22 was wedged on a branch nearby. There was other blood. Mac and Eileen were standing by the tree, talking and gesturing, and near their feet lay a large pit bull, motionless and covered in blood.

Doc pushed past and looked up at his wife. "Annabelle, get down. You need to get down from there."

"Yes, I do. I think it's time." She turned and stuck a foot down, feeling for the next branch below her.

Moving to get under her, Doc cried, "Careful! Be careful!" his voice thick with stress.

Annabelle turned her head to speak over her shoulder, but she addressed Garrett. "Sheriff, I need to show you something when I get down."

Several of the more intrepid, or perhaps aggressively curious, neighbors had now located the tree. Maureen Macklenburg, eyes wide with excitement, notebook and pen in hand, was taking in the scene. Ronald Gump arrived. Garrett was dismayed, especially as he realized that Doc's stance had become less protective of a potential falling woman, and more an attempt to shield his wife from the gathering crowd. In a low voice, he spoke to the elderly veterinarian. "It'll be okay, Dr. Clary. We'll get her away from this as soon as we can."

Gump had shoved forward. He was looking down at the

bleeding dog. In the fuss of the moment, no one noticed him, nor did they notice the look of horror on his paling orange face. "Damn," he murmured. "Damn." Only Mac heard him, and then she saw him back slowly away and fade into the cover of the forest.

"Whose dog is that?" Mac pointed at the bleeding pit bull.

Maureen declared, "Oh, that's Arnold Clenting's dog, Killer. I'd know that beast anywhere."

Lew Harris had been looking up, his eyes searching the thick branches of the pine, and suddenly he burst out, "There you are, Lucky! Where you been? What the hell you doin' up there? Get down!" Turning to the group around him, he shouted, "My dog is stuck up there. He must have followed Buddy up, but he really doesn't know how to climb. Can somebody help him get out?"

Everyone looked up in the tree, trying to spot the invisible dog. It was Mrs. Marco, the tow truck driver, who stepped forward. "Take it easy, Lew. I see 'im. Let these other people get down first, then I'll go up and get 'im."

To Doc's relief, Annabelle had reached the low bifurcation of the tree trunk, and with a short drop, her bare feet achieved the ground. He prepared to shield her from the neighborly human onslaught, but to his surprise she was smiling, and to him she said, "Just a minute." Turning, she reached up, saying "Hand me Sneaker."

Taking the little dog from Junee, she passed her to Doc, who said, "Be careful! You've hurt your feet, Annabelle."

"Yes, but I'm okay, Edgar." All eyes had turned toward the tree again, where Junee was making the drop to land, then reaching up to help Sophia, who made a run to reclaim Sneaker, as Mrs. Marco told Marco to give her a hand up so she could get Lew's dog. Everyone was distracted, not seeing Annabelle take her husband's exhausted cheeks in both of her own tired, blue-veined hands, and then she looked straight into the worried, red-rimmed old eyes, and said the words he had been needing to hear for so long. "I really am okay, Edgar. I have remembered. I remembered at last. I know everything. I know who you are. Who we always were—I found us, you and I. And I love you. I have always loved you."

It was Garrett, keeping his attention on the whole rescue

scene, who glanced over and saw that the tired old man was going to faint. A quick step, and the sheriff had put a steadying hand to his elbow. "Right here, Doc. Behind you, there's a log. You sit on this log."

Doc Clary had Annabelle's hand so fiercely that Garrett was afraid he'd break the fragile, elderly fingers, but he sat, bringing his wife with him, and sitting, said, "I'm okay, Sheriff. Just a little woozly. Gonna be okay."

Sitting by him, Annabelle was a different woman. No longer did her expression look withdrawn and closed, her head down, her eyes avoiding all contact. She was watching the activity by the tree with great interest, eyes sparkling, smiling as Mrs. Marco climbed up several branches, appeared to take a struggling animal into her arms, consoled it, then, apparently with difficulty, came back down to hand the invisible Lucky to Lew.

Garrett looked at Annabelle's bloody legs. "Your legs are hurt, Mrs. Clary. We need to get them taken care of."

"Oh. Yes, of course. In due time." She transferred her smile to the sheriff. "Thank you. But Sheriff, there is something you need to know. Those dogs were digging by the tree... "

Garrett interrupted her. "Dogs? There were more than one?"

"Yes, yes. There were two dogs. They dug and dug and dug, and when I jumped down to get my gun, I saw something where they had been digging. I think they were digging for something, but that dead dog is lying over the hole right now."

"I see." Frowning, Garrett walked back to McCracken. "Look, Mac. We need to move this dog. Give me a hand?" Overhearing, Marco and Bennie stepped over.

They all grabbed a leg, starting to drag the dead dog off the hole, when Bennie exclaimed, "Wait a minute! Take it easy. This dog is alive!"

Junee's face fell and Doc mumbled, "Shit," starting to stand, but Garrett had become brisk. "Look, Doc, why don't we transport him to the clinic and put him in a cage until you can give him some attention. Right now, I'd say you need to take care of Annabelle."

The group had quieted, the reality of Annabelle's bleeding legs and the dog's moving eyes now sinking in. Patch's rumble was uncharacteristically quiet as he said, "That's right, Doc. Let's get you and Annabelle onto my four-wheeler and I'll get ya' home. I'll drive easy, and Buddy can run alongside."

"Yeah." Doc was still looking in amazement at his transformed wife. "Yeah, we better go. If somebody gets that dog there before we get there, you put him in that big cage in the southwest corner, then you lock it and be damn sure the lock is secure. Who's taking him?"

Bennie's was the only other ATV nearby. "I'll take him. Don't worry, Doc, we'll lock him up good and solid." Clearing logs and brush from the way, they brought the four-wheelers closer. Bennie's had a roll of heavy irrigation plastic in the front work box, and they laid the plastic down and slid the wounded dog onto it, then lifted him up onto the vehicle itself. The dog removed, Garrett stepped over to look into the hole.

Maureen Macklenburg put her hand over her mouth and said in a dramatically shocked stage whisper to Eileen standing next to her, "I heard them say that the dogs were digging. Remember, I told you that that Arnold Clenting was burying meat with Billy Ray's clothes, teaching it to dig for her body, he said. He said he needed to have that Killer be able to find Billy Ray if she ever had an 'accident.' Oh, my god! What if Arnold made Billy Ray have an 'accident,' like he said, and he put her there! You know, I mean, not a real accident..."

Garrett had motioned Hobbs and Mac over; the rest of the group were now keeping a nervous distance. Looking into the hole, Hobbs grunted. "Well, I'll be damned. There she is." This caused the group to gasp, shuddering backward a step. Hobbs crouched down and began to push more dirt away, saying, "Yup, here she is, all right. Our pretty little M39. Right here, just a little bit lost, magically lost, in the middle of the forest."

SOPHIA HAD TUGGED on her anxious mother, dragging her over to look at the limp dog on the back of the ATV. "Mom, he hurts so bad." Then, thinking she needed emphasis, she stressed, "He hurts so *damn* bad. You gotta do something. You need to fix him."

Her face grim, Junee snarled, "I'm not so sure I want to undo Mrs. Clary's good work in shooting that mean devil."

"Oh, no, Mom! You got it wrong. I don't think he's so mean,

not really. Maybe confused or curious. And she didn't shoot him. I did. It was an accident. I think Annabelle scared him when she jumped down, and he was biting her, and I wanted to make him stop. I thought I could scare him back, but I didn't have the barrel pointed right, so I shot him. I need some lessons in how to use that damn gun, 'cause I hurt him, and now he's crying."

Junee stared, first at her daughter, then at the dog. Sophia was right. It looked hurt and sad. It did have tears running from its mournful, ugly, animal eyes. It seemed to think it was being punished for having tried to do the right thing.

36

"SO YOU FOUND THE MISSING PARTIES, but really you aren't any closer to knowing who shot that Russian woman?" That was Jenny, summing up. It was mid-afternoon. Garrett and McCracken were taking a break after dealing with the events at the pinyon tree. They needed lunch, and of course Garrett had headed for the Cowpath and Jenny. Hungry as a bear, Mac skipped the salad and gobbled a burger while they told Jenny about Annabelle and Sophia being found in the tree, not to mention the gun buried beneath. Garrett skirted his conversation with Doc, and Mac understood that they shouldn't bring up the dog whistle yet, not even to Jenny, but that still left a lot that they could tell her if she was to be kept abreast of the general neighborhood buzz. Now Garrett had fallen silent and thoughtful, his usual mode, as Mac, a little defensively, reacted to Jenny's comment.

"Hey, we got the gun, at least. If it matches the bullet."

"Right. That's good. Is Hobbs on it?"

"Yeah, he went on down. Shouldn't take CBI long to sort out if the gun and bullet match."

"But can you find out who owned that gun? Fingerprints? How long will that take?"

Garrett let his brain return to the table. "Hobbs will trace it for ownership. It can take fifteen minutes to find the person who bought it. Or a week. Or Never."

"Oh, wow!" Jenny exclaimed. "Can't they put it on a computer somewhere or... How do they trace it, anyhow?"

"Asa'll send the gun particulars on into the ATF. He has the manufacturer, model, caliber, and serial number now; nothing had been defaced. The ATF will take it from there."

McCracken was working her phone. "There isn't any computer, like you say; no national gun registry. It says here that federal law bars that kind of registry. NRA opposition, you know. It says here the ATF processed more that 344,000 gun trace requests last year, and that those are primarily done with phone calls and manual labor."

Hesitantly, not wanting to show her ignorance, Jenny said, "So, ATF. That's the Association of... of... "

Quickly, to forestall a gloating reply from the knowledgable Mac, Garrett said matter of factly, "Oh, ATF stands for Alcohol, Tobacco, and Firearms."

It didn't work very well; Jenny blushed, thinking she should have known. Fortunately, McCracken was busy, pleased to be on the Internet and the one still in the know. She filled in. "It says here that the information goes to the Bureau of Alcohol, Tobacco, Firearms, and Explosives National Tracing Center in Martinsburg, West Virginia. That is the only place in the country that can trace it."

"Just one place." Jenny was impressed. "But they can eventually find the owner, then?"

Garrett finished his burger and his second cup of coffee while McCracken worked her phone, then he said, "Well, they start with the manufacturer, who can identify the wholesale distributor that bought the gun. Then the wholesaler can take them to the gun dealer. The retailer is supposed to be a federally licensed gun dealer who keeps a record of each purchase made from him."

"Complex," Jenny offered.

"The thing is," Mac added, "The gun can keep changing hands from that first retailer, or get stolen, or the dealer might have gone out of business, place burned down or something. Some dealers resent the federal rules, so they keep bad records, write the stuff down on paper towel or toilet paper. I guess that stuff ends up in West Virginia, too. You're right. It does get complicated."

Jenny stood to step to the counter for more coffee all around. Sitting, she said, "So, if they succeed, who do you think they'll trace that gun to?"

Mac and Garrett exchanged glances. "I dunno," Garrett said. "There were a lot of people out there wandering around above that settlement this morning who I guess you could say don't have alibis. Can't help but wonder what they were all doing up there, really."

"For example?" Jenny waited.

"Well, both Annabelle and Doc, of course, and that Will Yelets we told you about from the settlement that took off early to sell some kind of carvings." He hesitated, then said, "We aren't sure where Carol, uh, Carol Haddon was this morning. You know, I got the impression she thought it was Maarika Yelets that hit her dog, was maybe trying to run over her. Maybe Haddon got it in her head she'd strike first, before the Yelets woman tried something else to maybe kill her. But I don't know what the dispute was about."

Mac said, "What about Ronald Gump? He seemed to be all over up there for no good reason."

Thoughtful, Garrett said, "Red and Louie found him at home, in his dressing gown, sipping coffee. That was at 8:30 this morning. The murder was at 6:00. It's possible, but does he have a motive?"

Sighing, Mac said, "Yeah, I'm having trouble with motives here. I can't see strong motives, especially not Doc or Annabelle. I don't see Annabelle as that crazy, and I can't imagine a scenario where Doc would step in somehow to protect her from Maarika."

"Back to Gump's motive," Jenny was frowning. "You know, he really wanted that piece of land up there. He's a developer, and it is plum. It has the spring, borders the BLM, and is set in a beautiful pinyon-juniper forest itself, with lots of wildlife all around, and views. Maybe if he makes those Vedrussians' lives miserable, they'll decide to sell out."

Garrett pulled at his mustache, recalling the stories of harassment he had heard from Grisha and the other Vedrussians just a few hours ago. "Mmmph. Here's one thing. The rifle itself, it would be a treasure to a hunter. Or a military man. And you know who is both, fella that lives not far away from the settlement?"

Mac laughed. "Arnold Clenting."

Laughing with her, Jenny said, "So we may as well pull them all in. Politics. County commissioner candidates. What about Billy Ray? Or Bennie? Where were those two at six this morning?"

Garrett smiled, but his eyes were distant. "Dunno, do we? Well, I guess we'd better get moving. Already four o'clock. You'll be in your suppertime rush here pretty soon, Jen." He kissed her cheek, leaving the lips for later.

37

WHEN McCRACKEN AND GARRETT entered the clinic, Junee was peeling off surgical gloves while Bennie, Lew, and Patch hefted the pit bull, made a dead weight by the anesthesia, and hauled him to the secure cage. Junee gave the officers a big smile. "So, there you are again, officers. We've already had a nap, or I'd call this harassment, these excessive visits from the sheriff's department." She chuckled, feeling happy, looking fondly at her retrieved child, who had curled into a waiting room chair, gaming and projecting an aloof attitude of absence.

The officers chuckled, too, and Garrett said, "So, how's Doc?"

"He came down to do the surgery, but we sent him back up to the house. He has a lot of catching up to do with Annabelle."

Bennie added, "And they both looked bushed. We closed the clinic down for the weekend so they could rest. I'll bet that's a first; the man hasn't had much rest in fifty years."

Patch rumbled, "Junee told him she could do the surgery herself this time."

"That is surely true," Junee said. "If I'm going to buy this practice (She looked significantly at Sophia, who feigned absorption in her game) and if Doc is going to retire to ply his new-found profession as co-grandfather with you other yahoos (Now her significant look included the three old men, who, like Sophia, played innocent), then I need to start doing things around here without having Doc hold my hand." Despite herself, a pleased smile had crept to Sophia's lips. Garrett took the chair next to her.

McCracken asked, "So how's the dog?"

"Well, for somebody that was just trying to scare something

off, my daughter managed to do quite a bit of damage. One shot caught him in the upper front leg, then the next one glanced off his skull. That last one is what made him so limp and goofy while we were talking under the tree. But he'll live." Her eye on Sophia, her eyes twinkling, she added, "Unfortunately."

This time Sophia reacted. "Mom!"

This brought Junee up to spin, ready to giggle. "It didn't help, you know, that on the way down here the poor old dog started to wake up and wiggled and Bennie and Lew, here, saw fit to whack him on the head with a heavy rock."

With guilty shuffles, the two men said, "Didn't wanna get bit," and "Save some on the anesthetic bill."

Sophia was glaring at them. She put down her iPhone and started to get up, but Garrett put a gentle hand on her arm. "Just a minute, Soapy. Before you go, I need to ask you a question."

"And what would that be, *Officer?*" she snapped.

"While you were out hunting Sneaker, did you see anything unusual, anything that surprised you, any people besides Annabelle?"

Sitting back down, Sophia said, "Not really. I just hunted Sneaker nearly forever and got really tired, and then I thought it would be easier to walk in the road awhile, but there was a man coming down, so I hid in the bushes."

This was the first time Junee had heard about this man, and she exchanged glances with the law officers. "What did that man look like?"

"Mom, I don't know. He was a stranger, so I hid. I guess I'm kind of like an ostrich—I stuck my head down in the bush so I couldn't see him, which would make it that he couldn't see me. He was going on down the road just as I saw Buddy and Sneaker."

Junee began, "Can't you tell us anything else, Sophia?" but Mac said, "You were a smart kid to hide, Sophia. That man could have been dangerous. Did he have a gun?"

Looking from grownup to grownup, Sophia said, "I really didn't know him, and I didn't look at him. When I did look, I looked at his dog."

Garrett said gently, "So he had a dog?"

Sophia fixed him with a serious, worried gaze. "Yes, Mr. Garrett. He had a dog following him. It looked just like that dog in there. I think I shot his dog."

"I see."

"And he didn't have a gun. I am thinking now; I'm using my powers of thinking, and the man who I shot his dog didn't even have a gun." She was chewing on her lip. "Does that help?"

Garrett smiled at her. "Yes, indeed. It helps a lot, Soapy. He shouldn't have let that dog loose so that it might hurt you or Annabelle. And he might have had a gun before you saw him, you know. So thank you for the very helpful information."

38

"TELL YOU WHAT, MAC. You take the car, head back up to the settlement, see what needs to be done to get things squared away for a while. Maybe the Stoney City bunch sent up some reinforcements and Red and Louie can catch a break."

McCracken raised her eyebrows. She didn't need to ask, but she said it anyhow. "Jenny?"

"Yeah, I'll call 'er. But I was going to have you drop me off at Carol Haddon's."

"I can..."

"Nah, Mac. Not this time. We need you worse to check up at the settlement. They been short-handed most a' the day."

Patch, like the rest of the exhausted crew slumped in chairs around the clinic, had been listening in. He rumbled, "Well, Sheriff, looks like I 'bout done all the damage around here I can manage for one day, so I'm headed on home. Want me and Buddy to drop you off at Carol's? Save your deputy a little?"

"You bet. That'd be good." Garrett paused, thinking. "You know, though, I'll need my car tomorrow. Mac, if you could, work something out with Red to get that car dropped off at Jenny's by morning, okay?"

"You bet, Chief," and there was a general stretching and shuffling as everyone made their way out the door. Junee locked it behind them, then turned to talk to her daughter.

Sophia was fast asleep, slumped over her iPhone in the awkward waiting room chair, Sneaker stretched flat on her own side, asleep on the floor by the child's dangling feet. Junee looked down at the angelic face of her sleeping daughter and whispered, "Ah, you little bullhead. Just what have you gotten us into now?"

GARRETT HOPPED DOWN from Patch's truck, made his way up Carol Haddon's walk, and knocked. It was dusk again. He sighed. It had been a long day.

The door began to edge open, but the first thing that appeared was the barrel of a pistol, aimed out the tentative crack. Garrett stepped to the side, away from the shaky aim, saying, "Hey, easy there, Ms. Haddon. It's the sheriff here."

The gun lowered, the door opened, and Carol Haddon babbled apologies. "I'm sorry, Sheriff. I'm just so nervous. I don't feel safe anymore, even in my own house. I probably couldn't shoot you anyhow—I don't use guns. Please, come in."

"Yeah, well, you're making me a little edgy, too. Maybe ya' oughta lower that damn barrel."

Looking down at the gun, surprised, Carol lowered the barrel. "Oh! Oh, I... Yes..."

She laid the gun on a stand by the door, then said, "There. Now. Would you like to come in, or...?"

His big ears seeming to move forward to seek out possible sounds from inside the house, Garrett said, "Yes, I think I would. I think I would like to speak with you for a few minutes, Ms. Halabi."

"Oh! I see! Halabi. Oh, you know, then. Please sit, then. I'll explain. Please. There, a chair..." It was a cozy room, not large, but furnished with a couch, easy chairs, healthy plants, and pictures of sheep dogs on every wall and surface. "Let me get you something to drink. Coffee? Or a soda? Whiskey?"

Garrett studied her. "I wouldn't have expected a Muslim to have whiskey."

"I'm not Muslim." Her expression was regretful. "You see, Sheriff Garrett, people have stereotypes. This time, I did the stereotyping, I think. I want to live in this community, and I thought that rural people like around here would hear my name, Halabi, and decide I was a terrorist or something. I figured they would ostracize me. I didn't want it to be like that—I want to be part of the community and have friends here. I couldn't change how I look, but I changed my name. I thought..." She caught herself. She had almost said, "I thought I would be Mrs. Will Yelets soon, anyhow, so I wouldn't have to worry," but she wasn't sure she wanted the sheriff to know all this. Instead, she finished, "I just thought I could fix the name change once I got settled here."

"Hmmph," Garrett said, still suspicious. "How about a Pepsi? I'm dry as dust." She had foregone the protective kaftan, thinking she was alone and at home, and she was wearing a sleeveless tee shirt and pants designed to accommodate her belly. Garrett noted the baby bump. He added, "And there is more to the story, right?"

She nodded, shot him a rueful smile, and went into the kitchen. Garrett studied the pictures. They were well done, some paintings, others photographs. This woman really liked her dogs, all right. Then, tucked unobtrusively among a row of framed dog photos along the top of a bookcase, was a photo of a dark-haired woman that looked very much like Carol, the same beauty, but older. "Well," Garrett thought, "Here's mama. But where is papa?"

Carol reappeared with a tray bearing a glass of iced Pepsi, water condensing on its cold sides in the dry evening heat. Aware of his parched throat, Garrett couldn't wait to get his hands on that glass. There were two plates, a thoughtful choice between the sweetness of sugar cookies or the saltiness of peanuts set amidst chunks of cheese, crackers, and baby carrots. Garrett helped himself, his thanks sincere. Two dogs had followed Carol into the room, nudging Garrett for a handout, but when she chided them they minded, going peacefully to lie near her on the rug.

Carol and the sheriff both relaxed, Carol pleased to have successfully accommodated a guest. She began to talk at once. "You see, Sheriff, my grandparents are Christian. They immigrated here from Saudi Arabia. There is an ancient tribe there, the Banu Taghlib, that were some of the earliest Christians. In fact, in Jubail, in Southern Arabia, you can find the ruins of the oldest Christian church in the world. My family are descendants of that tribe, but their beliefs have been forced out. Most were converted to Islam long ago; we were just remnants. In 1956, my grandfather realized that political interests were using Islam and Sharia law to tighten their hold on the people. He gathered our family and brought them to America to escape persecution. A good move, as long as we can avoid the likes of Ronald Gump."

"So you are a Saudi, but Christian?" Garrett affirmed.

"Well, not really. I'm third generation American agnostic. You know, about like everyone else in this country. Our family still has some ethnic values, cook ethnic food, and so-on. Like me, we're sometimes a little jumpy about prejudice — they really torture and kill Christians now, in Saudi Arabia.

"Anyhow, I also look like my grandma and my mom. See her, in that picture? She is Qamar Halabi, a good American woman, but she looks Saudi enough to trigger xenophobia in some places. She used to belly dance in a restaurant near the army base — I think she must have given off an exotic aura."

Garrett smiled. "She's beautiful, like you. But why pick this community? Why not go somewhere a little more open to outsiders, if you saw this place as being so, well, so narrow about foreigners?"

A piece of cheese disappeared behind Garrett's mustache as Carol fumbled, "Well, I... I, uh..."

Garrett smiled. "The father?" He indicated the baby bump.

Carol smiled back. "Two fathers. Mine and baby's."

"I see." Garrett was interested. "So, tell me about these fathers. Who is your father?"

"That's the problem. I don't know. My mother says he's dead, and that she was never married to him anyhow. She won't tell me who he was, nor anything about him. She just told me that he came from this area, from Croissant or nearby, and that before he died he arranged for me to inherit his land when I reach my twenty-fifth birthday, but he didn't want me to know who he was. She said that when I was born, he wanted to provide for me, so even though he didn't marry her, he made sure I would someday get his land. He left it as a trust with some law firm, and they will notify me on my birthday. Only a few months now!"

Garrett could see that this great mystery made Carol Halabi very excited. Her face was animated, her hesitance and fear gone. "So, Ms. Halabi, that sounds very motivating. You came here because of this promised piece of land, this upcoming inheritance from your father. And, as you said, that's why you feel you need to become part of the community. You hope to settle here."

"Oh, yes, Sheriff! To me it is a beautiful place. At first, I had such hope here."

"But your deceased father. That's not the only reason you came, is it? There is the other father."

Sobering, Carol sighed. "Oh, yes. Will." She raised her lovely eyes and spoke with piercing intensity. "Sheriff, Will Yelets from the Vedrussian settlement is the father of this child. I cannot tell you how much I love that man, and we thought we were married, but then that Maarika showed up from Russia. I'm talking about the woman that tried to run me down, the one that hit Sassy. He had married *her*, in Russia, years ago. He doesn't love her, and I hate her. He didn't think it was a real marriage, but she..." Carol stopped abruptly. Both she and the sheriff had heard a car pull onto the gravel in the driveway, then running steps toward the house.

Carol started clumsily to stand as the door burst open. A young man, blond and rumpled, burst into the room. "Carol! Oh, my darling, Maarika is dead! Someone has killed Maarika! I had our papers, determined to at least get the legal proceedings started for a divorce, but Zhora reached me before I even got to Richfield. I rushed back. He said someone shot her this morning! I've been frantic about you! Are you okay?" He reached out to gather her into his arms, then he saw the sheriff.

Garrett heard another car enter the driveway, an engine he recognized. Jenny's timing, as usual, was spot on.

39

PILLOW TALK, dappled early sunshine, coffee, and Jenny. What more could a man want? Garrett wiggled the skinny toes on the feet that perched just inches beyond the end of Jenny's queen-sized mattress and enjoyed playing with a strand of Ms. Jenny Threewinds' long, silky, black hair, wild and loose across her lovely back. She was tickling at the broad, ugly scar that ran from his left jaw, down his neck, and across his chest. As a toddler, he'd climbed up the stove and pulled a pan of flaming grease onto himself. He used to hate the scar, partly because it didn't come from an act of heroism in the line of duty, just from consistent neglect on the part of his substance-abusive mother, but now Jenny's constant and steady appreciation of his deface-ment gave him a new perspective on its value.

Jenny was telling him some of the scuttlebutt she'd heard from customers after he and Mac left the Cowpath yesterday afternoon. He felt tickles puttering around on his bare chest as she talked; he half listened to her. "Those people up in the settlement, they're part of a big partly social, partly religious movement that is spreading all over the world. It started in Russia. It has to do with a sort of prophet, a Russian woman, kind of mythic, called Anastasia, who believes that creation is happening and it involves dark energy and light energy. Humans can bring in light energy, the good energy, by living the right way with nature. There are cedar trees in Russia, Siberian pines, that get filled with the good energy and ask to be cut down and have their wood given away in little pieces to help distribute that good energy everywhere. These trees tell people that they are ready to be distributed by ringing. They are called the Ringing Cedars of Russia."

To be polite, Garrett repeated, "Ringing Cedars of Russia." The tickly little fingers had escaped the scar and were migrating across his stomach. It made his eyes blur.

Jenny said, "Right. So these people up there, up Forest Road, they think they have found ringing cedars here. Our trees are Colorado pinyon, but the Yelets guy you just told me about, he is an especially strong believer, and he is convinced that some trees here are ringing, and it is his job to protect them. You can imagine how they feel about Ronald Gump and his slash and build concept of the countryside. Plus, I guess the currently dead Maarika thought it was all a crock of shit. I heard that last night, too."

Tickle, tickle, tickle. Did this woman know no boundaries? No, she did not! She knew perfectly well what she was doing. Garrett, clearly having filled with good energy, gave up on the lock of hair and made a grab for the rest of the delicious, succulent, naked body, his only issue being where to start first. Jenny squirmed in delight. The telephone rang.

Groaning, Garrett said, "Oh, my god! Let it *go*. Who cares?" The caller was persistent. The rings continued, and the spell crumbled away. Finally, sorrowfully, Jenny crossed the room to get the phone and answered, then turned to the sheriff.

"An invitation, my sweet. Dr. Clary would like you to come at once for coffee and breakfast rolls."

"Whaat! Coffee and... What! At once?"

Smiling ruefully, Jenny nodded. "As soon as possible. Annabelle was there when Maarika was shot, and neither she nor Doc are fully confident in her memory yet. They want you to come before she forgets the details of what she saw."

"Oh, Jesus Christ." Garrett swung his lanky body out of bed.

Commiserating, Jenny murmured sadly, "Yes, murder won't wait, will it?"

EVERYTHING HAD SETTLED DOWN by the time Garrett reached the Clary house, and he had begun to wonder what the observations of a woman with a notoriously faulty memory might mean, especially if she had information they might need to use in court. When he knocked on the door, he was surprised to have it opened by a smiling, gracious

Annabelle Clary.

"Come in, Sheriff, come in. We're so sorry to bother you so dreadfully early, but I think Edgar explained our reasoning to Jenny. I can't help but think this is very important, but it has all been such a shock to Edgar, I needed to see him back up and running before I told anyone else."

As it was, Doc was on the phone and seemed to be in fine fettle, having ignored the attempts of Junee and her cohorts to give him a weekend break from clients and vet work. As he entered the room, Garrett heard him say, "What's going on, you old s.o.b.? You just wake up and crawl out from under a bush to cause trouble this morning?"

Silence, then uh huh, uh huh, then, "Well, feed her some of her own shit."

Apparently this prompted a startled reaction on the other end of the line. Annabelle handed Garrett coffee, smiling indulgently toward her husband, who was saying, "No, I am serious. A heifer gets into the grain like that, maybe eats too much, gets a little shitty, you get a syringe and get some of that shit back down into her stomach. It'll act as a probiotic. Ever heard of a probiotic? Like yoghurt. Helps get the right kind of bugs back inside ya'. She's shit out all the good bugs, so you need to put some of the good ones back in her."

Annabelle passed sweet rolls and napkins, telling Garrett, her softer voice tracing across Doc's loud one, "It's all back. I was sure yesterday, but after a night of sleep, I'm even more certain. I remember everything, and I feel like I am the person I was long ago; I remember that dog fight and the child, too. It's okay. It's all okay."

Doc had hung up the phone and sat down. If anything, he had changed as much as Annabelle. No longer a man with a secret burden, he was beaming. Having at a sweet roll, a fulfilled host in his own domain, he said, "Thanks for coming so soon, Sheriff. We talked it over and agreed it was important to tell you as soon as possible. Have another roll."

Having agreed that it was important to tell him as soon as possible, they now made extensive small talk. Frustrated, scrubbing away at his miserable mustache, Garrett finally ventured, "So, Mrs. Clary, I understand you have information about this murder?"

"Not Mrs. Clary. Annabelle." She became serious. "Now you see, Sheriff, I saw it. I suppose no one will believe me, the condition I have been in, but I think you need to know what I saw. Then you can decide what to do with the information." Garrett leaned forward encouragingly.

"Here is what happened. I went up the Ute trail; I was thinking about suicide. I'd screamed at Sophia because she tried to show me her dog, and I just felt like I couldn't take Edgar through all this anymore. Sophia is special to him, and I couldn't believe that the monster I had become, that monster I couldn't control, would do something so stupid and dreadful and damaging. I spent a long night up there in the spruce, up in the BLM, and a lot of things happened that I won't go into here. Dreams and so-on. I was wandering back down the trail yesterday morning, still confused, still trying to sort it out, when I arrived just above the Vedrussian village. Just as I came down the hill and in sight of the settlement, a man stepped out from behind a tree in front of me, raised his rifle, and shot. I was terrified. I had my own rifle, but I couldn't believe it was enough. I shrank back against the tree I had been passing, but I could see the man clearly. It was Arnold Clenting."

"Clenting!" Garrett exclaimed, sitting up straight, slapping down his coffee mug. "Clenting? That was who you saw, for sure?"

"Absolutely. If I had a reputation as a sane woman, I could testify in court without a qualm. After the shot, I looked into the settlement. I saw the fallen woman and people running toward her from the various buildings. I watched them, in shock. I was very afraid. I didn't know what to do, and when I looked back at where he had stood, Clenting was gone, and I finally left, too. All I could think was to get home, that Edgar would take care of it all."

Before Garrett could ask more, there was a brisk knock on the door. The conversation was suspended as Doc opened it to admit Junee Bailey, who entered while apologizing for the intrusion. "I'm really sorry to butt in, but the thing is, I see the sheriff's car up here and, Mr. Garrett, I just found out something I think you should know, and I wanted to catch you. I'm not sure how important it is, but it could be, I think." Without waiting for an invitation, she sat, now addressing Doc Clary.

"Doc, remember when Ronald Gump came by, that time we were all out in the clinic yard, trying to cool off from this awful heat? You were there, too, remember, Sheriff? Gump came in spewing a lot of trash talk about those people up in the settlement being terrorists and cultists and stuff? Remember?"

The two men nodded, and she continued. "Well, remember that he wanted us to remove a growth from under his dog's left eye? That dog, his dog Cuddles, had quite a growth there, and we removed it that day.

"So, anyhow, just now Cole and I were working with that pit bull down there, the one Sophia shot, and I suddenly realized that we all had overlooked something rather important in all the excitement yesterday. That is a female dog. That dog is not Killer, like everyone said. That dog is female, and she has a goodly scar right where Doc and I put it, under her left eye. It is Cuddles, Ronald Gump's beloved pit bull, not Killer—it is Cuddles who doesn't have an alibi."

40

GARRETT REALLY NEEDED THE MOUNTAINS. He needed altitude and isolation, the whisper of aspen, the sigh of air being breathed through spruce. He was so close to sorting all this out, and the mountains always cleared his head. He needed them right now, though, so they were not an option. East or west, it would take at least an hour to achieve the quiet he required. The nearest ones, to the south, would take him past the Vedrussian settlement. Passing by that would be like a mammoth trying to tiptoe across a tar pit. Sighing, he let his car drift north into Peaseford. He seemed to recall that it had a town park or two, maintained by the Lions Club or something, possibly quiet at this time of day. Somewhere in this valley was a very dangerous person, a person who had gone off kilter enough to murder. He or she might do it again. He was not going to feel that people were safe here until he had figured out who this person was.

Muddling about the listlessly paved streets of the little town, he considered his suspects. He supposed he could still include Will or Annabelle, but this would involve believing one or the other of them to be deceitful, and from what he had seen, that would be a stretch. On the north side of Peaseford he passed a tidy brick ranch house, roses at the door, the lawn kept bright green by heavy water usage in the dry, baking August heat. The sign at the mailbox said, "Clenting," and a large sign in the yard proclaimed, "Billy Ray Lives Here! Vote!" Ahhh. What about Billy Ray, the other politician? Should he suspect her? He could see no motive.

Not far from the Methodist Church he found the kind of little park he sought: shady, pleasant, and, best of all, empty. He pulled in to find a parking space under a huge elm, stepped out of the car, leaned against the tree, and messed with a plucked twig while he thought. So, probably not Will or Annabelle. Doc unlikely. Billy Ray, no reason to even consider. That left a much narrowed list. The problem was, sometimes the closer you get to untangling the string the tighter it knots up.

First of all, Annabelle swore it was Arnold Clenting she saw shoot; with any other eyewitness, that would be heavy evidence. But this was Annabelle. You had to be careful. Second, what was Cuddles doing up there by that tree? Cuddles, the dog Ronald Gump swore never left his side? The dog that wasn't visible when Louie and Red visited Gump? The dog with no alibi? No alibi. Well, what about Gump's alibi? Surely he knew where his dog was. Why hadn't he retrieved it from the clinic? Maybe it was Gump that Annabelle saw instead of Clenting. Did Clenting and Gump resemble each other? Garrett had never thought about it, but he didn't think they did. And where was Killer?

What about Carol Haddon aka Halabi? She seemed to be a woman of secrets, and he was bothered by that sheep dog whistle found near the shooter's tree. Now, Carol was a woman with a motive, all right! She not only had declared that she hated Maarika, she thought she was being stalked by her, so she feared her, too. It would be to her every advantage to have Maarika removed from the world. Despite all the lovely hospitality last night, and Will's explosive entry, the bottom line was that Carol Haddon didn't have a real alibi. No one knew where she was yesterday morning. It wasn't clear that she even knew Maarika had been shot — Will didn't seem to think she knew — but didn't he recall Bennie mentioning that Carol had called him about hearing poachers in the area? What was that about, an attempt to set up an alibi?

Pulling out his cell, Garrett dialed Bennie Senderson. Abby answered. Bennie was shaving. Bennie felt he had to present a favorable aspect to voters now that he was running for commissioner. She was happy about this. She'd fetch him, though. Garrett waited. Finally, Senderson came on the line.

"Ben, didn't I hear you say that Carol called you yesterday morning about poachers, said she heard a shot? Could it have been that shot from up there at the settlement, the shot that killed the Russian woman?"

Abby was clanking dishes in the background. Benny grunted.

"Hell, I don't know what you're gettin' at, Sheriff. What difference would it make?"

"I don't know either, Bennie. Just trying to clean things up a little, get some facts, tidy up my thinking."

Those were definitely chewing sounds, then a noisy swallow. "Well, I can see that. Bottom line is, I don't see how she could've heard that shot clear down at her place. I think she was out walkin' the dogs or something. Honest personal opinion, DOW experience, I doubt she heard a poacher. I think she told me she was walkin' dogs. Probably coulda been up that direction, though." More chewing.

"Well, thanks, Ben. Ya' been helpful. Enjoy your breakfast." Garrett snapped his phone shut and headed for the car. He was recalling something his grandfather once told him. "Pat," he had said, "If you want to run with the big dogs, don't pee like a puppy."

In the car, he contacted McCracken. "Catch me up, Mac."

It threatened to take a few minutes, details about the arrival of Stoney City deputies, the departure of most of the neighbors after the coroner picked up the corpse, the attempts by the Vedrussians to tend their plants and animals in peace. She and Red were on scene; Louie had headed back to Riversmet to check on her kids and get some shuteye. Garrett was patient, listening. Finally, he told her about the information at the Clarys. "Look, Mac, I want you and Red to go on down, move in close to Gump's place, and just keep an eye on it. And him. I'm going to drive to Arnold Clenting's; I want to locate him and Killer."

Garrett was pulling out of Peaseford when he got the land line call from Edith Oviedo, the secretary at the Riversmet sheriff's office. "Hey, there, *Señor*. Your buddy Asa Hobbs has got the trace on the gun."

"All *right!*" A private high five and a grin. "You gonna tell me, Señora A-deet, or you just gonna sit on it?"

"Whatcha gonna pay me?"

"A big kiss if you don't hurry up."

"Ah, no, *Señor!* No torture the poor woman, please! No *beso grande* from the sheriff. Your retail guy is called Gary's Guns. He's small, he's licensed, and the part you're gonna love best is, he's right there in Croissant, on Dirty Kid Alley."

"Whoof," Garrett said. "So good all around! *Gracias*

mucho." It probably wasn't good Spanish, but whatever. He was just five minutes away from the seller, and he wouldn't need a G.P.S. Croissant only had about ten streets, none more than a few hundred yards long. Just for the heck of it, he put on his flashers and hit the accelerator.

41

NOT IN THE STEREOTYPICAL craggy mountains of peaks and spruce and cliffs, Croissant was, even so, a mountain town. This meant that one didn't start with a flat place on which to build a home. No, one started with a bulldozer and flattened the slope of the intended building site. Results from this weren't always foolproof. Gravity enjoyed toying with the structures it found in its midst. Driving along the streets, searching for Gary and his guns, Garrett noticed several houses where parts of the foundations had slipped downhill, leaving structural cracks and flaws where the rest of the foundation and the frame had failed to go along for the ride. A tough place to settle, even in this day and age, Garrett thought, prowling along streets, looking for their names.

Croissant was small. It didn't take long. Dirty Kid Alley proved to be a real street with a legible sign at the intersection, and the gun dealer's house was not one of those which struggled so valiantly with the mountainous inclines. Instead, it sat next to a large irrigation canal that wound its way around the bottoms of the slopes that fed it. The gun dealer's house was at least a hundred years old, a log house, but the logs had been squared, no doubt using axes and hand saws, then stacked like Lincoln logs into place. Somewhere along the line, an owner had decided that a white house would be best, so the logs had been thoroughly whitewashed. Perhaps a little embarrassed by this white covering, the house had sunken into its surroundings, making itself invisible among fat lilac bushes, uncontrolled wild roses, and two large, very pushy weeping willows near the canal. There was no house number. No problem. A neat, carved wooden sign protruded from a nearby fence post, proclaiming that here, indeed, was "Gary's Guns."

Inside, Garrett found Gary himself, a monstrously big man with heavy freckled hands and red hair that was so rusted it seemed to have leaked, dripping across the open, friendly face and leaving splatters of freckles everywhere in its wake. The first room Garrett encountered was tiny, primarily a chair and a counter, but through the open door he could see another room filled with guns, gun cabinets, equipment designed to do gun repair, presses to aid in loading bullets, and long boxes that must have contained gun shipments. In fact, it was a small house, and Garrett couldn't see a living area. Where did the man eat and sleep? Did he have a wife, or family?

Garrett thought not, for Gary was lonely. He liked to talk. As Garrett explained to him about the gun and why he needed information on it, Gary interjected judgments, opinions, and stories of his own that went far afield of the business at hand. It was only after a wearying forty-five minutes or more that the dealer pulled out a record book and, with a patient Garrett looking on beside him, ran a finger across many lines on many pages. At last, they came to it, with Gary saying, "All right, Sheriff. I think this is the information you want. I can go back in my files and find receipts and so-on, if you'd like."

Thanking the guy, who walked him to the car, still talking, Garrett waited until he was well away before calling Mac. "Look, Mac, I'd like you and Red to pick Gump up for questioning as soon as possible. You might get hold of Edith and get some arrest legalities into place, too, but don't waste time. Let me know when you've got him."

"Ten-four, Chief," and it took far less time than it had taken to chat with the gun dealer. The next call was Mac. "We got him, Chief. We picked him up in his driveway; he said he was just going out to get some supplies. What do you want us to do with him?"

Garrett said, "I tell you what, Mac. I'm up here at the Croissant Community Building. The town clerk, Kelly, is here, and she's found us a private room where we can talk to him. She'll show you where it is. Just hold him awhile; don't take any B.S. off him."

"And just where will you be, Chief?"

"Don't worry, I'll get there pretty soon. I'm gonna run out

and pick up Clenting. We've got a few questions to ask him, too."

This time it was Mac's turn to say, "Mmmmph." Then, "Arnold Clenting, you say."

"Right. If nothing else, I'd kinda like to say hello to his dog, Killer."

42

THE OLD CLENTING PLACE was an ancient, shambling ranch house set a hundred yards back from Highway 46. Originally white, it sat just at the boundary where the irrigation allotments from the mountains ended. Green irrigated pasture and farms devoted primarily to raising hay lay to the south and east; to the north and west, dobies drifted to the horizon. Around the house were broken cars on blocks, cast off pieces of ranch equipment, and tired outbuildings, worn and crumbling, all contributing to the general sense of dishabille emanating from the place. Garrett knocked on the door. It wasn't locked. He stuck his head inside, noting the stale odor of fried bacon, and yelled, "Clenting? Clenting, you in here?" No answer.

Outside he poked among the outbuildings. A big caged area contained three floppy hounds that set up a general hulla-balloo as he passed, barking and slobbering. He made his way to the back of the place, and, leaning on a rickety gate made of graying wooden slabs, he looked out across the pastures and dry hills that would culminate in Old Grand Road, and tried to think what to do next. He was loathe to search the house without a warrant. The guy could be dead in there, but he'd smelled old bacon, not death. So where would Clenting have gone? Ranch supplies? Groceries? On the lam?

A movement in the distance far to the southwest caught Garrett's attention. Shading his eyes from the glare, he squinted toward it. Hard to tell. Could be a person, walking. It shimmered along. Could be a deer, for all he could tell. He jogged back to his vehicle, pulled out his binoculars and his rifle, ran to the gate, and had another look at the receding figure. Ah, better. It was indeed a man, a lone man, walking rapidly across the unfenced dobies.

Grunting to get the gate open enough to squeeze through, then laboriously pushing it shut behind him, he set off after the retreating figure at a brisk trot. By the time he had closed the space between them enough to be sure it was Clenting, they were approaching Old Grand Road and the sheriff's ribs ached from the pace. Clenting had stopped, and Garrett stopped, too, bending to suck air.

Looking up again, he realized that they had veered far enough west to reach Carol Haddon's house, just across the road from where Clenting stood, transfixed. Carol was in her yard playing with two of her dogs, sending them across the lawn with commands, laughing, praising them.

It was then that Garrett realized Clenting had a rifle. He was raising it, taking careful aim. Carol was unaware. Bursting into a dead run, Garrett shouted, "Hold it! Clenting, put it down!"

Clenting turned frantically and fired toward Garrett. Garrett hit the ground and scrabbled behind a scraggly rabbit brush. Cautiously raising his head, he adjusted his own gun, leveling it at Clenting, who was staring wild-eyed at the bush. He located the sheriff and took aim, and Garrett yelled, "Buddy, I got you in my sites. Don't do it. Put down that gun."

Carefully unfolding himself, standing, and stepping into the open, Garrett let him see the rifle trained on him. "It's the sheriff, Clenting. Put that gun down."

Hesitant, Arnold Clenting slowly put the gun on the ground and raised his hands. His face had gone sullen. "I coulda took you."

"Yeah, probably." Garrett approached him and kicked aside the rifle. "For Pete's sake, put down your hands. What the hell do you think you are doing, Arnold?"

Clenting put his hands down. He tried to face Garrett, but his eyes shifted. "Well, I... Well, I thought you was Gump. I was out huntin' prairie dogs, then I spotted you back there, and I thought you was Gump. He's dangerous, you know." Garrett glanced up at the house. There was no sign of Carol Haddon or her dogs. Seeing the direction of the sheriff's eyes, Clenting added, "I came up this way because I thought I ought to warn Carol Haddon. I think Gump is after her. I had my rifle ready in case I saw she was in trouble. It was him, you know, tried to poison those dogs with wienies soaked in rat bait."

"Yeah, well, it seems from what I saw that you might be causing a little trouble yourself. I just came by to ask you a couple questions, but now I think maybe I need to run you on in to get several things sorted out. Hold out your wrists, Arnold. Now we gotta walk all the way back to your place to get the police car." Scowling and reluctant, Clenting obeyed and Garrett cuffed him. "I think you better lead the way. I'll be holdin' my rifle, and I got a couple deputies'll pick up your fancy gun."

As they trudged toward the old ranch house, Clenting looked over his shoulder. "So what kinda heavy shit was it you wanted to ask me, Sheriff?"

"I got a few things. We'll talk about it when we get there. One thing, though. I keep wonderin' where that dog of yours is. That dog you call Killer. I don't see him around."

Clenting stopped dead, turned to face the sheriff, and said with disgust, "That's a helluva stupid question. I got no idea where that damn dog is. He just goes visiting. He's a good dog, wouldn't hurt a flea, so it ain't gonna hurt anybody if he runs around a little. That's what livin' in this great country of ours is all about, isn't it? Bein' free? Bein' free, and lettin' your poor damn animals have a little freedom, too. I hope you got better ideas than that for talkin' when we reach the station."

43

THEY WEREN'T HEADED FOR THE "STATION." Garrett turned right instead, drove east, and radioed McCracken, who met him outside the Croissant Community Building, where she gathered up Clenting and escorted him inside. While she did, Garrett relaxed his shoulders, took a pinch of non-nicotine mint chew, and stared thoughtfully into his rear view mirror.

There had been a car waiting in the pull-out just past the Old Grand Road and Highway 46 intersection, and it had clung behind him all the way as he drove into town. He was sure it was Carol Haddon, and he expected her momentarily. She did not disappoint. She pulled in beside him and he unfolded himself from behind the steering wheel to meet her. "Please, Sheriff. Could you give me a minute before you go in there? I need to speak to you in private."

Garrett nodded down at her. "Yeah, good idea. Let me know what you got on your mind, Ms. Haddon."

"Well, as you know, this is Will's baby. I've always considered myself to be Will's legal wife, but of course I was living in a fantasy world. His sham marriage to Maarika was the one legally recognized by both Russia and this country, and he couldn't get out of it very easily. She wouldn't let him. She didn't love him; she just wanted to control him. She didn't believe in any of his hopes and dreams, like I did. Will talked to a lawyer about it, and it looked as if it could take months, maybe years, to get through the red tape, if she fought the divorce, and she assured him she would. Our baby is due in less than four months. We were desperate for resolution. We wanted to begin building our own life together in the village." She was quiet, trying to decide how to proceed.

Leaning against his vehicle, Garrett studied her. "So, go

ahead."

"Will thought he had found a ringing cedar right between my place and the Vedrussian property and he... uh, do you know what I'm talking about? The ringing tree?" Garrett nodded, and she went on.

"We met there twice a week. We called it the tryst tree. So, anyhow, we were there Thursday night, the night before Maarika was shot. We were trying desperately to think of a solution to our problem, which was, of course, Maarika. It was odd. Patch's climbing dog, Buddy, had followed us up, and then in the middle of the night another dog showed up. I think it was Arnold Clenting's pit bull, Killer. Him, or maybe Gump's Cuddles. Anyhow, the dog seemed threatening. Buddy thought so. He climbed, and Will and I hid. The dog didn't try to find us, though. It could have sniffed us out if it had wanted to. It just fiddled around by the tree, then someone called it with a low whistle and it took off.

"By then it was late and we were exhausted; Will walked me home. We still hadn't come up with any plan as to how to deal with Maarika, and I couldn't sleep. I lay awake the rest of that short night, and by 5:00 in the morning Thursday— Yesterday! It feels like a century ago!—but yesterday morning, I just decided I couldn't take it any more. I got it in my head that maybe if I went to Maarika myself and she could see Will's child coming and I'd throw myself on her mercy, ask her to free Will, offer her money... Now I realize it made no sense. I, of all people, knew how heartless she was, but I was exhausted, and afraid for Will and me and our baby.

"I drove up to the pull-out above the village, parked, and tried to get my courage up. I thought it would be best if I walked on in, just a funny feeling about driving in unannounced that early in the morning. It might alarm them. They were already jumpy, had had threats, from Gump, I guess. Besides, I wanted to look in and get a feeling for what was going on before I just blundered in. So I worked my way through the trees to the hilltop overlooking the village and stood studying it to decide how to approach it all, when I heard voices."

"Voices?" Garrett repeated.

"Yes, two male voices. I could see down into the village, but the voices were very, very close to me, soft, almost whispered, but clear. I froze. I couldn't see who was speaking. The sun was just coming up, and the shadows were still thick around the trees, so I just listened to what they said, and my blood ran cold. The one man was telling the other to shoot into the village. At first it sounded like they just wanted to scare people down there. The one voice kept goading, saying things like, 'Shit, I didn't buy the damn gun for a lily-livered coward, did I? That's a freak nest down there, a bunch of terrorists; you need to give 'em a good scare so that we can get rid of them. That was our deal, wasn't it? I think of stuff to do, you do it.'

"The other voice said, 'But what if I hit a kid?' and the first said, 'Ain't no kids there. Big crack-shot hunter like yourself, you won't hit anything you don't wanna hit.'

"That's how they talked, Sheriff, the one pushy, the other kind of whiny and hesitant. And then the part that has me so scared, why I pointed that gun at you last night. See, pretty soon the goading one said, 'Look, you do your part in this and we can get rid of these tree huggers and that neighbor woman of yours that you hate so much, all in one blow.' Then he said, his voice raised a little, kind of excited, 'Why look, there she comes right now, Carol Haddon, coming out of that building over there.'

"Sheriff, I had no time to react. The shot went off and I saw Maarika fall and I was totally gripped in terror. I ran like a rabbit, reached my car, made it home, locked every door and window in my house, and loaded my gun. The one I pointed at you. I've been terrified out of my mind ever since. I don't think they saw me, but I'll never know. I can't even bring myself to tell Will! What could he do? That man acted like he thought.... Why would whoever it was be so keen to shoot *me?*"

She was shaking. Her voice had thinned and risen an octave, and Garrett, uncharacteristically, placed a comforting hand on her arm. His cell rang and he hit 'talk,' then barked "Hold on" into the phone.

Turning back to Carol, he said, "Ms. Haddon, thank you for the information. It helps, and it took courage to tell me. Now I need you to do one more courageous thing. I want you to go into that building and locate one of my deputies. Tell them that the sheriff wants you to be present when he talks to Mr. Gump and Mr. Clenting."

The look Carol gave the sheriff was appalled and pleading,

but he held up his hand. "No, no, don't misunderstand. You shouldn't have to be in the room with them. Just tell the deputy that I'd like you to wait for me outside the room in that little hallway in case you should be needed."

Carol nodded, numb.

"Good woman. I won't call you unless I really need you. Now, I also need you to tell whichever deputy you find that I need to return a call from Detective Hobbs. Then I'll be in."

44

GARRETT RETURNED THE HOBBS CALL, grunted his greeting, then listened. After a minute he hung up, saying, "Thanks, Asa. It fits." Closing and opening his phone, he stood scowling down at the highway that meandered through the town. The dog-that-always-sleeps-in-the-street was there, and he wondered why no one had run her down yet. Then, abruptly making a decision, he opened the phone again and made a second call before going in.

They sat at a folding table, Gump attempting to appear accommodating, Clenting sullen, and now Garrett taking a chair opposite them. The two deputies in the room leaned, arms folded, against nearby walls, but Garrett had neglected to close the door. Kelly, the town clerk, walked slowly by, busily shuffling papers, then for some reason walked by again, still shuffling, casually looking into the room and taking in the scene. McCracken got up to close the door, but Garrett said, "Nah, Mac. Let it go. It's hot in here — we're gonna need a little breeze before we get done."

Glad to comply, McCracken resumed her place. Garrett studied the two men, and Arnold Clenting shifted in his seat, waiting. Finally, the sheriff spoke. "You know, Mr. Clenting, I've just heard from my detective. There were some fingerprints on that gun that shot Maarika Yelets, and I think you know who those prints belong to, but I'll make it clear up front. Those fingerprints are yours, Mr. Clenting."

The expression on Clenting's face had gone from sullen to agitated. He started to stand, but Red's firm hand pressed him back into his chair. "Easy there, cowboy. You better sit and hear what else the sheriff has to say. Don't look like he's done yet."

Sinking back down, Clenting snarled, "I thought you said this was going to be about dogs. It wasn't my gun that shot that woman."

"You're absolutely right, Mr. Clenting. The gun that shot Ms. Yelets was purchased by Mr. Gump, here."

Gump smirked, his voice oily. "Why, Arnold, how in the world did you get my gun?" Then a gesture of phony enlightenment. "Oh, I remember you admiring it, Arnold. Why, Sheriff, he must have just borrowed it; it's a beautiful firearm. I suspect he borrowed it, then one of those terrorists stole it. Isn't that what happened, Arnold?"

Before Clenting could reply, there was a strange scratching sound from the vicinity of Garrett's lap, and he produced his phone, looked at it, and said, "Oh, excuse me a minute. I need to answer this text."

McCracken stared at him dumbfounded. It wasn't just that the sheriff never used texting; he was annoyed by the "new" mode of communication and had never learned how. What startled her was that his cell phone was outdated. He couldn't text on it if he wanted to. Before she could gather herself, Garrett had slid back his chair and stepped into the hall.

He found Carol Haddon there, sitting quietly, hands folded on her lap, face worried. She looked up at him to see him pointing to his lips, his ears, and, holding up two fingers, the room behind him. She frowned in puzzlement. He repeated the gestures, and suddenly it dawned; a wave of comprehension washed over her face. Nodding vigorously, she shook her finger toward the room, held up two fingers, pointed to her ears. She wanted to say it aloud, but resisted, instead mouthing, while she nodded, "It's them. It's the voices I heard."

Garrett grinned, shot her a thumbs up, and went back into the room, offering a polite apology. "Sorry to hold everyone up. Sheriff business. Couldn't wait. Now, where were we?" Sliding into his chair, he said, ""Oh, yes, we have Mr. Clenting's fingerprints on Mr. Gump's gun, which just happens to be the gun that killed Ms. Yelets. We found that gun in the woods, not far from the Vedrussian settlement. But Mr. Clenting, we have something even more damning. We have a witness to the actual murder, a person who saw that it was you who raised the gun, shot, and then left."

Clenting's mouth opened, but before he could say anything, Gump said, "Ptah," and made a dismissive gesture. "Really, sheriff, you should know that word travels fast and mysteriously in this community. I've already heard about your witness; it's that doddering old Doc Clary's crazy wife. You know that her testimony wouldn't stand up five minutes in court."

"I see." A little smile played under Garrett's mustache. "The problem is, we have other witnesses who can also place you at or near the scene of the crime."

Gump had had time to regroup, and he was settled comfortably back into his seat. "Well, I don't know about Arnold, but as you well know, Sheriff, I was at home Thursday night. Your deputies can testify to that. They came by yesterday morning to see if I had seen that lost child."

Clenting was staring at Gump with loathing. He wasn't sure what was happening, but he was getting the distinct sense that he was being thrown to the wolves. He opened his mouth, but before he could speak, Garrett was saying quietly, "And where was your dog, Cuddles, when the deputies dropped by? Remember Cuddles? The dog you say loves you so much she won't ever leave your side — where is she now, Mr. Gump? What I think is that she witnessed your crime, and I think she is at Dr. Clary's clinic, recovering from bullet wounds that she incurred when she was trying to follow you through the forest as you hurried to get home after a murder."

Gump's face had gone livid, his fury uncontainable. "You leave Cuddles out of this, you son-of-a-bitch. She likes to be with me, and she would be here right now, if she could, if your Nazis had let me bring her. She's at home. That dog in the clinic is Clenting's dog, Killer. That stupid, wandering mutt of his was out making trouble that night, like always, and Cuddles was with me. I was at home all morning with Cuddles, *including*, mind you, at the time of the murder."

Arnold had begun to babble, but before he could gain the level of coherence he needed to apply to Ronald Gump, there was a sound in the hallway and a healthy, friendly pit bull trotted into the room, wagging his tail and pleased with himself, hoping to greet everyone present. He was sadly restrained from doing so by the person holding his leash, Ms. Billy Ray Clenting.

45

"HERE'S YOUR DAMN DOG, ARNIE. You know he always comes to me when he's scared, poor baby. And you know that gun shots scare him to death. Sit, Killer." Killer sat, then lay down and put his paws over his nose.

"And as for you, Ronnie, you know you weren't home with either of those Cuddles you like to claim. You're lying, as usual. I felt you sneak out of bed at 3:00 a.m., and I watched you head down the driveway in the moonlight, the doggie Cuddles wagging along behind you. Oh, I can testify to that in court, Ronnie, my love."

For the first time that morning, Ronald Gump looked shocked and horrified, but Billy Ray continued. "Oh, you thought you had me under control, didn't you? You thought you had me treed. You thought if you got put on the spot that I'd back up your story like some weakly, needy, lovesick wimp. That I'd say you were with me Friday morning. Ha! Are you nuts? I'm absolutely fed up with you—I am not your toy!

"You and your little buddy, Arnie here, may as well come clean, because I figured out your little scheme right after I moved in with you. You didn't plan to gather support and then throw the election my way, like you told me. Oh, no. That was just the bullshit boy's bedroom sweet talk. You planned to take the election yourself and then use the powers of the office to gain ownership of all the property around you and get a monopoly on the resources in the area. County commissioner may not be president, but every public office is significant, and there's a lot of damage you could do once you got the power—mess with eminent domain, adjust the budget, harass landowners... you'd have used everything that you could throw at them, and then you would have had Haddon's land, the Vedrussian land, the old Clenting place, and that was just for starters." She gave an ugly laugh, turning toward Arnold.

"And as for you, Mr. Clenting, you better not gloat. He didn't plan to cut you in if you helped him scare everybody off, like he told you he would. He had plans to go for you, too." She turned to the sheriff. "I've been waiting to see if those two connivers would offer to cut me in." She snorted. "I'd have turned them down, of course, Sheriff. But political rivals? Ha! Neither of these baby boys are friends of mine. They're just the usual greedy, two-faced male assholes."

The glare which Arnold Clenting had fixed on Gump would have melted steel. "No, she's right. Mr. Gump wasn't with her yesterday morning; he wasn't home at all. He was with me, up above that Vedrussian settlement. He'd told me to meet him up there, and to bring that Russian rifle he bought me."

Gump interjected hurriedly, "Now Arnold! Think carefully what you are saying."

His gaze fixed on Garrett, Clenting would no longer be stopped. "Look, I didn't want that rifle so I could kill somebody. I just thought it was a damn nice rifle, a collector's piece, and Gump has plenty of money. He said he'd buy me the gun if I'd use it once in a while to scare some of those people with, so when he kept pushing me, I figured why not. Why not? It wouldn't hurt his pocketbook to shell out a little, and I would get a kick out of shooting it. The thing was, up there yesterday morning he just kept pushing and pushing, telling me I had to shoot into the village if I was gonna earn his respect. What he was sayin' made me feel like a coward."

Gump had drawn himself up and the corners of his mouth were so far down they reached his jawbone. "I didn't tell you to shoot anybody. I told you to scare them, not shoot them."

Clenting wheeled on him. "That is a fucking lie. You told me to shoot her. You told me to shoot Carol. I didn't think I was shooting that Russian bitch. I knew we needed to get rid of Carol, and I thought it was her. They look alike, and that other cunt just got in the way."

Garrett's voice had become very, very cold. "Mr. Clenting, look at me. I think you had better explain to us why you were gunning for Carol Halabi."

Clenting dragged his eyes back to the sheriff's face.

"Because she claims to be my daughter. At least, her mother claims she is. I don't think she is; she sure as hell doesn't look like me. She only looks like that cunt, her mother, Qamar. But no matter that I don't know her from Adam. In a few months she's going to take possession of my land, what little is left of it after that dirty bitch that's hanging onto my dog over there took me for all I'm worth. If Halabi gets the rest, then the old Clenting place will be owned by a bra-burning fanatic and a fucking Arab. My granddad would turn over in his grave."

His voice still cold, Garrett asked, "So how is it that Carol Halabi is going to be able take possession of that property, Mr. Clenting?"

Clenting's voice sank to a barely audible mutter. "Qamar Halabi blackmailed me."

"Please continue."

"She lived near the base where I was stationed. She was a student, but she earned money on weekends, belly dancing in a Middle Eastern restaurant there, supposed to be giving it atmosphere. Her and other women brought in more customers, I guess. We talked, and eventually we hooked up. I was a young fool. I couldn't keep my hands off her."

Billy Ray's eyes had narrowed, and she said angrily, "We were married then, you bastard. I thought I loved you then. I was sending you reams of lonely mush letters through the APO."

Clenting looked at her, shrugged, and turned back. "Whatever. To make a long story short, Sheriff, when Halabi came to me to tell me she was pregnant, I asked her if she was sure it was mine. That really pissed her off. She screamed at me, told me I was calling her a slut.

"You see, she was like a snake. She was beautiful, but deadly. When she had me in her coils, I lost my senses, and on the nights we spent together I confided stuff in her. I told her about my life, my home, my doubts about my marriage. Then, worst of all, I told her about how I had embezzled from the Peaseford treasury while I was on city council. I guess I kind of bragged about it; not everybody can get away with that kind of complex operation."

A smile flickered across his face, but he was into his story now, and oblivious to the expressions of distaste around him. "So when I asked if it was actually even my kid, that really turned her around. She gave me what for about how belly dancing is an art form, not some prostitution thing. Then she got real mean, and she told me she wasn't a whore, that I had deceived her by not telling her I was married, and that she never wanted any more to do with me, but that whatever else I did, I was, by the mighty will of God, going to provide for that baby. If I didn't, she would see that it came out about me taking the money. Shit, I had already spent that money; there was no way I could pay it back, much less afford going to court.

"Like I say, long story short. She got it all together, went to attorneys, drew up the papers, followed it through. I didn't have enough money left by then to suit her; my regular income was tied up already trying to deal with the beast over there, so Halabi got her teeth into my land. It's set up as a trust or something. When my supposed daughter reaches twenty-five years of age, she will automatically own it.

"And you know what? That fake daughter, she ain't my blood. Her ancestors never settled this land, fought Indians for it, grubbed to make it yield a crop. She didn't drag logs from the mountains to build the house, the sheds, to fix it all up. She's nothing. She's just a foreign imposter. You know damn well we should nuke 'em all."

Into the deathly silence that had fallen over the room, Garrett said, "Mac, Red. Please arrest Mr. Clenting and Mr. Gump. They will be charged with murder. Read them their rights."

Gump spluttered, "Hey, hold on. I didn't shoot anybody. It was that little coward there. You heard him. He fired the gun — I never touched it."

Turning hard eyes toward the bully, Garrett said, "Mr. Gump, under Colorado law, your actions have made you fully culpable as an accomplice to murder, which means you are as culpable as the person who pulled the trigger. It will benefit you if you hear the deputies out as they read you your rights."

Sighing, suddenly deeply exhausted, Garrett faced Billy Ray Clenting. "Ms. Clenting, you will also need to stay. I will call in the other deputy, and you will have to be held in Riversmet for questioning. I'm afraid some issues have arisen with respect to your being an accessory before the fact in this affair."

Before she could respond, he left the room. He glanced at

the chair beside the door where Carol Haddon had sat to over-hear the exchange inside. It was empty.

46

GARRETT SPENT THE AFTERNOON in the Croissant area tending to loose ends, but by evening Mac and Red had returned, having deposited their prisoners in Riversmet and needing to tie up some loose ends of their own. To facilitate that, Garrett took them to dinner, the Cowpath, of course. Jenny, having this night off, sat with them. The place was busy. Bennie and Abby Senderson had a table near the door. The Weinant-Anderson family, Duz, Carmen, Gritty, and even old Alma, sat nearby. It wasn't all that private for discussion, but the lawmen were happy to have tied up the case so quickly. Feeling celebratory, they ordered the best: barbecued ribs, fried chicken, chicken fried steak, apple pie....

"So, Chief. What was with the texting, anyhow?"

"Elementary, my dear Watson. I thought you'd have that all figured out by now. I wanted to find out if the voices Carol Haddon heard in the room matched with the voices she heard at the scene of the murder. Not hard evidence, but her confirming it gave me confidence." He grinned.

"Nah, Chief. I did get that one. What I'm trying to figure out is that sound."

"Sound?"

"You know, the incoming text sound. What was that, anyhow? You don't text."

"Oh, that! You know, you do text, all the time, and I realized that those incoming text notices can be anything from a braying donkey to a Mozart minuet, so I figured a scratchy noise would work, too. I just scratched my watch hard against the bottom of that old table. My watch survived; may have defaced the table."

Still chuckling, Red said, "Well, I have a question. Won't

Billy Ray have some kind of entrapment issue, since you called her to come in and bring Killer?"

"I didn't call her. The only people I talked to were Hobbs and Duval, our D.A. I wanted to be on solid footing with those charges; I needed to be sure that Gump could go down for murder as an accomplice, and we'll still have to see what Billy Ray comes up with when they question her, to find out whether the accessory charge will hold. But at any rate, Ms. Clenting waltzed into that room all on her own. She doesn't live far away; maybe she was on her way to get groceries, saw the activity, got curious, and came up to check it out. Or maybe the town clerk, Kelly Gallowup, tipped her off. News always gets around here, one way or the other."

Then the sheriff looked up to see Maureen Macklenburg, and thought, "Well, speak of the devil."

Maureen had approached with notebook and pen in hand. After a breathless, friendly greeting, she got down to business. "Sheriff, I heard you made several arrests today?"

"Yes. Yes, Ms. Macklenburg, we did."

"These arrests were with respect to the murder?"

"Yes, the arrests had to do with the murder." Garrett looked longingly and significantly at the meaty rib that was suspended half way to his mouth.

"We can assume that you will be having a press conference about these arrests very soon?" She asked this with great satisfaction at the weightiness of it all. She knew she had a scoop.

"That would probably be a good idea." Garrett took a bite of meat.

"And it certainly clears out the electoral field. Hmm. I do believe I see the presumptive county commissioner and his wife sitting right over there." Casting a 'thank you for the information' goodbye over her shoulder, Maureen headed toward the Senderson table.

Jenny waited until she was gone, then asked, "Where is the dog?"

"The dog?"

"You know, Arnold's dog. Killer. Where is he?"

McCracken laughed. "Oh, he turns out to be a big pussycat. Carol Haddon agreed to keep him. Will was with her, sorting things out, when we dropped him off. She'd been crying, but when she saw the dog she laughed and said, 'Well, I may as well take him in. It looks as if he is my orphaned little brother.' I think she's going to be all right."

At the next table, old Alma Weinant had been sitting, hunkered and apparently oblivious, working with difficulty to dispose of a roll and a cup of bean soup. There were spills. Suddenly, like an ancient tortoise awakening from hibernation, she raised her head, turned it toward the sheriff's table, and said, loudly and distinctly, "Well, Lyle, that's quite a crime you've been working on."

Garrett was so taken aback he couldn't answer. She still called him by his older brother's name, after all this time! His irritating, obnoxious older brother! Good grief, what to make of it? Her family, which had been pretending not to listen, was smiling, nodding, trying to distract her, making embarrassed sounds, but Alma continued, loudly. "Well, from what I heard today, it just goes to show what they always say. Politics makes strange bedfellows."

Now back in possession of his wits, Garrett replied kindly, "Why yes, it does, Mrs. Weinant. It certainly does."

"And, Lyle, I was just thinking about Patch's dog, Buddy. Uh huh. Old Patch's dog, that's right. That dog, it climbs after those squirrels, but he's got sense enough not to get too high up in the tree. You get too high, the branches get thin, and the squirrel just jumps to another tree. It takes a stupid dog to try and follow the squirrel too high. Stupid dog would fall. Looks to me like Mr. Gump lost control and his squirrel jumped."

She nodded, satisfied with her statement. She had the attention of the entire room by now, but she had begun to lower her head, prepared to address her difficult soup. As an after-thought she added, "Well, he thought he had her treed, didn't he, but when he got up there, she jumped."

Acknowledgments

First, most thanks go to Doug, Judy, Erin, and Sara. They found time to read the raw manuscript, all of it, to read it fast, and tell me what it needed to make it work. They were astute and kind. Thanks also to Tanya, who advised about emergency vehicle communication.

Cheyenne, thank you for the great Buddy photos to choose from for the cover. Roxanne, thanks for coming through again, on deadline, with another map of that mythical area, Croissant.

Kathy Little and Jan Ryan at the Crawford Community Library never, ever fail to deliver the goods as needed for research. Thanks!

My heart and gratitude to my good friends, the Bibliofillies and Fun Book Clubbers—we read the book, we share the feast, and I learn every time.

I'd be crazy to stop without thanking Ann Miller of Earth Star Publications. You, my friend, are the best person in the universe to work with.

Everyone that knows us knows who else: Dr. David G. Gallob, inimitable supporter of wifely writers. A veterinary fact here, a gun fact there, and unfailing encouragement on the down days. Words are inadequate, Dave. You're the best.

About the Author

Karen Weinant Gallob is a Colorado rancher and an anthropologist who taught for several years at Metropolitan State College in Denver. She is interested in the relationships among language, culture, and human perceptions of reality.

She has published articles, reviews, short stories, poetry, and novels. Her cozy mystery, *Baby Skulls and Fowl Odors*, was a finalist in the 2015 Eric Hoffer award competition, and her poem, "Aspen," was a finalist in the Colorado Authors' League 2016 Writing competition. She is a member of the American Anthropological Association, the Colorado Authors' League, and two rambunctious local book clubs.

The Climbing Dog Affair

A Pat Garrett, Leigh McCracken Mystery

by Karen Weinant Gallob

Not your copy?

If you'd like to order your own copy of this book,
or get a gift for a friend,
please use the order form below.

ORDER FORM

Please send me _____ copies of *The Climbing Dog Affair* by Karen Weinant Gallob.

Enclosed is my check or money order for $11.95 for each copy plus $3.00 shipping and handling (total $14.95 per book) *(Colorado residents please add 35¢ **state sales tax** for each book ordered.)*

Name _____

Address _____

City, State, Zip _____

Send a photocopy (or clip out) of this order form to:

KAREN WEINANT GALLOB		**EARTH STAR PUBLICATIONS**
2240 Clear Fork Road	**OR**	P.O. Box 1213
Crawford, CO 81415		Cedaredge, CO 81413

Also available locally at The Creamery and The Blue Sage
and from Amazon. Get the eBook version from Amazon Kindle

To find out where to order Karen's earlier books in the series,
Baby Skulls and Fowl Odors, and
All the Bad Stuff Comes in Threes,
visit **www.earthstarpublications.com/BadStuff.html**
www.earthstarpublications.com/BabySkulls.html